ROSEMARY A JOHNS

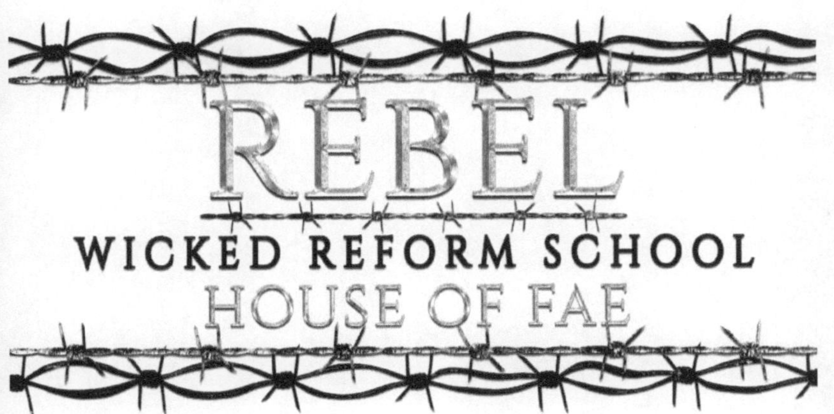

REBEL: HOUSE OF FAE

Stay away from Court Fae...

My dad drilled that into our Dark Fae tribe, trapping us in the forest. Court Fae are deadly, cruel, and believe that they're fated to mate for life.

But I'm also Lord Spring: a rebel with something dangerous and magical growing inside me...

Now I'm a prisoner in a supernatural jail with my two hot and protective fae friends, held captive because I rebelled against the Queen. They even kidnapped the beautiful shifters. How can I escape this hellhole with its trials, executions, and classes with blood-thirsty vampires, werewolves, and witches?

Go for counseling with the sexy succubus, my friends said. It couldn't be worse than dying, right?

Yet love could be deadlier than anything else in this reform school. Why choose just one bond when all are so temptingly hot? Yet will these new loves and friendships be enough to fight the system and the Court Fae?

If I fail to graduate…

…I die.

WICKED REFORM SCHOOL MAP

*Welcome to Wicked Reform School. Here is your campus map.
Escape attempts through the magical wards, disobeying professors,
and biting other students will all land you in front of the Dean.
Mandatory: Reform or die.*

MAGICAL BARRIER
HOUSE of MERMAIDS
HOUSE of ELVES
HOUSE of DWARVES
HOUSE
HOUSE of ELEMENTALISTS
HOUSE of DEMONS
HOUSE of DRAGONS
HOUSE of the UNDETERMINED
FOUNTAIN of WOE
STAFF HOUSING
TRAINING GROUNDS
M
DINING HALL
DETENTION CENTER
BEHAVIOR MODIFICATION CENTER

HOUSE of BERSERKERS
HOUSE of PHOENX
SHIFTER ALLEY
HOUSE of SHIFTERS
LIBRARY
HOUSE of VAMPIRES
HOUSE of WITCHES
HOUSE of NECROMANCERS
HOUSE
MEDICAL
HOUSE
HOUSE of NEPHILM
HOUSE of FAE
HOUSE of ZOMBIES
HOUSE of ALMOST HUMANS

VAMPIRE MAGE
VAMPIRE GOD
VAMPIRE SECRET: REBELS AND
RENEGADES

REBEL VAMPIRES - COMPLETE SERIES
COMPLETE SERIES BOX SET BOOKS 1-3
BLOOD DRAGONS
BLOOD SHACKLES
BLOOD RENEGADES
STANDALONE: BLOOD GODS

REBEL: HOUSE OF FAE - COMPLETE
HOUSE OF FAE

AUDIO BOOKS

CHAPTER ONE

**Wicked Reform School, Trial Area
Monday 26ᵗʰ April**

LORD SPRING

This morning, I either reformed and graduated or remained wicked and died.

At the Wicked Reform School, once you'd reached the end of your sentence, it was the only choice.

Yet I was Lord Quincey Spring, the leader of the despised Rebel Dark Fae tribe from the English forests, who'd walked in the shadow of death my entire life. After a decade exiled and locked up in this American prison of a reform school because my tribe had been sentenced for rebelling against the Unseelie Queen, I wasn't a model student.

This term alone, I'd had to sit a special lesson invented just for me: The Problem Prankster. How to think beyond *What Would Loki Do?*

Let's just say that I hadn't planned a graduation party.

My golden wings fluttered, and I wrinkled my nose at the scent of tangy blood that stained the wooden floor. I edged my foot away from the patch of scarlet (I'd spent ages polishing my boots), and glanced out over the Trial Area that'd been adapted into a stage for the graduation ceremony.

The fae were ranked like an army on parade, if that army were dressed in steam punk military uniforms with slashes in the sweeping coats for their burnished wings. Their emerald eyes were fixed forward, and their pale faces were as emotionless as we'd been taught to be.

Almost like they weren't here to be executed.

My heart clenched at the thought of what was about happen to *my* people.

Why hadn't I been able to save them?

If my older brothers had been here…if they hadn't been killed or exiled…maybe together we'd have led them to freedom. But what did I know about being a leader?

Please, even though I'd die today, let the rest of the fae survive.

When my wings drooped and my shoulders slumped, Radley (or Lord Brooke as I never bothered to call him…okay, as I sometimes *mockingly* called him…more like *Rads* for short), grabbed me by the scruff of the neck and pulled me straighter again.

Radley had a thing for manhandling me but then he had the muscles for it.

I peeked at Radley, as he adjusted my golden scimitar that was slung at my waist and then the swan clips in my hair, which had been digging into my scalp.

Somehow, he always knew what was hurting me.

Radley was my best mate. In fact, since I was a kid, he'd been like family. The type who were overprotective with a hint of psychopath mixed in. Like me, Radley wore our uniform, which was a long coat with glowing runes on the lapel that stopped us from flying without permission and the swan crest of the House of Fae. The same crest was emblazoned on the belt of our khaki pants, and could be spelled with either restrictions or rewards.

You knew that you were screwed when even your pants could punish you.

Radley was taller than me, and his gleaming emerald eyes were bright against the dark of his ebony skin. His sweeping wings arced over me like he could protect me, despite everything. I'd braided his hair this morning into a warrior style because this was a battle, even if it ended in our deaths.

The other paranormals in the reform school called this day *the culling*, but we fae knew it as the *Day of the Wicked*.

When you reached twenty-five in the reform school, there were only two options: *reform or die.*

The spring sun shone hot across my translucent skin; my eyelashes fluttered against the light. Clouds flew across the cornflower sky like swans. My heart ached at the phoenixes calling to each other, as the bird-like creatures swooped overhead, in haunting melodies.

I wondered if the phoenixes had ever tried to escape through the high invisible barrier, which trapped us in the school. There were rumors that a dragon once had, only to crash. There were always whispers in a prison like this. It was judging between the truth and lies that was hard.

"Brothers in wings," a soft voice said from my other side, as a wing brushed against mine.

I shivered.

Oh yeah, wicked.

"Brothers in wings," Radley and I muttered in response like answering a prayer.

I turned to Felix (or Lord River as I sometimes called him…*Lix* for short), and cold gripped me at the way that he forced himself to smile, pushing his tumble of hair out of his light green eyes. His caramel skin glowed in the heat. He was gorgeous but he was always too buried in books and intent on proving that a Forest Fae could be as bright as a Court Fae to realize it.

There were many tribes of fae, but only one Court ruled by a Queen, and she was a despot. The Court Fae were tyrannical and cruel, believing that you mated for life. If tribes rebelled against Court rules, then they were punished.

Like my Forest Fae.

Felix was as close a friend to me as Radley because the three of us had been sacrificed to the Court Fae as kids. At least we'd always had each other to love.

I scanned the Trial Area. The main campus with its modern buildings was behind, and the school's vast gates in front. Yet the gates were warded and guarded.

There was no escape from this.

"You know," I glanced at Felix, "I'm starting to seriously doubt the claim that you're as magically *lucky* as your name."

Felix grinned. "Hey, Felix does mean *fortunate*, and Fortune Magic is powerful."

Radley grunted. "It also means *fertile*. Is there anything that you want to tell us?"

Felix blushed, and I loved the way that it spread

down his chest. He circled around us. "Let's stick with lucky…"

When Felix stumbled, Radley caught his arm and pulled him to his chest.

The other Houses were right to fear the Fae Lords: *we were fierce.*

Felix gave a quiet laugh, scratching the back of his head, which was his tell for when he was nervous. He'd been trying to hide it for my sake like he always did, but I knew him like a brother. We'd spent our childhoods sharing a tiny room that hadn't been much more than a cell.

The Queen had made a mistake when she'd sentenced us to this reform school, which was meant to be for the wickedest paranormals of the supernatural world. How had she thought that it could break us, when we'd already suffered in a prison for most of our lives? Just because that prison had been called the Dark Fae Court, rather than a reform school didn't change the truth.

They'd made us too strong to be *reformed.*

Really, well done on the irony.

I swallowed, steeling myself to look out at the crowds. Staff and students had gathered to watch the ceremony. I avoided looking at the staff members, especially the stern-faced demon, the Dean of Discipline. Vampires, wolf shifters, and witches crowded the stage. I winced at the excited betting on who'd survive and how the execution would take place, which was led by huge shaggy-haired beserkers, (my odds to survive were currently 200:1, and the most hoped-for execution appeared to be flaying...*bastards*).

Well, this was what we got for making ourselves feared by the other Houses in order to survive. As the only all-male and English House, we'd always been the outsiders.

It took a serious crime to be sentenced here. Most of the other students, whether bear shifters or warlocks, were brutal and deadly. I'd learned to act like I was twice my size, just to stop myself from being torn in half every time that I stood in line for lunch.

A vampire pure blood with his chin tilted up arrogantly, even though he was swathed in dark robes to protect his delicate skin from the sun, sneered at me. His fangs glistened.

I snarled at him because I was having one of those savage moments that broke **Court Dictate 203:** *No snarling or growling.* I took a deep breath and then growled for good measure.

The Court Fae had taken Radley, Felix, and me as Hostage Lords as kids. We'd been the youngest (okay, *dispensable*), sons in our tribe. The Court had demanded that we be handed over and raised away from the forest, fostered at Court, and kept as a guarantee that the Rebel tribe would never rise up against the Queen's Court.

If they did, then we'd be executed.

Of course, my tribe had *still* rebelled in what came to be known as the *Love Rebellion*. Yet the Court Fae had fostered us Forest Lords for so long that they couldn't bring themselves to kill us. Instead, they'd sent us to the Wicked Reform School along with all the other male Forest Fae who weren't yet twenty-five.

But they'd made certain to traumatize us first by slaughtering our brothers in front of us.

I bit my lip hard, struggling to breathe.

In and out, in and out…

My lungs burned with their familiar illness, as I fought for breath. Next to me, Radley stiffened, and Felix swept in front of me to shield me from the view of the ghoulish crowd.

"You're okay," Felix whispered. "We've survived because you're strong. This doesn't make you weak."

Felix never let others see my sickness, which had grown in me since I was a kid. It weighed me down, settling on my chest and stopping me from trans-forming into my fae form. Something was wrong with my own magic, which attacked itself.

I truly was the worthless youngest son.

Radley pressed his hand gently to my chest, and at the same time, an unfamiliar scent like hot ginger warmed through me. My eyelids fluttered, and I sighed. The pain and tightness eased, and the attack ended.

Yet why did my magic feel more powerful and dangerous, rather than weaker after every attack?

My nose wrinkled. *Where was the aroma of ginger coming from?*

Felix gripped my hand. "We've still got about ten seconds before we're called up to *graduate*, Quince. We can think of some way to escape, right?"

I raised my eyebrow. "It's not as if we're guarded by armed ogres, on a stage surrounded with blood-thirsty witches, shifters, and dwarfs (the dicks), in a warded reform school, so I'm sure that we can make a break for it..."

"Lord of the Sarcasm, you're not cute." Radley gripped me by the neck.

"Yeah, I am." I leaned closer.

"Do you need a spanking?"

"Does anyone ever *need* a spanking...? Plus, who's the boss here, Rads?" I raised one elegant finger.

Radley's grip on my neck tightened. "Certainly not you, short wings. Has that pulling rank crap ever worked since we were kids?"

I cocked my head. "*Ehm*, nope. But hope springs eternal."

"We could pray to Belenus…" Felix said, thoughtfully.

Belenus, The Shining God, was our Celtic God. He was sacred to the Forest Fae, and hated by the Court.

Would he even recognize a Hostage Lord with my illness as one of his people?

"Never pray to a god for help." I crossed my arms. Quinn had taught me the cautionary stories late at night of the gods who were glorious but terrifying. "They're not there to do what we ask them, and what if we don't like their answer?"

This was our last time together. *Our last chance.*

My breath caught. I wouldn't…*couldn't*…say it. *But we all knew it.* "Whatever happens is the will of the forest. I'm honored that you've stood by my wing. I wish that I alone could die for you."

"Don't you dare say that." Radley's voice was suddenly rough with tears. "I'd burn the world to ash for you."

"I don't doubt it," I said, softly.

Radley smelled of wood and rich leather, as I pressed my lips to his. My heart clenched, as he wrenched away his head.

"I won't say goodbye," he whispered.

My eyes smarted with tears. "I rather thought that I was attempting to say it with my lips instead."

Radley huffed, but Felix snatched my arm, pulling me into a hug.

"I'll find you after death," he murmured against my neck. "They can't part brothers in wings."

I nodded, stroking across his shaking back.

All of a sudden, the ranks of fae began to beat their wings together like a drum roll. My heartbeat sped up — *thud* — *thud* — *thud* — to match its rhythm.

It's here now… any moment Wells, the Head of House, will call my name…

"The Marquess of Spring, Lord Quincey Spring, step forward. It's time to judge the wicked," announced Wells with a haughty flourish.

I pushed away from Felix, fixing on my Patented Sneer (see, *fearsome fae*), and staring across at the Head of the House, the Duke of Wells.

Wells was a Court Fae, who I'd feared taking my lessons from as a kid because of his dreaded pop quizzes on etiquette, manners, and other things that'd made me want to blow a raspberry in his face just to see his stunned expression. He'd spent the last decade in this school, attempting to reform me.

As usual, Wells appeared as unruffled and elegant as if he was taking tea with the Queen, rather than waiting to find out if today was an execution, rather than a graduation. He was old enough to be our father, and acted like he was merely guiding us out of kindness. His smart military outfit gleamed in all black; his scimitar was neatly at his side. He was tall, pale, and as snootily perfect as a swan.

Was it messed-up that I wanted to wreck his composure, break that cool mask of his, and prove that I was still a Forest Fae?

Around the stage, the school was as elegant and neat as Wells. Fountains *tinkled* between manicured lawns and trees, as if this was an academy, rather than a prison.

Yet it didn't matter how beautiful the setting, if the reality was your ugly death.

An execution could take place in a palace, as much as in a ditch.

I shuddered, desperate to smell the sweet scent of the wild forest just once more before I died, even though my memory of it had faded after so long away.

I missed the trees and my home like I'd been hollowed out.

If I was going to die today, then it'd be as a Forest Fae, and not a Court one.

I grinned. "You know, I'm not crazy about being labeled."

The fae broke off their drumbeat in shock. Wells' smugness wavered, and the crowd fell silent.

Okay, that wasn't good.

All of a sudden, the spicy ginger scent wrapped around me again, and I stumbled towards it like I was mesmerized. When I looked up, I met the ruby gaze of a succubus.

Who was she?

The succubus was beautiful with golden hair that coiled like snakes, and a white satin dress, which fluttered around her as if she was licked by wisps of frozen flame. But I should've recoiled from her because she also wore the swan badge of both the House of Fae and the Queen's Court. It meant that she was a new staff member, and I *hated* the professors who oppressed and controlled us.

Yet Professor Succubus wasn't watching this spectacle with excitement or dark enjoyment like the other staff. She shook with both rage and grief like it hurt her to witness it. When she offered me a sad smile, the burning inside me flared.

I smiled back, longing to march off the stage and instead, drag Professor Succubus into my arms. My dick twitched, hardening in my pants.

If I was going to die, I needed to hold her at least once. Yet I didn't even understand where those feelings came from, after all, I'd been kept *pure* and *untouched* by female fae for the sake of my future bonded. Except, I *did* know because it was her *smile* that made her truly beautiful. No one had smiled at any of us fae like that since we'd arrived in the Wicked Reform School. We were rebels, and we didn't deserve smiles that spoke of warmth and understanding.

Emotion was a weakness, and we had to mask it.

Bonding to a female was nothing but slavery: I'd soon been taught that at the Fae Court. Brotherhood was the only thing that I could trust.

Yet Professor Succubus' smile was like *hope* in the midst of the despair of this Day of the Wicked. I drew it close into the place that burned inside me.

Then I took a deep breath. My eyes glittered with a malevolence that blazed through me. Wells had battled to *tame* me.

But I was a Dark and wild Fae. I'd prove that I was free even at the end.

When I drew my scimitar, the ogres snarled and circled closer, but Wells waved them back. His cold gaze met mine.

Then I closed my eyes, humming "Don't Fear the Reaper."

How many times would I have to dance to this song and mean it? Although honestly, reapers were dicks.

I raised my scimitar, spinning across the stage and losing myself in the dance of my people. My skin prickled, and I was flushed with warmth. In front of the captive audience, I leapt and pirouetted, slicing my sword through the air in the age-old Forest Dance that Wells despised because it was the tradition of my tribe.

My heart swelled at the grins on the fae's once blank faces, as their feet stomped now in time to my own. I grinned too.

You could take the fae out of the forest, but not the forest out of the fae.

It felt like I was being burned alive from the inside; my legs were like jello. I knew that I was pushing myself too hard but when I was being killed in about…*hey, a minute now*…what did it matter?

Then my knees buckled, and I collapsed at Wells' feet.

Brilliant, I was just where he loved me to be.

I struggled onto my knees.

The fae fell silent.

My ragged breathing was loud, as I gasped after oxygen like a predator chasing prey.

You can do it…just one more breath…in…out… in…come on…

White lights danced in front of my eyes, and I slumped forward. My vision grayed.

Then Felix and Radley were kneeling either side of me, and their wings cradled me. Radley's large hand circled over my chest, as Felix massaged my back, and the pressure eased. When my breathing steadied, I raised my head.

"He only called *my* name," I rasped.

Radley shrugged.

Felix snuggled closer. "When weren't we wing by

wing? Sorry, we'll just have to…you know…together."

He meant die together.

I bit my lip to hold back my tears because I wouldn't allow Wells or the other students to see them.

I could act like a Marquess…sometimes.

When Professor Succubus caught my eye again, her jaw clenched. I expected her to look away, rejecting me after my dance. But instead, she determinedly held my gaze like she was saying that she too was with me *wing by wing*, even though she was pale like she was about to hurl.

The staff loved these public punishments. *Why was she different?*

"Now you have your moment of rebellion out of your system," Wells drawled, flicking imaginary fluff off his sleeve, "shall we get on with the ceremony?"

I inclined my head. "Your Grace, the most Noble Duke of Wells." Time for the *pious face*; he loved that one. "I await the will of the House of Fae and our most acclaimed Queen with bated breath." Now *holy face* (another one of Wells' favorites).

Wells scrunched up his nose. "Don't hold it too long, we don't want you passing out on us just yet, *hmm*? Can I be assured that you're not about to burst into a jazz improvisation, rock ballad, or exotic dance? Perhaps, you wish to entertain us with a Shakespearean tragedy before you graduate?"

"Give me another horse! Bind up my wounds! Have mercy," Felix deadpanned. "Shakespeare's kind of *my* thing."

Wells sighed. *It was brilliant to have shattered his perfect mask.*

He rubbed the bridge of his nose. "Lord River, enough of your tribe's savagery. I know that you were taught better at Court. I've spent years breaking you of such wickedness."

Felix frowned. "S-shakespeare's *c-civilised*."

I stiffened. When Felix stuttered, I knew that he *was* close to breaking. Lock us in solitary, whip our wings, or threaten to kill us, but *never* insult Felix's Shakespeare.

"It's from the non-magical human world, and you learning it goes against at least five of the Court Dictates," Wells snapped. "When you graduate from here, you'll become Court Fae. What would the Queen think if she heard you spouting nonsense? The fae who choose to bond to you will be much harsher than I, if you can't at least *pretend* to be reformed."

When Wells' cool gaze met mine, I knew what he was pleading for: he knew that I wasn't reformed enough to be married into the Court. Wells had been one of the fae who'd begged the Queen not to execute us after the rebellion and he didn't want to murder us now.

Instead, he was desperate for us to hide our true emotions and act like perfect dolls. If he ever experienced anything as messy as the feeling of being *desperate*.

Why did it matter so much that he save us?

I'd tried Wells' approach as a kid, and I'd still always fallen short. I couldn't manage it for the rest of my bonded life. I didn't have a clue what bonded love was…or if it even existed…but it *couldn't* be that, right?

"On my feathers, I'm just excited about bonding now. The ladies of the Court sound like *keepers*," I gritted out.

Wells stared at me. "Excellent. The Bonding List for the one hundred fae graduating today has already been vetted and decided. There's equal excitement at the Court to welcome you all to your new home…or in your case *home*."

He never had understood my sense of humor.

"It was never our home," Radley growled; his sharp teeth glistened.

Wells ignored him. "Let's just get your graduation officially over with, and then your new life can begin."

I battled to keep myself still.

I was the youngest son of a Duke. I knew that the

rest of the tribe didn't respect, know, or want me (*wow, that still smarted*), because I'd grown up away from them at Court. But I was still their leader.

If this was a war, then I'd lead them into battle. *But how could I lead them to their deaths, rather than a new life?*

If I'd known that becoming a grown fae meant decisions like this one, between condemning my tribe to death or forced bonds without love to cruel Court Fae, then I'd never have envied my older brother so much. I shook because to free them, I'd have to become the disappointment that they'd always thought me.

"That's all fascinating, Your Grace, but I won't make a choice for the rest of the House of Fae." I steeled myself, before I hollered across at the golden ranks words, which I knew would shame me forever, "I relinquish my Claim of Lordship over you. You're free to choose yourselves, whether you wish to graduate or are executed. I'm sorry, I wish more than anything that I could save you but instead, I grant you freedom of choice."

Silence.

Sweat dripped down the back of my neck and between my shoulder blades.

"What are you doing?" Radley hissed.

"You'll be an outcast." Felix shuffled closer; his light eyes were wide with worry and shock.

Amid the sea of disapproving faces in the crowd, however, Professor Succubus' expression flickered for a moment with admiration, before she schooled it to blankness. I blinked. No one but Radley and Felix had *ever* looked at me like that. When Wells wrenched back my head by the hair, agonizingly digging in the clasps, my moment of connection with her gave me the strength to meet his furious gaze.

"Your brother, Quinn, Duke of Spring, was one of the *best* fae that I've ever known. For his sake, I've tried to help you. Do you not see, wicked boy, how disappointed he'd be that you've abandoned your people?" Wells demanded.

I wet my dry lips. "I'm freeing them." Wells' fingers tightened in my hair, and I winced. "If you love my brother so much, why'd you let the Queen try to force him into a bond?"

Wells stiffened. "The Queen believed that your brother would be a perfect bond, just as you'd be for the Countess Pond."

Where was the Countess? I thanked Belenus that at least she wasn't standing next to Wells like I'd expected.

"Brilliant decision." My eyes narrowed. "Absolute *genius*. If you hadn't tried to force love on him… and me…then the Forest Fae wouldn't have rebelled. You know that we don't believe in a single partner for life, right? We love many fae in different ways.

But what does it matter what savage fae like us think? You *forced* my tribe into rebelling. It's your fault that my brothers died, and we're locked up." My pulse was too loud in my ears; and my eyes blurred with tears. "And my fault too," I added in a whisper.

I remembered the night that Quinn and my other brothers had broken into the Court to free me.

Radley, Felix, and I had already been huddled in the corner of our room, as sounds of battle had raged outside.

"W-what's h-happening? Who'd dare attack the Q-queen and Court?" Felix's hand had stolen into mine.

I'd clasped it to my chest, pulling him onto my lap. "They're stupid, Lix, whoever they are. She'll rip off their wings."

We'd all flinched.

"*I'll* rip off their wings first, if they try and hurt you." Radley had prowled to his feet, standing guard over me.

When the door had banged open, blasted off its hinges by magic, we'd jumped. Then an imperious Forest Fae had swept into our room; his scimitar had glowed in the gloom.

Radley had growled, and his fists had clenched.

Yet to my shock, the Forest Fae had grinned, dashing towards us and holding out his wing in familiar greeting. "I've found you!" *Why was he thrumming with joy? Why did his eyes gleam with tears?* "Come on, we have to go now."

And just for a moment, I'd hesitated. As Radley had refused to budge, I'd recoiled.

The Forest Fae's eyes had widened with a hurt that he couldn't mask, before they'd filled with a compassion that was even harder to take because I'd recognized him then like slowly rising from sleep.

How hadn't I recognized my own brother, Quinn?

I'd never even known our parents, but Quinn had raised me like *he'd* been my dad, until I'd been abandoned at Court. *And I'd hesitated to take his wing...*

"More apologies have wept through me than trees in our forest that I couldn't save you before. But are we not now brothers?" Quinn's sadness had shaken my own tears down my cheeks.

When he'd held out his wing to me again, this time I'd reached for it.

Only, now the soldiers of the Court Fae had been rushing into the room, overpowering Quinn and beating him to the floor. He hadn't taken his gaze from mine, however, like he'd never wanted to forget what I looked like and knew how precious those last moments between us would be.

I'd fought to reach my older brother again, but Wells had pinned me against the wall. Later, Wells had forced me onto my knees to watch as my three older brothers were executed and Quinn was exiled to a land of gods and monsters, so far away that I'd never see him again.

Today, I was on my knees in front of Wells once more, awaiting my own execution.

I slipped my scimitar onto the floor in front of me, caressing my hand across it. It was the only thing that I owned, which had belonged to my dad. In a fit of sentimentality, Wells had allowed Quinn to pass on dad's sword to me. I'd always seen it as a consolation prize for being sent away.

A fae was never parted from their weapon, except by death.

I bowed my head, and next to me, so did my best mates. I should've known that they would've kept their promise to never let go of my wings.

Dizzy, my heartbeat raced. Cold flooded me, as I sensed the green-skinned ogres circling closer with their swords raised. The largest guard caught me looking and winked.

Sadistic bastard.

The ogres' stench of mud and rotting flesh hit me, and I gagged.

Wells pulled out a graduation scroll from his pocket. "You're my flock of hundred wicked boys. I've spent a decade proving to the Court that there are more effective methods to control and curb rebellious impulses of youth than brutality. On the name of the Queen, reform now and graduate. Return as perfect bonded partners and proud members of the Court. Your Forest Fae heritage has been washed clean. You need no longer even remember—"

Radley touched the scroll, and his magic burned it to ash. It disintegrated in Wells' hand.

The crowd snickered.

"Well said," Felix muttered.

"I forgot once who I was," my voice was steadier than I expected, when all I could see was the memory of Quinn's hurt expression at the moment that I hadn't taken his wing, "and I won't again. I'm a Forest Fae, and I'll die as one."

"Then you'll die," Wells said, icily.

The ogre booted me in the back, holding me down, as he pressed his sword to my neck. I hissed, as its cold iron pressed against my skin.

Iron burned fae. *Didn't they think that decapitation was enough of a punishment?* Tears prickled my eyes at the smarting agony. But then, this was what they'd done to my brothers.

Wells truly was sick to choose this as his method of killing me.

Clack — clack — clack.

Wells' polished boots stepped around me. I hated that his boots would be the last thing that I saw.

"It tires me that you could even ruin my attempt to scare you into behaving. I'm not going to kill you." *Wait...what in Belenus' name did he mean?* When the sword eased at my neck, why did that scare me more than anything so far? "This was just the mock run of your graduation."

I sat up too fast in my outrage, and Radley caught me, before I toppled over.

"Like a mock exam…?" I growled. "Wonderful. Really, I didn't need the practice."

Wells clasped his hands smartly behind his back, and his smile was so malicious that it made me shiver. "Oh, but *I* did. Now I know that you Lords will sacrifice yourself as long as you're *free*, and your tribe have *choice*. This is your last week in the Wicked Reform School. It's my final chance to break you, and luckily for me, I have some interesting new methods." I groaned: *brilliant*. "Saturday is the first of May, the start of summer, and your *true* Day of the Wicked. You may have given up your Claim of Lordship, but if you're not reformed, then your entire tribe will be judged wicked. Just like you did with your brothers, you'll watch as they're executed. Only after they all lie slaughtered, will you get the chance to die as well."

"Wait, you *can't*." I staggered to stand, but Wells shoved me back onto my knees with a *crack*.

"I'm Head of your House: *I can*. How do you like being pranked for once?" *Did he truly just claim that staging our deaths was karmic prank revenge…?* Wells' lips twitched as he glanced at Felix. "Are you certain that you're not in fact jinxed?"

When Felix launched himself at Wells, Wells stumbled back. Radley caught Felix, pulling him into a tight embrace. I curled my wings around myself.

How had I allowed myself to be tricked?

Court Dictate 307: *Emotions are your curse, and a blessing to your enemy.*

I'd shown Wells just how he could hurt me. He'd tried to teach me for years to mask my true self.

Well, didn't I feel the idiot.

But still, at least a Forest idiot, rather than a Court idiot.

Yet now, I only had a week before the true graduation ceremony, where I'd no longer be merely sacrificing my own life, but risking every Forest Fae's execution.

CHAPTER TWO

Wicked Reform School, House of Fae, Orchard
Monday 26th April

I fell back onto the warm grass, as my swan shifter, Apollo, crushed me beneath him. He hissed, and his wings spread out, pinning my arms to the ground. His graceful neck that was trapped by an emerald collar, which stopped him from shifting back into human form, wound against mine. I breathed the scent of his feathers, which were sweet and intoxicating like wild daffodils.

My chest rose and fell rapidly. For the decade that I'd taken him as mine after my brother's banishment, we'd played these games, but he'd never looked like he meant to do anything but cuddle me before.

This afternoon, under the spreading branches of

the magical All Spells Apple Tree, I wasn't certain whether he was furious that I hadn't warned him about the graduation ceremony or that I'd refused to reform.

Probably both.

"On my wing, if I swear that I'm sorry, will you stop with the *I'm going to peck your balls* glare?" I winced.

Perhaps, I shouldn't have given him that idea?

I drew in my breath, as Apollo shifted. But then he grunted and rested his head against my throat.

I stroked the downy softness of his feathers. "You're my brother in the wing as well, and I didn't mean to scare you," I murmured. "Where are the cygnets?"

My friends each had a swan shifter that lived with them in the House of Fae as well, although theirs were only young: two sisters, Odile and Lil Swan. Radley's shifter had an urban edge, even though she sounded like she should be in nursery. But she did a brilliant rap about life on the wrong side of the pond.

"*I don't know, My Lord,*" Apollo's voice had a soft Scottish lilt and wound telepathically into my mind. "*The Countess took them away for training, and we all know what <u>that</u> means. You left me here alone, not knowing if you were dead...*"

I shuddered, grasping him tighter.

The Countess Pond was Deputy Head in the House of Fae. She was also a Court Fae, who'd been our tutor as Hostage Lords. The Queen had wanted me to bond with her, until Quinn had tried to rescue me. I was sure that the Countess had followed me to the Wicked Reform School out of revenge at the humiliation the rebellion had caused her.

I'd rather be dead, than live bonded to her. But Apollo didn't need to know that.

I soothed my fingers through his feathers. "*Shh, I'm alive. No one can separate a Fae Lord from his beloved swan. Forgive me…?*"

But what would I do on Saturday, when the graduation or execution would be real? Our swan shifters would be left behind in the hands of the Countess and Wells, and what would they do to them?

I sighed, turning to stare out across the miniature English farm that Wells had brought with him and seeded from the Court around the grounds of the House of Fae like a slice of Court life. Actually, not Wells: *us Rebels in Horticulture Class.*

It was Horticulture now, and fae were stripped to their waist, sweltering under the sun. They tilled, hoed, and planted the ranks of vegetables. There was no shade and their tired wings drooped. I could just glimpse the glimmering blue of Swan Pond at the far side. The silence was oppressive, apart from the *clink* of tools and the quiet *drone* of bumblebees.

Wells himself sat underneath a gazebo that shaded him, sipping on a coffee with affected boredom, whilst he was fanned by a fae. His black swan shifter, Lincoln, sat snootily on Wells' lap but his gaze glittered maliciously.

The garden was enchanted. It wasn't controlled by the seasons, but by Wells. He could produce any plant, whenever he pleased, in order to create magical properties to add to potions.

Weren't we just the lucky ones?

Although, I'd heard stories about deadly Gardening Lessons in the rest of the Houses that were more about murdering students than reforming them, so maybe we *were*.

It shook me that sometimes, I believed Wells when he said that he was *protecting* us from the rest of the school.

Yet even though he didn't want to slaughter us each lesson (my expectations really had been lowered), Wells intended to *break* us as much as the soil. He wished to tame the earth, like he'd tame the Forest Fae.

I snorted. *Was cuddling a swan part of his lesson plan?*

"Aye, I forgive you," Apollo's voice shook, *"but when your daft arse prepares to die on the Day of the Wicked, don't leave me behind with Wells next time. Kill me first."*

"Thanks for the input." I clenched my jaw, struggling to keep my caresses gentle down his neck. "But on the other hand, not a flying fae in hell's chance, you overdramatic swan."

Felix whistled. "I'd listen to him, Apollo. That's his stern voice."

Apollo turned up his beak. "*Overdramatic but beautiful*."

Felix threw himself down on the grass next to us, dropping a wicker basket by his feet. He drew out a miniature book from his pocket and shook it, which enlarged it to its proper size. He shot me a cocky grin (his easy magic was impressive but nope, I wasn't telling him that), then settled back to read.

I've spent as much time dragging a book out of Felix's hands, as the Countess has spent it pushing one into mine. I'd never touch *this* one, however, because it'd been given to him by his brother…the one who'd been executed alongside my own.

"You're so smart," I said. "Do you know how hard that makes me?"

When Felix startled, I chuckled.

"And this is *my* stern voice." Radley shot us both a glare as he took off with a ripple of muscle to hover amongst the branches of the All Spells Apple Tree. "It's our duty as Lords to pick these psycho fruits. Instead, you're snuggling a swan."

"Guilty." I grinned.

"*Snuggling a beautiful swan*," Apollo muttered.

"Why is it that you rascally blue-blooded fae always leave off the <u>sacred</u>?"

Radley ignored Apollo, who was doing the swan equivalent of pouting, and pointed at Felix. "What's your excuse?"

Felix stretched. "Oh, I hate getting my hands dirty. If the Duke of Wells intends to break us with manual labor, then I'm just protecting myself."

Radley banged his head against the branch. "By escaping into some fairy tale…?"

"Shakespeare's "A Midsummer's Night's Dream"," Felix supplied with a helpful smile that wasn't fooling me. "I can't decide if this non-magical bard was actually captured once by a Court Fae and wanted to take revenge on them in play form. Maybe I should write a book about Wells…?"

I grimaced. "Brilliant idea. Then we can at least kill him off on paper. Anyway, most fae have just as messed-up a view of the non-magical."

I glanced across the farm and out over the school. In the distance, the blue-haze of mountains shimmered.

What did humans think was hidden away up here in the forests and mountains?

I bet the non-magical reckoned that the academy was a cult.

Radley flew higher into the branches of the vast apple tree. Even though it was spring, ripe apples grew amongst the delicate pink blossoms. Apples grew all year round on the All Spells Apple Tree and many different types together: glossy green, pink-and-green striped, smooth pink, and deep red. Each one had a spell woven into it, but you never knew what it was until you took a bite…

Yeah, like I ever willingly took a bite.

This unnatural tree was grown from an apple taken from the orchard at Court. It made my balls want to shrink back into my body.

Radley plucked a scarlet apple and dropped it into the basket.

Thunk.

I winced. "That'll bruise."

Radley glowered. "I'll bruise something else in a minute. Get your lazy fae ass up here and help."

"*Pfft*, my ass is notoriously bad at picking apples without the rest of my noble self. And when I'll be dead in four days, why spend them working?"

Silence.

I peered around at my friends who were all now glaring at me. "Too soon to joke?"

"It's not as if the Court Fae haven't been trying to kill us for years." Radley's smile made me shiver.

I trailed my fingers across Apollo's downy feathers. "On Belenus' prick, it's different than before. Can't you feel it? They truly mean it this time."

I wished that I could kiss away the worried frown

that creased Felix's brow, even though I'd been the one to put it there. *Should I've lied?* But I'd always told my best mates the truth before.

It didn't matter how we schemed against others; we were each other's truth.

A second, green apple tumbled into the basket.

Thunk.

Followed by a third, pink apple.

Thunk.

As if in protest, when Radley reached for the next one, the tree yanked the branch to the side. The bees that'd been buzzing between clusters of apple buds swarmed at Radley, stinging his hand. He howled, flying backward, but the tree caught him in its branches, slamming him against its scaly trunk.

Pink blossoms rained down on Felix, Apollo, and me like confetti. I laughed (breaking **Court Dictate 506**: *Never laugh, whilst working*). Then I plucked a petal out of Felix's hair. I placed it back, as he studied me with dancing eyes, because he looked beautiful like he'd been crowned.

I shivered with the desire to kiss him. I'd almost lost him today…*almost lost all of them.* I rested my forehead against Felix's, and petals tumbled from my head to his and across Apollo's feathers.

This was what the Court Fae would never understand. The power of such small moments.

The battle for love, rather than false bonds, had

started the Love Rebellion. I didn't know how yet, but I could sense it burning through me that it'd be our salvation now.

If not, it was the only thing worth dying for.

Radley struggled, before collapsing against the tree. Then he cleared his throat. "*Ehm*, I *might* be trapped up here. Did I ever let your pampered ass off working just because you're the leader?"

I smirked. "You shouldn't have upset the poor tree." The All Spells Apple Tree sighed, and the branch loosened around Radley. If I waited for Radley to play nice, then he'd be trapped up there until nightfall. Wait, make that *all week*. "Anyway, I am working. I'm scheming."

Radley rolled his eyes. "Snuggling."

Apollo preened, curling his wing more firmly around me.

I nodded. "Snuggling and scheming. But since I *was* almost brutally executed today, I need the touch."

Touch was essential to fae. To Court Fae, it meant hierarchy and dominance. To Forest Fae, it was love, family, and brotherhood.

Apollo's feathers ruffled in distress. *"Don't say that like nobody would miss your elegant behind. I wept all morning thinking that..."*

I smoothed Apollo's feathers. "*Hush*," I whispered, "I'm still here." Gently, I pushed Apollo off me, even though he hissed his protest, attempting to cling tighter. "I have a damsel to rescue who's tied to a tree, before a dragon turns up for the sacrifice."

Radley's growl made the hairs stand up on the back of my neck. *Yeah, I was in for a spanking.* Perhaps, I shouldn't let him down just yet…?

Felix snickered.

"You're no help." I booted petals into Felix's face, and he spluttered, throwing them back at me: *blossom fight.* Then I sauntered to the base of the tree. Sweat slicked my chest; it stuck my coat to my back. I slipped my arms around the broad trunk and rested my cheek against it like I was slow dancing.

"Who's a gorgeous hunk of wood then?" I licked along the grooves, which tasted tangy. The sweet scent of the apples smothered me. "I love the way you taste."

Behind me, Felix gagged.

He could only judge me, when he made sweet love to a tree in order to free his friend.

Now that was brotherhood.

The branches loosened even further around Radley.

"I just…" *Come on, use your honeyed tongue and no snickering Quincey,* "can't hold it together around apples as fresh and round as yours."

When the tree let Radley go with a gasp of delight, Radley landed on me.

Of course he did.

Perhaps, Wells was right that Felix was really a jinx…?

"Well, I don't know about the tree but I'm turned on now. I'm claiming Quince tonight." Felix's pupils were dilated, and to my shock, he'd even shrunk and pocketed his book.

He must be really serious.

I lay with the air knocked out of me beneath Radley, staring up at him with startled eyes. His chuckle was low and dangerous, as he sprawled on top of me like he'd arranged this to happen. Then he shifted, rubbing our crotches together (he was hard because he was *always* hard), and pushing me more firmly into the dirt.

"He's mine *right now*." Radley's lips curled around his gleaming teeth. "You look good beneath me."

"The words that you're struggling for are: Thank you, Your Lordship, for rescuing my unworthy damsel wings."

Radley cocked his head, as one strong hand crept up to pin my wrists above my head, and the other worked to undo my belt.

Okay, that didn't look like *a thank you*. Why hadn't I learned never to tease a psycho fae?

Oh yeah, because it was fun…

When Radley's hand slipped into my pants, teasing at my cock and balls, I bit my lip. "The words that I'm struggling for are: You're going to regret calling *me* the damsel."

Good job me at pissing off the only Fae Lord who the other Houses truly *should* fear. I'd watched Radley take on a lion shifter, demon, and a zombie in our Fighting Lessons all by himself and be the only one left standing.

Although, if pissing him off led to the firm way that he was now stroking my prick, then I was all for it.

I shuddered, relaxing into his hold.

Then I flushed. *Wait…could Wells see what was happening?* I was already in disgrace but I wasn't an exhibitionist and being wanked off in public was a step too far. Plus, Wells would probably have a heart attack.

Wait, now we were back onto the *positives*.

Felix crawled closer, shielding me from the view of the other fae by stretching out his wings. He always protected me. I smiled at him, even as I panted, battling not to arch. Radley twisted his hand along my hardening prick in the way that he knew I loved.

A decade as the only male house and unable to trust the women in the rest of this prison was too long to go without *some* relief.

I shivered, and a scent caught at my mind of hot ginger: *the golden-haired Professor Succubus from the graduation ceremony.*

All of a sudden, I was lost in her again.

My prick pulsed, and my balls ached. I imagined that she was here with us in her flaming white dress and with her soft smile. Then that her small hand joined Radley's large one around my prick.

Perhaps, she was just a *little* disapproving like I hadn't handed in my assignment and now she'd punish me, along with the pleasure…

Where'd you like this naughty Lord to bend over, ma'am?

I gasped, and my eyelids fluttered shut.

On the Fair Shining One, I needed her…

Radley's hand squeezed my balls, and I hissed.

"It's rude to not be entirely present, when I'm putting in all this work. Who's attracted your attention?" Radley's eyes narrowed, and his thumb swiped warningly over my balls. He knew me too well. "Drain the gold from my wings, it's not one of those *fish hugger mermaids*?"

Jealousy alert…

I swallowed nervously, as Felix leaned over me and licked my neck, before kissing up my jawline. "Don't be greedy, Quince, share your fantasies."

I gave a sly smile. "I really can't wait to do that, if Rads would just remove his fingers from around my balls, so I'm certain that he won't bust them. They're the only pair that I have."

Radley grunted but returned to stroking my prick.

Here goes… "She's a succubus."

Felix's brow furrowed. "Who is?"

"The new professor and my fantasy bond. I saw her just before we were mock executed."

Both Radley and Felix stilled.

Then Radley leaned down, so that his lips grazed mine on each word, "You know better than to fantasize about potential bonds. Plus, there aren't any succubi staff, and even if there were, why would you bring her into this…?" He twisted his hand, and I gasped into his mouth. Our lips touched, and he kissed me with as much passion as if he could claim me and vanish all thoughts of the succubus.

Felix sank his sharp teeth into my collarbone at the same time, and the delicious pain added to the sensations that were tearing me apart and remaking me at the same time.

Felix was a biter: he loved to mark me.

With difficulty, I pulled back. "Convincing as that argument is, clearly a succubus *is* now working for the House of Fae. It's the will of the forest, I can sense it. And you didn't see how—"

"Hot she was?" Felix sat back on his knees, crossing his arms defensively.

"*Kind* she was," I retorted. Felix looked at me, shocked. "It's astounding that at last they've employed someone who doesn't want us hurt or dead."

"If that's true," Felix played with the hilt of his scimitar, "then maybe we've discovered our Save the Fae Scheme. No one else in this hellhole would care to put into that fund but…what if this *new* professor would…?"

I grinned. Could I help it if my malevolent side was shining through? I wasn't my brother, Quinn, but I had brilliant mates. Together, we'd find a way to take on the challenge of saving my tribe.

A new and innocent professor could be the perfect mark.

"You all talk too much," Radley growled.

Radley crushed his lips to mine again, as his hand rubbed across the head of my prick. Then he edged his thumbnail into the slit, and I came in my pants. My cry was swallowed by his kiss. He stroked me through the orgasm, until I was oversensitive and squirming.

"Mean fae." Felix bumped Radley's shoulder.

Finally, Radley let go of my prick with a final swirl along its head, as if to be certain that I wouldn't forget him.

How could he think that I would? No bond would ever break what we had, right?

Then he slid his hand out of my pants with a satisfied smirk.

I rested my forehead against his and raised my wing to touch Felix's knee. "We live for our brothers," I whispered.

Radley and Felix's eyes widened, before their expressions softened with desperate understanding, as they chorused, "We live for our brothers."

Then Radley muttered, "Just be careful. I don't trust succubi, and she won't trust you."

Felix brushed his hand nervously through his hair. "Everything that I've read makes their Court sound as frightening as the Fae Court. They don't mate for life, however, but take multiple incubi bonded. But the male partners still have no choice. What if she just wants you as another one of her harem?"

My fantasy of Professor Succubus exploded. *Why did that hurt so much?* I'd hoped that she was differ-ent. I should've known that I could only trust my two friends.

Oh, and my sacred swan shifter, of course. I'd better not forget the *sacred*.

Apollo bustled over to join our cuddle pile, forcing his head on its long neck between Radley and me.

I laughed, and Radley snarled but allowed Apollo to lay over me in a feathery blanket.

"No fair, you always sneak your sexy times when I can't join in. I hate being trapped like this. Couldn't you at least have waited until you took my collar off tonight?" He grumbled.

I ran my finger over Apollo's collar that stopped him shifting back into our lover; I wished that I could remove it now. "We'll just have to make tonight special then, won't we?"

"If you're lucky," Felix winked.

Even now, however, the memory of Professor Succubus ached through me like she'd been etched into my bones. The way that she'd *shared* the intense moment, when I'd believed I was about to die, *had* bonded us but in a way I'd never imagined possible. It wasn't a planned bond, but one that called to something deep inside me.

How could I pretend that I wasn't desperate to see her again?

Perhaps, this was the first lie that I'd ever told my mates. All our lives, we'd feared *bonding*. How could I tell them that I might've found mine?

Despite that, however, in the shade of the All Spells Apple Tree in the bright spring morning, with my lovers and friends in my arms, it was possible to forget that this was a prison and we were under order of execution.

Yet when I caught sight of the three bruised apples in the basket (which should've been full by now but failing Horticulture wasn't high on my *regrets* list… okay, maybe I should get on with writing that list), I knew that I had as little time left as those apples.

I assure you, that was a sobering thought.

All of a sudden, a buzzing grew above my head,

louder than the bees. I stiffened, squinting up through the light, which shafted through the branches.

Wings glittered in between the blossoms, along with the tips of spears.

We were being hunted.

Radley twisted around to cover me, and Apollo hissed, but it was too late.

There were other deadly paranormals, who lived on these lands that'd been stolen. The woods had belonged to the myrmidons for centuries before the Wicked Reform School had even been built. The myrmidons were fierce warriors with many different tribes just like the fae, and as we'd encroached on their territory, *they wanted it back.*

Honor dictated that they fought with the Fae Lords. No matter how I'd tried to broker peace, ever since we'd arrived a decade ago, we'd been at war with them.

At least this tribe *had* honor. The ones who lived deeper into the woods were used in general classes, which at least Wells helped us avoid as much as possible, to murder students. I shuddered at the number of shifters and vampires who'd been flayed.

Then my eyes widened, as the myrmidons attacked.

CHAPTER THREE

Wicked Reform School, House of Fae, Orchard
Monday 26th April

The myrmidons with transparent wings that glistened in the sun, like a wave of armed insects, dived out of the All Spells Apple Tree. The leader, who glittered purple and orange, narrowed his oval eyes and shook his floppy ears.

The tiny bastard was calling me out.

Perhaps, I shouldn't have pranked him by hosting a rave in *his* section of the wood last weekend.

Okay, I now had Number One on my Regrets List.

Felix rolled over, sheltering behind his book, as the creatures landed on top of him, battering at the cover. Apollo reared back, flaring his wings and hissing. The myrmidons circled him with sneers but they didn't dare to attack.

Don't let them work out that my swan shifter was bluffing...

Apollo would lose in a fight against a kitten. In fact, he *had*.

"When you're ready, guys, I'm over here." I waved, stretching with a sensual wriggle. "This is all really exciting. What are you going to do with me now that you've caught me? I mean, it's not like I haven't been taken hostage before. Come on, make it interesting."

When the Chief Myrmidon launched his spear at me, I yelped (breaking **Court Dictate 707**: *never show emotion in the face of danger*). I twisted to the side, and the spear whistled past my ear, *twanging* into the grass. A new spear magically grew out of his hand like a vine.

My pulse pounded, and my breath hitched.

There was *interesting*, and then there was simple ill-manners.

By my wing, this meant war.

The tips of the myrmidons' spears were dipped in hallucinogenic poison. The myrmidons weren't messing around.

It was lucky that we'd been allowed to hold onto our scimitars within the school because it was such strong tradition not to part a fae from their weapon. It hurt to know that the fae prince who'd tried to help me at Court was suffering in the English reform school, Rebel Academy. Yet it'd *crushed* me, when I'd heard that in Rebel Academy they were even crueler and had taken Prince Lysander's sword away from him.

It would've wrecked him.

Radley, on the other hand, never needed his scimitar either in a fight or to wreck somebody.

Radley launched himself up; I forgot how hot he was when he blazed into protective mode. "You're dead, bug-face." When he crooked his finger at the leader, the warrior paled. *I didn't even know that myrmidons could do that.* "If you're brave enough to ambush us, why not come over here?"

The Chief Myrmidon shook his head.

Radley's dark grin grew. "Why not? I only want to be friends…with your insides."

There was the psycho who I loved.

The Chief Myrmidon squeaked.

"You shall not defeat Shakespeare," Felix proclaimed, whacking the divebombing myrmidons with his book.

Radley winked at Felix, before they both transformed in a spray of glitter into their fae form: large white butterflies with wings that glistened like polished metal.

My breath caught, and I pushed myself to my knees.

On my feathers, they were dazzling. They looked like white apple blossom amongst the pink.

Why couldn't I...just once...transform alongside them?

The familiar burning built in my chest, until I struggled for breath, as I fought to transform.

Just once...if this was my last week...just this once...

I hated being marked out as different to every other fae. *If I ever managed to become a true fae, would it kill me?*

Radley and Felix fluttered between the myrmidons, nipping at them with their sharp teeth. The myrmidons scattered with terrified squeaks.

My lungs closed up, and I gasped.

Bright Belenus, I couldn't breathe...

I slammed my fist against the ground in frustration. What kind of leader (or even fae) was I, when I couldn't transform and fight wing by wing?

Apollo nudged his head against mine. *"My Lord, stop it. Why do you always push yourself like this? Being different, doesn't make you weak. Will you leave off trying to kill yourself for one hour at least? Please, for me?"* If he'd been in his human form, he'd have been weeping. *"Right, like I don't know what it is not to be able to shift as I please. Should I break both my wings to show you how little I care that you can't fly the same as the others? For your sake, I'll never fly again."*

Brilliant. I'd incited a swan to grand acts of martyrdom.

I gripped Apollo by the wing like that'd stop him running into the tree and cracking his own wing bones (okay, I was never imagining *that* again), and gave up trying to transform. The burning died down inside me, until my breathing steadied. I slumped over Apollo, resting my head on his feathery back.

"Wing breaking may be romantic in the swan world," I whispered into his feathers because it was easier than saying the words to his beak (and how much did I wish that he was in his human form right now), "but firstly, I adore your flying. You should never clip your wings for anyone's sake (even mine). And secondly, I'd rather that you simply said *I love you.*"

Above my head, I heard Radley and Felix's tiny war cries as they battled the myrmidons. A battered insect warrior tumbled out of the air to land by my nose, and I flicked him away with malicious joy.

"*I love your daft self.*" Apollo's words were soft and careful. "*Just as you are.*"

Court Dictate 18: *Tears are nothing but drops of shame.*

My lips curled into a smile. "That'll work."

Then something pricked me in the ass.

I glanced over my shoulder in shock to see the Chief Myrmidon perched on the hollow of my lower back with his spear balanced dangerously on my ass.

For the first time in the spring heat, I was glad for the thickness of my coat and trousers, which protected my skin from the poison.

Felix and Radley hovered mid-air, fluttering their wings in agitation.

I arched my brow. "Well played, my buggy nemesis, but this isn't over."

The Chief Myrmidon twirled his spear with a smug smile (he was just showing off now), before flicking me off.

There was a reason that we'd been at war for a decade.

When I spun to grab him, he snickered, whizzing back into the air.

"Have you forgotten that this is Horticulture class and not Exterminating Insects for Idiots?" Wells' cold voice boomed across the farm.

I flinched, pushing myself to my feet. Felix and Radley transformed back in a spray of gold.

"*Shoo*," I hissed at the myrmidons, who'd frozen in fear; they knew by now that us Forest Fae were only playfighting, but the Court Fae would wipe them out like the other tribes who they'd conquered, "unless you want Wells to serve Myrm Soup for supper."

The myrmidons were our enemy, but no one deserved to be Wells' target.

The Chief Myrmidon waved his spear defiantly, before retreating with his warriors into the branches. I wished that I could follow their glittering path between the apples.

But I couldn't even fly.

I glanced across at Wells, who sat frozen in his chair. Behind him, towered the golden turret of the House of Fae. Our *prison* for the last decade appeared to have been modeled on our burnished wings. It was as pretty as the rest of the grounds. The Queen's crest of two swans bowing their heads in a courtship dance, which would mate them for life, was hung above the arched gateway. Its thatched eaves were a quaint joke, when if you looked closely enough, the turret had no windows.

The House of Fae wore a glamour of serenity. But underneath, torrents raged.

Wells was no different.

Wells pretended to find the depths of his coffee fascinating. "Lord Spring, would you hazard a guess at how many Dictates you've so far broken this afternoon."

He'd been watching us...? Of course he had.

In turn, I pretended to count on my fingers. "Four...five...does the rude limerick that I thought up about the Queen and the skunk shifter count because that was only in my head…?"

Crack — Wells' hand tightened so hard around his cup that he broke it.

Coolly, Wells threw the cup to the side. When Lincoln hissed at me, Apollo hissed back in a *swan off.*

I swallowed.

So, insulting the Queen was traitor territory and would've probably led to my execution inside the Court. Yet Wells hadn't raised to the bait. He'd worked out how to hurt me, and I still didn't know what truly hurt him.

Was there even a way to wreck him like he intended to wreck us?

Unexpectedly, I met the haughty gaze of the fae, Beau, who'd paused in his fanning of Wells. I flushed, as warmth coiled through me. Beau was ethereal, pale, and the hottest fae that I'd ever seen. He was also a mystery. He was the only Court Fae who wasn't a staff member. Sometimes, he visited the House of Fae and then, he was treated just the same as if he was a Forest Fae and a student.

Yet he never spoke to or touched any of us.

Beau was emotionless, poised, and perfectly behaved. In fact, the snooty bastard was everything that the Forest Fae weren't.

What crime was so bad that he'd been sent here?

Yet it didn't matter because like the rest of us, Beau was trapped now, and sweat plastered his hair to his forehead. He was ashen and swaying. My brow furrowed with concern. Fae weren't meant to live in the cold or the hot. All the seasons here were too harsh for us compared to the mildness of England.

Exile was crueler than merely losing our home.

Wells elbowed Beau, and he started fanning the Head of House again. "Twenty-nine Dictates," Wells answered like I hadn't made the crack about the Queen, and he hadn't had to dispose of a corpse cup. "I taught most of them to you myself, along with the Countess. I don't think you appreciate how enlightened I am. All of you," the other fae glanced up from their work nervously, "should be grateful that I employ such gentle methods compared to the other professors. Hard work in the fresh air will teach you to act like *proper* fae. If you can manage that in this false court, then I'll know that my flock of hundred are ready to be allowed to fly into the real one."

"But by my feathers, *we* won't be real," I insisted.

Wells waved his hand like that was a small matter. "Do you know what the Queen asked when she approached the Wicked Reform School to establish our House here?"

My guts clenched. "Let me think…"

"Don't try too hard will you now, *hmm*? It'd be a terrible shame if your brain exploded, before I had a chance to try out my new methods of reform this week."

Less than a week to the ceremony, and Wells was finally getting creative.

Beau's gaze darted to mine again, before he staggered. I took a step forward, but then he straightened, tightening his hold around the swan-feather fan.

My jaw clenched. "Did she ask if they'd cut the prices and throw in some spa days if we did our own gardening?"

Wells smiled. "As the swan swims, we should've had you as lead negotiator. In fact, the Queen asked the Dean if he thought that an all-male House, something that had never been done before, could be tamed. Despite what you still appear to think, she doesn't want you *broken*. She has fae who are experts in that beneath her own Court." I shivered, remembering the screams. The Fae Court was a place of nightmares. "Instead, she desires me to train your emotions, until there's no rebellion left in you. Does it shock you that all she hungers for is your undying love?"

I wanted to hurl...

All of a sudden, Beau's fan clattered to the grass, and he swayed. He grasped onto Wells, but Wells batted Beau away in disgust.

Beau passed out with heat stroke, hitting the ground hard.

Radley growled, and Felix looped his arm around my waist in distress.

I tried to launch myself forward to help Beau because Court Fae or not, he was still hurt. Wells smartly pushed himself up, however, straightening out his uniform. Lincoln swooped off his lap, landing on the grass. To my shock, Wells snatched Beau by the hair and dragged him to the water trough.

"You're a disgrace, boy," Wells sneered, dunking Beau beneath the grimy water.

What in the winged heavens was Wells doing?

Our Head had disciplined fae over the last decade, but he'd always done it with military precision, rather than this brutality.

It wasn't Beau's fault that he'd been overworked in the heat.

At last, Beau spluttered awake, choking and coughing on the water. His wings beat weakly. Wells yanked him out casually by the scruff of the neck and then shoved him back under again.

Would Beau drown?

CHAPTER FOUR

**Wicked Reform School, House of Fae, Orchard
Monday 26th April**

My eyes narrowed, as I watched Wells hold Beau's head under the water again. Beau's hands clawed at the grass, and his wings flapped. The sun beat against the two Court Fae, lighting them up, so that I didn't miss a single struggle or choked convulsion.

"I have to stop this. He's drowning him," I hissed.

My hand slid to the hilt of my scimitar, and Felix's hold on me tightened

"It's a punishment for making Court Fae look weak." Radley's voice was tight.

"Really great job Wells is doing on proving the non-emotion rule because right now, it's *Wells* who's lit up with a thousand ugly emotions." My lips thinned. "It's fascinating that the Court want to suppress the good but are okay with the bad. After all, they sent away their own *prince* to the Rebel Academy because he wouldn't execute our brothers as rebels, and that's about the only school that's more deadly than this one."

The morning that the Queen had ordered my family to be murdered, the only thing that'd stopped me from hating all Court Fae (and honestly, allowed me to have compassion for Beau), was Prince Lysander. He'd refused to prove himself to his Guardian and Queen by wielding the executioner's sword.

That'd taken balls, especially as I knew how brainwashed Court Fae were.

In turn, the Prince had been deposed and sent away to the Rebel Academy as punishment.

Court Fae could be rebels as well.

I hoped that Prince Lysander was okay. If we both survived, one day I'd thank him. It was strange to be in debt to a Court Fae prince. It made me all squirmy inside.

Wells raised Beau's head out of the water again. Beau was soaked and shivered. His eyes were glassy.

"Please, my apologies," Beau gasped.

When Wells prepared to duck Beau back under again, Felix whispered, "Let's see if we're lucky…"

I blinked. "What…?"

Suddenly, a banshee wailing broke out from the opposite side of the farm. I winced, slamming my hands over my ears. The fae groaned, dropping to their knees.

"Blasted magical carrots. You need to be gentle with them. Who's been upsetting them again?" Wells demanded, dropping Beau in a crumpled puddle.

Wells strode away between the trees towards the carrot patch. Lincoln followed at his heels.

I twisted in Felix's arms, until we were nose to nose; his smug grin was deserved. "You're claiming that was your Fortune Magic…?"

He nodded. "That earns a kiss, right?"

I licked across the seam of Felix's lips, before pushing my tongue into his mouth and twining it with his. I settled into his safe scent of old books and ink. His body was as familiar to me as my own. He moaned, kissing back with equal joy.

Then I pulled back, dragging him after me. "Come on," I called to Radley, as I strode towards the farm, "we have a drowned fae to save. Apollo wait for us."

Radley swaggered next to me. "Are you sure…?"

"He's a snooty Court Fae…? Yeah, I am. But I'm still helping him."

"Would you help the Queen if she was about to drown too?" Radley demanded.

"Theoretical moral questions, how fun." The tips

of my ears heated at the glares of the other fae, as we passed. I was used to being seen as the pampered Hostage Lord who wasn't truly one of the Forest Fae any longer. But *outcast*, wow, that smarted. "If the Queen was drowning, I'd yell for one of her own people to save her. Then we'd see how *real* their loyalty was."

Radley snorted. "She would be so dead."

"Ah, such a sweet dream." Felix sighed.

I stared down at Beau, who was gasping and pushing the hair out of his eyes. He stared back like I was there to finish off what Wells had started. It wasn't like I'd shown him any kindness before. I'd gone out of my way to ignore the Court Fae.

"Time to catch a ride into the shade." I grinned.

Beau's eyes widened, and he scrabbled backwards.

Sometimes, I forgot how malevolent my grin was.

Radley merely grunted, before he grabbed Beau and threw him over his shoulder like a…particularly handsome…sack of potatoes.

"I insist that you let me down." Beau's cold voice reminded me so strongly of Wells that I had to bite my tongue hard enough to taste blood not to tell Radley to do what Beau wanted, as long as he dropped him on his head.

Why was I helping a Court Fae again?

I led our procession back to the All Spells Apple Tree with Beau attempting to look like he'd chosen to sprawl in a damp fireman's lift over Radley's shoulder.

When we reached the shade, Apollo flapped around us in nurse mode. Radley dropped Beau far more gently than I'd been expecting.

Instantly, Beau huddled against the trunk with his wings curled around himself. His eyes were like olive green pools in his pale face.

You'd have thought that *we'd* been the bullies holding him under the water.

I lowered myself to my knees in front of him. His breathing was too shallow, and he was worryingly pallid.

"Sexy as you are, I'm only going to take off your wet coat now to help you dry out." I slipped my hands into Beau's coat, and he flinched.

When I pulled the coat off Beau's shoulders, revealing alabaster skin, he panted. I brushed a stream of water away with the pad of my thumb, and he arched like I was stroking his prick.

I knew the signs: *he was touch starved.*

How long had it been since anyone had touched him kindly? Fae couldn't survive without touch. It was torture to be denied it. I knew because I'd been punished like that as a kid.

I crushed Beau to my chest in the tightest hug that I could manage, before I could stop myself. My wings curled around him. He smelled of the sweetest peaches. My mouth became moist, and my tongue darted out, desperate to lick along his neck.

Beau pushed me back, and his gaze was anguished. "Do *not* touch me."

Since when did a fae not want to be touched?

It couldn't even be the dick Court rules on touch hierarchy because I was a Marquess, which meant that I had dominance.

I frowned. "I mean, you're only shaking from touch deprivation, but sure, I won't *touch* your haughty ass. I wouldn't want to dirty you with my Forest Fae hands. And you're welcome, by the way."

"You didn't have to help me." Beau looked down, as his hands balled in his lap.

"Nope, I didn't." I caught his startled gaze with mine. "But that's what it truly means to be a fae and not…" I gestured at the ranks of the neat farm and the gleaming House of Fae beyond. "*This* is make-believe. It only pretends to reform us. Your Court isn't civilized, and the truth is that if I give in on the day of Wicked, we'd only be going from one prison to another."

Apollo shouldered his way onto Beau's lap. To my surprise, Beau allowed it, stroking Apollo's wings.

Apollo preened. "*All he needed was a beauty like me.*"

I fought to smother my smile.

Beau cocked his head, and his hair tumbled into

his eyes; I longed to brush it behind his ears. "*Life* is a prison, you know."

"Oh, you're a dark one, aren't you?" When Beau blushed, I leaned closer. "You only think that because you've never experienced the wild joy of the forest or the non-magical."

"What could possibly be so joyous?" His voice was curious in a way that I hadn't expected, rather than contemptuous.

"Music, dancing, and *love* for starters…" My malevolent grin was back, and I couldn't hold in the thrumming wave of magic that pinned Beau to the tree.

He shivered at the same time as me.

The non-magical world was all around us in this reform school. There was even a House of Almost Humans just across from us. They held rowdy parties with music like I'd never heard before, which blared through their windows. It'd taken a combination of Felix's Fortune Magic and my own sweet talking of one of their Prefects (he had a thing for fae, and I'd never turn down a wing stroking), to sneak across and steal an iPod.

Apart from my sword, I treasured the music trapped inside that tiny machine more than anything but my mates. With my magic, I could free it for everyone.

When I slid my finger across the iPod, Tricky's

"Wash My Soul" wound around the All Spells Apple Tree with a hypnotic and agonizing rhythm. My fingers clawed into my knees, as inside I writhed.

With a shudder, I remembered Professor Succubus as she'd been both watching me from the stage and in my fantasy as Radley had wanked me.

What would she feel like touching me for real?

What would it feel like to touch *her*? By my feathers, I longed to sink my prick between her thighs and gift my virginity to someone who I'd chosen…and desired.

Yet who was she? And why was someone who was so distressed by the execution of us wicked Forest Fae, working for Court Fae?

"What in the Queen's name is this music?" Beau gaped at me; his pupils were dilated.

Radley flashed his sharp teeth. "It has nothing to do with the Queen."

As the song played like the heartbeat of a new birth, I spun to my feet. Then I closed my eyes and simply let myself *feel*. The music swept through me, catching me in its riptide.

I lost myself then, dancing with the beauty and violence of a battle. It was a desperate plea for the cleansing fire of redemption in every leap and spin.

Why hadn't I taken hold of Quinn's wing? Why had I forgotten where I'd come from?

Round, and round, and round, and…

Radley caught me, as I fell. He always did. I knew that he always would.

My eyes snapped open, and I laughed. I hadn't laughed like that for a long time. Radley's eyes twinkled; I loved the way that they creased at the edges.

Felix stroked his hand down my hair, before pulling out the swan clips that marked me as belonging to the House of Fae and the Queen. I laughed again, as my hair tumbled to my waist.

"I insist that you stop this." Beau struggled to his feet, and Apollo flew to settle beside the basket. Beau stared between us like we were crazy. "You've broken Dictate 41, 506, and 709…"

"You missed 425. Don't worry, I always forget that one." Felix examined his nails.

Beau raised a shaky finger. "End this madness at once."

Radley pushed me into Felix's arms, before storming to Beau and cracking him into the tree. He towered over Beau, holding his arm across Beau's throat.

Radley's muscles made him look twice the other fae's size. "Watch your tongue, soft wings. I wouldn't want to make you faint again." Beau reddened. "Who are you to *insist* anything? This is the Marquess of Spring you're talking to, even if he forgets it himself half the time."

"Don't, Rads," I said, quietly. "He's only a Court Fae. He doesn't know any better."

Beau's eyes flashed. "How silly of me. I forgot that I'm nothing but a lowly, ignorant Court *peasant* in your eyes, beneath your notice and not worthy of attention or even to be remembered."

Wow, that had been *way* more personal than I'd been expecting.

Had I insulted Beau before today? It was true that I'd barely paid him any attention. But then, as far as I knew, on his visits to the reform school, he hadn't spoken to anyone.

Felix's expression hardened. "Rads is right. The Court Fae should show you some respect. We're Hostage Fae but we're still entitled to the deference owed to our positions. Plus, they believe in all that hierarchy stuff more than we do."

Beau ducked his head. "Then, *Your Lordship*, please stop it, otherwise we'll end up in trouble that we can't escape by dancing."

When a black butterfly of a fae circled my head like a shadow sprung to life, I pushed Felix behind me, straightening my shaky legs.

Yeah, I couldn't dance myself out of this trouble.

The Countess Pond, Deputy Head of the House of Fae, transformed in a golden spray back into the sophisticated woman, who'd tormented me as my tutor at Court as a kid and haunted my nightmares.

She'd planned to make me her bonded *and she still did*, if I broke on Saturday.

I shuddered.

The Countess' face was hidden behind a veil of black swan feathers; I could only catch flashes of her eyes and her scarlet lips, which were pursed and thin. She wore the same military uniform as Wells, but a swan brooch was pinned over her heart like a promise.

The Countess would hand that brooch to her bonded...*to me*. She'd forced me to play act that moment enough times that even seeing it now, made my throat burn with bile.

The Countess swung her hips, until she brushed against me. When she stroked her lace glove across my cheek, it was scratchy and dry.

I stiffened, wishing that I could tell her *not to touch me* like Beau had said to us.

When the Countess suddenly reached up to a low branch, I jumped. Then she snatched something by its wing and tossed it to the floor.

I caught a glimpse of glistening purple.

The Chief Myrmidon...

"I beg mercy," I gasped.

The Countess raised her boot, (still caressing my cheek), and stomped down.

The other myrmidons wailed in distress.

"Fly away home," Radley hollered at them. "It's too late, stupid bugs."

But he was as furious at the Countess as me. We'd never been able to fight her, even as kids. If we did, then we risked our tribe being punished. Now, we risked the punishment of the entire House.

Behind me, Felix flinched, and his hand bunched in my coat.

I bit my tongue to stop myself biting the Countess' fingers or kicking her to see how *she* liked to be stepped on. But the curses and wards woven into the belts on our own pants restricted us fighting back against our professors.

Wells said that he was only protecting us from ourselves because the Dean of Discipline had his own special *deterrent* for students who fought with professors. They said that if you injured a staff member, you were marched to the Detention Center and locked in for twenty-four hours with flesh eaters…or worse.

I didn't like to think about the *worse*, and Wells had a point, although I thought that his rivalry with the Dean of Discipline (who he hated because he had the power to punish us), was the real reason that he protected us.

My magic hissed and seethed at being restrained.

The Countess' fingers curled tighter into my cheek, until I winced. "You forget the true dangers all around you. Myrmidons are killers. Bugs can flay you, fountains can drown you, and the other students are locked up because they're deadly. So, why such emotion over an enemy, hostage boy? You don't love those who could offer you security and respectability, but you throw away your tears on those who'd slaughter you. Fascinating." She turned my head from side-to-side, scrutinizing me. "Will you cry more that you've earned the entire House two hours extra weeding tonight without magic or tools?"

My chest was tight, and I darted a glance at Beau, who wasn't sporting an *I told you so expression* like I expected but rather the same disdainful mask that he always wore around Wells.

It was no wonder that I thought Court Fae looked the same. They'd been taught to act haughty since birth. Yet no matter what they'd tried with me, I just hadn't been able to wear a mask.

I got why they called us the Rebels.

"Sure, you could go the cruel collective punishment route." *Come on, killer combination of both pious and holy face...* "But since it was *me* who broke the Dictates with (why be modest?), my truly brilliant dancing, punish me alone. You seem to get a kick out of that."

Apollo raised his head and shot me a hard look. "*Will you leave off sacrificing yourself. Didn't you already promise me?*"

But that's what a leader did. I'd learned that much from Quinn and Prince Lysander. They protected the fae, no matter what, even if they were hated for it.

My breath hitched, as the Countess moved her face uncomfortably close to mine. Her hot breath through the veil ghosted across my mouth. I winkled my nose at her cloying scent, which was sweet like marzipan; it choked me.

"You'd suffer for them?" She asked.

"I'd suffer anything to save my people."

Beau shot me a grudging glance of respect.

The Countess' lips curled into a smile. "Then you've earned a session with our new Emotions Counselor."

That didn't sound good.

Was this Counselor Wells' new method to tame us?

I squared my shoulders. "Counsel away."

The Countess' smile widened. "I didn't say that it would be your session, did I?"

My brow furrowed. *What had I missed?*

The Countess turned away from me, yanking Felix from behind me by his wing. He gasped, but she twisted his wingtip, until he stilled.

"I hope you understand that this shall be the last day of your defiance." The Countess narrowed her gaze at Felix. "Professor Emerald will change the way that you—"

"*Emerald?*" Felix arched his brow, unimpressed. "Did she need an alias when she was filling out the application form and just looked into Wells' eyes or admired his hair? *Emerald,* she thought, that'll do."

When Radley laughed, the Countess twisted Felix's wingtip again.

"He has a point." I licked my lips, wishing that I couldn't taste the marzipan sweetness of the Countess that shrouded the orchard. "Look at me, feathers all tingly in fear from the terrifying counselor who named herself to sound like a unicorn."

Radley snorted. "Take that back. Unicorn shifters are badass."

"My apologies." I mock bowed to Radley. "Named herself after your *dream* fae. I know your wank fantasies."

Radley flicked me off.

"If you behave like that in your sessions," the Countess glanced between us, "the succubus will eat you alive."

Did she mean literally eat me alive, and wait, succubus...?

I fought not to meet Felix's gaze because I knew that my own would blaze with jealousy that he was meeting Professor Succubus...*Emerald*...before me, and his would gleam with excitement that our plan to scheme and save the House of Fae could start.

Yet there was a cold ball in my gut that I didn't understand. I remembered Emerald's sad smile, and the urge to protect her the same as my own people surged through me. At the same time, the need to make her smile with joy.

I'd die or *live* to make her happy. I'd only ever been prepared to die before.

Was that a bond?

I cringed at what the other Fae Lords would think of me if they discovered that I'd betrayed them. We'd sworn never to bond and enslave ourselves.

My hands tightened into fists, and I steeled myself.

What if the succubus had been sent here to break us up and trick us into bonding? I could resist her and turn the tables. She might be a succubus, but I could seduce her into saving us all, instead.

The Countess misunderstood my expression, letting go of Felix and waltzing to snatch up the basket of apples. "Why so melancholy, hostage boy? Are you feeling left out? There's no need to worry, the three of you will be punished as well."

Beau straightened. "Three?"

"Didn't you choose to stand wing by wing with these Forest Fae?" The Countess' lips pinched. "Then you deserve to be treated just the same. How about a round of the Apple Game?"

"That sounds fun. But on the other hand, I'm allergic to apple." I backed away. "It makes me transform into a neurotic snake who goes around tempting people to *eat the fruit*, and you don't want that in this orchard."

"You will each *eat the fruit* in my game. Then we'll see what spells the tree has woven today," the Countess' voice was ice-cold. There was never any escape from her, as much as there wasn't from the reform school. "I shall teach you to control your emotions, as shall the new counselor. I wonder who shall tame you first?" The Countess' eyes gleamed maliciously. "I'll show you how it should be played beside Swan Pond. I believe that *I* will win."

The Countess shoved the basket into my arms and then transformed into a butterfly. Her wings glittered as she wove out of the shade and into the sun, towards the pond.

I shuddered, glancing at the magic apples in the basket. Then I stalked after the Countess and towards punishment.

CHAPTER FIVE

**Wicked Reform School, House of Fae, Swan Pond
Monday 26th April**

The Countess knew how to wreck me with her punishments. She always had. How could the Apple Game sound so innocent and yet be so wicked?

Dizzy, my heart pounded in my ears, drowning out the calls of the songbirds and the buzzing of the bees. I could only feel the feathery reassurance of Radley's wings outstretched next to mine on one side and Beau's on the other, as we stood in a circle beside the teardrop pond. I shifted, crushing the yellow carpet of gillyflowers under my boots, which curled around this side of the farm; their spicy, cinnamon scent grounded me.

I took a deep breath, and Radley shot me a cocky

smile, before schooling his face to blankness again. Beau already looked like he'd been transformed into a wooden toy soldier.

What would happen if I ever yanked the stick out of Beau's ass? *Would he turn into a real boy?*

Yet I knew the Court's methods for creating their perfect warriors because they'd tried with me as well. As a teenager, I'd walked for hours by the Countess' side through the corridors of the Fae Court with my hands behind my back and the same posture as Beau. The polished black Court had warped and shifted around me.

The Countess had led me in front of the curious and contemptuous stares of the Court Fae, and I'd been conflicted about whether I'd wanted to fit in or spit in their eye.

What instinct won out varied day by day, but it'd torn me apart.

"You can be reshaped the same as the Court," the Countess had told me, pausing one day as the walls had bulged into monstrous shapes as ugly as the Queen's heart. "I'll civilize you."

My eyes had burned with tears. "You promised that if I was good today, then I'd earn a reward. I want to let Lix and Rads out of our room."

The Countess had given a long-suffering sigh. "You're surrounded by riches and still you're on about *them*?"

I'd nodded.

Please, don't be unfair. Don't trick me again…

"You scuffed your feet too much like a peasant. You haven't earned a reward today." The Countess had twirled away from me dismissively.

I'd reddened. My wings had exploded out in an automatic show of rage and dominance.

I hate you… hate, hate, hate…

The Countess' eyes had widened, and she'd turned back.

"When I grow up," I'd growled, "I shall make a list of my own rewards, and you shan't receive a single one."

The Countess' expression had frozen. Then she'd snatched my wing, pinning me against the wall. My heart had hammered in my chest. Her smile had choked me with dread.

"When you grow up, hostage boy, you shall belong to *me*." The Countess' eyes had glittered. "You shan't be allowed a single reward that I don't grant you. I could make you happy. But do fight me now because it'll make breaking and remaking you more satisfying in the end."

I panted from the terror of the memory, which had taught me what *bonding* would truly mean. Radley caught my gaze with a concerned tilt of his head, and I lifted my chin.

Brilliant idea, Quincey, let your obsessive stalker get to you, before the game has even started.

Okay, *game* or *punishment.* This was a reform school: they liked to hide behind academy styled titles for brutalities because if they thought that they were reforming supernatural bad boys and girls, then anything was justified.

Who got to choose who was bad and who was good?

When black swan shifters with collars around their necks *honked* like bugles, I glanced across at the pond. The flock of swans were gathered at the edges in the reeds, watching us with beady glares.

You'd think that the fae had forced them into shifter form and then stolen their kids from them.

Oh wait, we did.

Two bundles of gray fluff quivered on either one of Radley's ankles: the cygnet shifters, Lil Swan and Odile. Radley had cussed enough to make most Court Fae blush, when the Countess had freed them from a net, which overhung the pond. But the Countess was too used to *me* to be most Court Fae.

Their parents had swum sadly beneath the net, guarding the cygnets. The swans had brushed their necks against each other in comfort. This was the only time that they were allowed to see their own daughters. The swan shifters were as imprisoned as me.

I had to find a way to allow the sisters to visit their mum and dad. It must be agony to be separated.

The Countess hadn't allowed Radley to pick up the cygnets and carry them in his pockets like usual, which meant that now they sheltered on his boots.

At least Apollo had flapped back to the golden tower, rather than following us to the pond. We had a standing agreement on him getting ready for comfort mode after these punishment sessions. Since I'd arrived at the reform school, the strength that I'd received from Apollo's touch alone had kept me from breaking. Felix once told me that humans were the same with their cats. It was nice to know that as the Fae Lord leader of my people, I had the same cuddle needs as a non-magical woman and her pussy.

Okay, that might've come out wrong.

"Why are you standing around holding your dicks? Kick the bitch's ass." Lil Swan's voice exploded telepathically into my mind like the slash of a knife. I always wondered if you received the shifter to match your personality. Lil Swan certainly suited Radley. *Wait, had my prick slipped out of my pants?* I flushed, subtly cupping myself to check. Lil Swan snickered. *"It's a saying, right? It means: why are you here doing nothing? The bitch who hung us in a net like she was going to make a roast dinner out of us is standing just behind you. Brooke could take her on his own."*

Radley gave a careful shake of his head, and Lil Swan huffed.

The hairs on the base of my neck lifted. I could sense the Countess close behind me. My friends had only received their shifters this year. The cygnets were young, no matter what they pretended. So far, we'd been able to shield them from the worst truths of the Wicked Reform School.

Lil Swan had the same pride in Radley as a kid had in their dad, when they boasted that *their dad could kick anyone else's ass.*

I hated that her faith would be stolen from her.

"*I want River,*" Odile wept; her voice was soft like Apollo's and suffused with grief. "*Where is he? Please, please, please. I want him.*"

When Radley's gaze met mine, it was filled with the same fear, which crept through me.

Was Felix safe with Emerald? Who was this succubus who chose to work in a fae reform school to counsel their *emotions*? I'd heard tales about succubi because they were deadly creatures. They could mesmerize and control, taking pleasure and feeding on it.

After all, a paranormal who forced another to give them pleasure and cared only about *taking it* was exactly the type who Wells would employ to prove that the love we Forest Fae believed in wasn't real. Yet surely it couldn't only be because I was *mesmer-*

ized that I craved to run to her now and felt through every feather in my wings that she was the emptiness inside me that I'd been running towards my entire life?

The Countess trailed her fingers along my lower back, and I flinched.

"No mistakes, reactions, or emotions," she whispered like an icy wind. "The first one to err, takes a bite of one of the apples. Won't it be exciting to see what spells the tree has grown today?" *Yeah, thrilling.* I gritted my teeth. "The game ends when all three of you play the game with your emotions governed." She assessed Beau. "Only one of you is even trying right now."

"Hit me with the first round. I just love the Apple Game." I winked over my shoulder at the Countess.

She curled her fingers around my neck.

Maybe now wasn't the time to play the sarcastic card.

"Dictate 44," she ordered.

"*Mate once and for life,*" I forced out the words.

I held my hands behind my back, gripping my wrist until it was sweaty. There were a thousand Dictates to choose from, and she'd just happened to pick the one, which she'd made me recite at Court every…single…morning.

The Countess nodded, before prowling to Radley. "Dictate 987."

Radley's expression soured. *"Laugh quietly."*

Beau stiffened, and the Countess' gaze narrowed. Why was I more nervous for his turn, than I'd been for my own? He was a Court Fae and not one of my mates.

Why did it twist something in me that the Countess was targeting him, as much as me?

"Dictate 782," she demanded.

When Beau hesitated, my heart clenched.

Had he failed?

The Countess had played this game with the Dictates every day to teach all one thousand of them to us Hostage Lords.

It was why Felix stuttered.

Felix, Radley, and I would line up, the Countess would shoot a number at us, then we'd recite the Dictates back. Except, as we had, we'd be magically attacked by invisible pinches, burns, or spanks to distract us, just enough to make us forget the words. If we'd hesitated, stuttered, or forgotten the Dictate, then we'd been punished.

Felix was brighter than any one I knew. But he was a perfectionist. He hated to fail, which meant that being forced into error had wrecked him.

At least, being with the succubus meant that Felix wasn't here now. Whatever was happening in his counseling couldn't be worse than this, right?

"*Always act with decorum and as a proper fae,*" Beau forced out in a tumble of words.

I held my breath. *Would the Countess allow that?*

Beau was ashen, and his breathing was too rapid.

At last, the Countess nodded, stalking behind me again. As she did, she leaned down, scooping the red apple out of the basket and onto her wing.

"We'll play this the traditional fae way." She bounced the apple up and down like a warning. At the same time, she traced her swan brooch, and I tensed. The Countess had chosen each Dictate to humiliate us. She might consider that I already belonged to her, but I never had. She'd no idea who I truly was, and I wouldn't allow her the chance to hurt others, whilst I stood here emotionless. *If that was being a proper fae, then I was fine with being a scandalous one.* "Dictate 887."

Only bond with permission of the Queen...

Of course, she'd listed one of my most hated Dictates.

Yet if she thought that I'd continue to recite Court Fae propaganda, then she was the one who'd been eating spelled apples.

Instead, I slouched, crossing my arms. Beau hissed in frustration.

"*Love whoever's in your heart.* Wait, that's not in there... *Fight the establishment!* Nope, that's wrong as well, okay, give me one more chance, I've got this:

Never bond with ugly Countesses. Wow, that one's scarily specific."

Radley laughed…loudly.

The Countess' wing *thwapped* across my face. I cringed at the sickening aroma of marzipan.

"Take a bite out of the apple." The Countess' voice coiled with dark anger and desire.

I lowered my mouth to the fruit. When my lips caught the Countess' feathers, she shivered. Then with a *crunch*, I bit hard into the apple.

The sweet flavor hit me, as the juices ran down my chin. I took three defiant chews on the apple…and then swallowed.

All of a sudden, the bright day around me in the House of Fae darkened with a lurch. I closed my eyes, grasping my aching guts.

Never trust a fruit, which tasted so sweet.

When I opened my eyes again, my mouth hung open. I was no longer trapped in the Wicked Reform School. I'd been transported into the shadowy coolness of a forest, and I was alone.

I stumbled around in a circle. My feet kicked up wrinkled leaves.

Here it was fall.

The seasons had changed as well.

Except, it *hadn't* because this must all be part of the Memory Spell… Nope, probably a Relive It Spell… I mean, it *could* be a Dream Spell…

So, I didn't know what spell it was that'd been woven into the apple, but I didn't care because I knew what forest this was: *Hope*.

My dad had named Hope Forest, when he'd hidden my tribe from the Queen after the first rebellion. This was the same forest that I'd played in every single day as a kid with my friends, before I'd been taken away to Court, and it was the one place that I'd missed like my soul had been ripped from me.

I stared around the tangle of trees with their white bark. At once, my breathing became easier, and my lungs took in the fresh air like I hadn't truly been breathing since I'd stepped into the Court. The scent of damp moss and wet tree trunks caressed me like a welcome home. I fell into the hush. Shadows played across my face.

I felt safe, for the first time in a long time.

For once, I didn't care that this wasn't real because it simply felt like too much of a *blessing*.

I grinned, throwing myself down on a bed of leaves, before windmilling my arms and legs through them like I had as a kid. The leaves *crackled*.

Belenus above, I was alone at last. Why shouldn't I enjoy it?

I tossed a handful of leaves up, laughing as they fell back down on me. Then I froze. I shouldn't be alone for my dream bonding. How about Emerald in a non-magical bridal dress?

Felix had described the elaborate weddings from his beloved Shakespeare. I edged my hand towards my prick.

Yeah, I'd just imagine her walking towards me in a white dress and sweeping train...

In a spray of love-heart confetti, Emerald materialized in a wedding dress with a train so long that it wound like a snake between the trees. Her hair was coiled on the top of her head, *and she was beautiful.*

She was also younger than I'd been able to tell at the culling. She couldn't be much older than me, surely?

My breath caught. *This must be a Fantasy Spell.*

I was either the luckiest or unluckiest fae ever because when this spell faded, it'd hurt like being punched in the prick.

A prick that was perking up and taking serious interest in my imaginary bride, who'd hiked up her skirts to stop them catching on the leaves and was stalking towards me with a frustrated expression that made me frown.

I didn't know that I had a thing for succubi with a dominatrix vibe. I'd imagined that my fantasy would've been sweeter and more romantic.

I was kinkier than I thought.

When Emerald leaned over and yanked me up by my wing, I mouthed *oww* at her.

Okay, *way* kinkier.

"I was in the middle of a session," Emerald huffed, soothing my wing without seeming to think. Her voice was American and as soft as smoke; it was also edged with melancholy. "You're under a spell and you've dragged me into it. Some of us can't just take time off work to lie around and…whatever *this* is." She scrunched her nose at the dress. *Hey, that dress was fit for a princess.* "Look, let's just get on with it, sexy wings."

I blinked. *Sexy wings?* I'd spent many nights wanking to my ideal partner because it'd been taboo: the one thing that us three friends had sworn we'd never willingly take. Yet not one night had it included pet names.

I swallowed. *It was time to take back control of this spell.* "That's fine with me, Emerald. Lose the clothes, and I'd rather that you called me *My Lord*." I shot her a smug grin.

At least I could have some fun.

Emerald arched her brow. "Seriously, call me *Professor* Emerald. You know, when I watched you up on that stage about to be parted from your gorgeous head, you appeared nobler than this. Plus, Lord River has been trying to convince me how *reformed* you are." Her tongue curled behind her plush lips, and I shivered. "But you're all bad, aren't you?"

Why didn't I just cut off my own head while I was at it?

I stumbled back, tripping over my feet and landing on my ass in the leaves. "You're *really* here."

Her lips twitched. "Uh-huh."

"You're the *actual* counselor, and I just commanded you to…"

Emerald's eyes glittered, as she slunk closer.

Felix had been working our scheme with her to save the fae because he was smart, but now I'd jeopardized everything.

Don't let her hate me. Love me, love me, love…

Why did the bond settle around me, as heavy and certain as any wedding band? Did she sense it as well?

I turned away my head. I didn't want Emerald to read the desire in my eyes, or the way that my skin tingled for her, and my feathers were aflame.

Yet she dropped to her knees next to me, leaning closer and turning back my head with greater gentleness than she'd shown me before. I recognized this side to her from the Day of the Wicked, yet now there was a playfulness bubbling beneath the melancholy.

"…Get naked, My Lord," Emerald murmured.

I couldn't suppress the shiver, or the way that the tips of my ears reddened. Then the bodice of Emerald's dress vanished, and my cheeks flamed as well.

No, no, no…this could not be happening.

Had my subconscious done that? *Bad, bad mind… or prick…whoever's doing this, I order you to stop it.*

Although, Emerald did have the most delicious

tits. *Burn my feathers, was I even staring at her tits now...?*

Emerald cocked her head. "My eyes are up here, sexy wings." *I mean, I was only a guy, after all. I had needs.* I darted my tongue over my lips. Would it be breaking etiquette if I licked just one nipple? Why hadn't my tutors taught me anything useful? "You'd think that you'd never seen a female's naked body before."

"I haven't," I muttered, before blushing. "Did I undress you? On my feathers, I don't make a habit of stripping my professors..."

Emerald pressed her finger against my lips; it was warm, just like her scent of ginger that heated me inside. "Stop panicking. I'm messing with you. I did it myself. I need to hurry this along."

I stared at her blankly. "And they're the romantic words that every guy longs to hear."

Emerald rubbed herself against me like a snake, before straddling me. "Your Pleasure Spell summoned me, but since I'm meant to be in a counseling session right now, and you're rather hot and distracting, I thought that I should free us. The spell traps you, until we both receive pleasure." She nibbled on my ear. "Hey, I find it flattering that you thought of me."

I'd never expected that my first meeting with Emerald would go like this, or that we'd be caught together in a Pleasure Spell. Why couldn't it have been a simple *Self*-Pleasure Spell?

I'd had decades to perfect that.

There wasn't any point in playing it cool, when Emerald already knew that having her in my arms in Hope Forest was what would bring me the greatest pleasure.

Then I froze. *Oh, brilliant.* She'd been wearing a princess style wedding dress for her grand entrance as well.

I raised my gaze to her amused expression: time to bluff. "You're my counselor. Is it appropriate for us to be together like this? Anyway, I rather think that you won't be able to cope with my dark desires."

Emerald's eyes narrowed. "I'm not your counselor now. But here's an interesting theory: do you think that Lord River will witness what happens between us? What if he's even caught up in the spell?"

She stroked her fingers through my feathers, until I ached. A fae's wings were as sensitive as his prick, and my prick was now pulsing and hard in my pants. I panted, arching against her.

In turn (because never let it be said that Lord Spring was a selfish lover), I rubbed my fingers experimentally across Emerald's nubs, and she gasped. Her nipples flushed and peaked. I circled them, swiping them in time with her caresses across my throbbing wingtips.

I could come from this alone…

Then Emerald whispered hot into my ear, "What if Lord River is acting out every stroke of your fingers across my tits?"

I pulled my fingers away from her like I'd been burned. "I don't want him to touch you," I blurted out. "What we're doing right now is mine…ours…not for other students."

First a wedding dress and then a declaration of…*what?*

Possessive emotions belonged to Court Fae's bonds. *Why was I surging with them?*

Emerald pulled back in surprise, scrutinizing me. "*Right now,* is only a spell. It's not real."

To you maybe…

I shrugged, avoiding her gaze. "Everything in the Wicked Reform School looks false but wow, is it *real.*" It was more painful than the flames licking through my lungs, but I still managed to force out, "I don't know why you came to work for the psycho Psychology Department, but you should leave. It's not only deadly for the students but the professors too. If you're in danger somehow, then just tell me, and I'll protect you."

Emerald tangled our hands together. "You're under sentence of death and you're offering to protect *me?*"

I chuckled. "Thanks a lot. I needed that boost of confidence."

When she played with my fingers, it felt more intimate than when she'd been stroking my wingtips (and they had a direct line to my prick). "You honestly did look like the noblest leader up on that stage. I hated that any of you were being forced into such a choice. I wish that I was even half as brave."

Warmth coiled through me, and her gaze was so intent that I could've lived forever in it. Then she flushed as well, looking away and pretending to busy herself with brushing a leaf out of my hair.

"The Day of the Wicked is sort of what this reform school is all about," I said with an edge of steel.

Help us…

I bit my lip to keep in the plea. Perhaps, I'd found the way to save my people, after all.

Except, Emerald ducked her head. "As you said, I'm new here. All I know is that we escape by bringing pleasure to each other, and you'll feed *me* at the same time." She finally raised her gaze to mine. "I take it that you've heard that if you give me pleasure, then I'll feed on it…? Well, I don't take from the unwilling. So, would you get a kick out of that because talking about your gory death just isn't a turn-on?"

"I'd do anything for you because you're my…" I snapped my mouth shut, biting my own tongue to stop *bonded* spilling out, instead, finishing lamely "…professor."

"If only all students were so keen to please. I was way too harsh on you before; you're a good boy."

With a growl, I twisted her, pinning her beneath me. "I'm no boy."

Emerald rocked her hips up against the hard prick tenting my pants. "I can feel that. So, what do you desire, My Lord? Chains, knife play, or something more adventurous?" I paled. *Could I take back the comment about being <u>no boy</u>?* She misunderstood my silence and laughed. "I've heard stories about fae."

I rested my cheek against hers.

Emerald's heat was so different to the Countess' coldness. Her fire leaped across to mine; it seared, and yet, I never wanted the flames to go out.

What was she doing to me?

"You're hotter than any creature who I've ever eaten," she whispered.

"Kiss me and never let me go."

"You promised something *dark*. At last, you're being honest."

Then she bit my lower lip.

I sucked on her lip in turn, and she moaned. I pressed my tongue into her mouth, and her tongue danced with mine. Beneath the tall trees of my childhood, in the hush of a forest, which I was exiled from and would never see again, the kiss was bittersweet and perfect.

I never wanted it to end.

I closed my eyes, losing myself in the terrifying sensation that I'd discovered love and home and everything that I'd been searching for since I was a kid.

Then Emerald cooled, her scent faded, and there was a sickening lurch that shocked me.

I opened my eyes, only to stare into the Countess' icy gaze. Her fingers were clutched so tightly around her brooch that the edges bit into her palm; scarlet trickled around the edges.

Remember what I said about *possessive…*?

I gasped, swaying.

Of course Emerald let go… everyone but the other Hostage Lords always did.

Emerald had only kissed me to escape the spell.

My guts twisted with disappointment. I should've known that it'd be a wicked punishment. The Countess always managed to wreck me.

This time when I fell, I wanted to hit the ground.

Only, like always, Radley broke position in the circle, as Odile and Lil Swan scrambled off his feet, to encircle me with his wings before I could.

Radley's concerned gaze caught mine, but I only shook my head. I'd never talk about Emerald in front of the Countess, when my lips were still tingling with our kiss, and my eyes burned with the tears of her loss.

When the Countess eyed the hard-on *still* tenting my pants, I realized why she was bubbling with such jealousy. "How could you corrupt this game with your depravity? Who were you dreaming about?"

"It was an orgy beside the mermaids' lake." I palmed my prick through my pants. The Countess' eyes widened. Sometimes, she was too easy a mark. "First, there were the Nephilim, the glorious half angels, because who doesn't fancy a glowing asshole? Wait, can I take back that image? Then, the mermaids sauntered out to join us. I'd always wondered if their hair below matched their rainbow locks. But that's a secret I'll never tell. I'll just say this: with their talent at kissing, there's no doubt that they're the offspring of Aphrodite. Finally, the kraken felt left out, so he came bursting out of the water, and who'd have thought it, but he was the tenderest lover with all those tentacles exploring so many holes all at the same time…"

Radley bit on his thumb to smother his laugh.

"You're lying." The Countess tossed down the basket, and the remaining apples rolled towards the cygnets.

"*Apple attack!*" Odile squeaked, sheltering behind Lil Swan.

Beau shot out his foot to block the apples, before it

hurt the shifters. Radley nodded his thanks across the circle.

Why would Beau risk breaking position to help us? Although, that meant we'd *all* failed the game…

The Countess smiled, frostily. "You still believe that you don't need to tell me the truth. Fascinating. But now the Apple Game begins again. How many rounds do you think you'll have to play?"

Beau doubled over in as much frustration at himself as us. "Why can't you learn? Just hide your feelings. Stop—"

The Countess snatched Beau by the wing. "You're the worst out of all of them." Her tongue flickered out. "I can taste your disgusting emotions: Jealousy, anger, and unrequited love."

My eyes widened. *Unrequited love?*

I stared at the way that Beau's beautiful face had pinked, and his chest rose and fell too rapidly like he was struggling to hold in the emotions, which the Countess was accusing him of… like *loving me.*

How had I missed him caring for me for all these years? Were Court Fae truly so good at hiding their emotions, even if it hurt them?

"You're wrong," Beau's voice was tear-tinged. "And even if you're right, *no more than you.*"

He. Was. Dead.

To my surprise, however, the Countess laughed, low and dangerous. "So, you do have the same bite as your father." She twisted his wingtip, and he howled. "Are you going to weep now?"

Radley and I circled the Countess.

Beau was a snooty Court Fae, but if he loved me, then that made him *mine*, and we Fae Lords always protected what was ours.

"Let him go," I ordered. "If making fae cry is one of your kinks, then save it for when we're bonded." *Yeah, like I'd ever spend eternity in tears with her, when I'd tasted pleasure with Emerald.* Yet by the way that her breath hitched, I knew that she was imagining it. "He's off-limits."

Beau stared at me in shock, before his eyes lit with tentative hope. When the Countess let go of him, however, and he curled his wings around himself, he'd already frozen back into haughty indifference.

The Countess' gaze slid between us. "I'm ending this game."

When she snatched up Lil Swan, Radley cried out in alarm. I didn't dare move, in case the Countess crushed the shifter.

Odile huddled behind Beau's boot.

"*Let me go, bitch.*" Lil Swan's feet pedaled through the air. "*I'll kick your skinny ass.*"

"One final round of the Apple Game." The Countess' lips curled upwards, smugly. "If you lose," she glanced at Beau, "then I'll take great delight in telling the Duke of Wells that a Court Fae performed worse than a Forest Fae at controlling his emotions. How do you think he'll discipline you this week?" Beau shuddered. I didn't blame him because the consequence of such a failure would be swift and brutal. "If either of you Hostage Lords lose, then…" Her fingers tightened around Lil Swan, and the cygnet hissed. "I'll kill your swan."

"If you hurt my shifter, I'll rip off your wings and beat you to death with them," Radley snarled.

He meant it.

The Countess merely turned her back to him like he was no more dangerous than Odile. "You *won't* because the wards won't allow you to, and even if they did, it'd mean your *much* more agonizing execution. But now that you have the impotent rage out of your system, shall we begin? Dictate 7," she snapped at Beau.

Control yourself…

She'd given Beau an easy one. She wanted him to win, and our shifter to die. Was she punishing me for turning my spell on its head and taking pleasure in my punishment?

Was this my fault for not breaking?

Beau was staring at me across the circle. His expression was inscrutable.

Control yourself…

Why wasn't he saying it?

My hands clenched, and sweat dampened the back

of my neck. I forced myself to nod reassuringly at Lil Swan, as she hung in the Countess' hands.

Control yourself...

Beau swallowed. "*Don't raise your voice.*"

But that was Dictate 56.

I studied Beau's shuttered expression and I knew: he'd deliberately got it wrong.

"Why would you...? The Duke of Wells will make you regret that tonight." The Countess hurled Lil Swan at Radley, and he caught her.

"Be careful, you're breaking the Dictate," I drawled.

I smiled at Beau. He wasn't simply a Court Fae any longer. He'd risked himself for Lil Swan and that made him my mate.

Even though Beau was shaking and pale with fear, the corners of his lips lifted in response almost like he wasn't quite certain how to form a smile. But also like it was the most precious thing in the world to him.

The Countess pointed at each of us in turn. "Nobody can say that I didn't try, but I was wrong. You *do* need the special methods of the new Emotions Counselor. You're the wickedest students in the House of Fae. This week you'll have sessions, and then you'll see that *love* is nothing but a myth. It won't save you from Professor Emerald and on Saturday, it won't halt your deaths."

CHAPTER SIX

**Wicked Reform School, House of Fae, Dormitory
Tuesday 27th April**

I glanced around the House of Fae's dormitory. Even though it was pitch-black without windows in the bottom of the turret, I was so used to the dark that I could still make out shadowy outlines and movement.

It was the hour before dawn.

I'd always been able to sense twilight, as if the sun was singing to my magic. If I hadn't been flooded with such unease about Beau, I'd have thrilled with the call of the coming dawn.

But Beau had been missing all night.

Last evening, the Countess had sent Beau to report directly to Wells, and Beau had never returned.

Had he been sentenced to the Detention Centers with their flesh eaters or…worse?

I knew that it was down to the same possessiveness, which had surged through me ever since Emerald had become my new obsession, but Beau felt like *mine* now. I hadn't grown up with him like Felix or Radley, but he'd still risked himself to save our shifters.

On my wing, did loving me always lead to punishment or death?

Step right up, ladies and gentlemen, the catch of the century (warning: risk of decapitation and flaying).

I shuddered. Beau would survive. He was a Court Fae; they were tough. They had to be.

I squirmed, shifting on the cold, golden floor. Would it've killed the staff to have granted us blankets? Although, if this was an imaginary list of privileges, then why not think big and throw in some mattresses?

The basement room was empty apart from feathered piles of naked sleeping fae, cuddling each other for warmth, touch, and comfort. As outcasts, us Hostage Lords had been banished to the far side. The cygnets slept in a fluffy pile next to us.

Walk through the dormitory doors… Come on, Beau, just return to us…

Yet every other night, I'd ignored Beau. I'd barely

noticed the way that he'd walked to a lonely spot to sleep huddled by himself.

No wonder he was touch deprived.

Who sent a Court Fae to serve their sentence amongst Forest Fae?

I should've noticed Beau before, but he'd been too well trained at not making a fuss.

Then I'd just have to make one for him.

My malevolent grin was back, as I snuggled down amongst my brotherhood of guys. It was my turn to stand guard over our nightmares. Each night, we took turns watching over each other in sleep. It was the ultimate test of both trust and love.

They saved me, even in my sleep.

I ran my hand over the discarded emerald collar in disgust.

Felix had run his hand over Apollo's neck, as we'd settled down for the night. The collar that was meant to be impossible to remove, had snapped open.

Felix had grinned. "How lucky."

Apollo had transformed back into his stunning human form in a spray of ivory glitter.

When Apollo's long leg twitched, and he whined, I edged closer. His eyes flickered behind his eyelids, and his strong hands clenched. I brushed his white hair, which was wavy and as soft as his feathers in swan form, out of his face. His cheek bones were high; his lips were so petal soft that I longed to kiss them. There was nothing soft about the hard muscles sculpting his chest, however, even if he chose not to fight.

He'd already witnessed too much death.

Apollo's breathing sped up, and he twisted side to side.

"Nay," he breathed, "stop, stop, *stop…*"

I hated this moment.

Shaking a mate out of a nightmare and into a reality that was just as bad was agonizing. Wells and the staff didn't understand that the pain of moments like this and the courage to overcome them strengthened us students, until we could face the trials that they threw at us.

Even spelled apples or flesh eaters.

I hoped.

My lips pinched together, as my own heartbeat fluttered in my chest in time with Apollo's. Then I leaned over him, stroking my hand across his cheek.

"You're having a nightmare," I whispered. "Come back to me, in the name of the forest."

It was all it ever took. Perhaps, our shifters were bound to us by more than collars and cruelty. I hoped so.

Apollo's startlingly bright blue eyes snapped open on a gasp like he was dying or being reborn. He grasped for me, as if it was instinct, hooking his arms around my neck.

"Ma!" His whisper was choked and frantic.

Apollo was caught in that moment between waking and sleeping, when the nightmare was still real. When he'd been taken from his mum as a cygnet, she'd tried to battle the fae.

They'd murdered her in front of Apollo.

We all had our reasons for our nightmares here in the Wicked Reform School.

At last, Apollo's cloudy gaze cleared, and he focused on me. Then he flushed with embarrassment.

I kissed him, before he could apologize. Then I rested my forehead against his. "We live for our brothers."

"Aye," he whispered back, "we live for our brothers." Then he wriggled closer to me, stroking across the hollow of my back. I shivered, as his fingers strayed lower. His scent of wild daffodils wound around me. "But I'm meant to be comforting your blue-blooded arse after that cold bitch took you away. At least let me give you a massage."

Why did I deserve one, since Beau was missing?

I shook my head.

Apollo's brow furrowed. "Did she hurt your rascally self?" His other hand reached to cup my balls, before exploring my prick with concerned strokes. "Are you damaged?"

I batted away his hands, at the same time as my wings drooped. "It's fine, I had a great time playing mind games with the fae who wants to force me into a bond."

Apollo's thick eyelashes matted with tears, but his expression hardened. "You're keeping secrets, My Lord. Why would you hide anything from the *sacred, beautiful* shifter, who'd give up his life, powers, and soul just to love you for a single breath?"

"Overdramatic," I muttered.

Apollo gripped my chin, and I met his bright gaze. "I'm not the one lying."

"Secrets? Lies? This sounds like the start to a thrilling book," Felix said, sleepily.

Felix was wrapped in Radley's powerful arms; even in sleep, Radley was protecting him. Except, they were both waking up now and studying me in the dark.

Although, we'd all been reduced to shadows.

Whoops, looked like I was outnumbered.

I sighed. Felix and Radley had been sleeping by the time that I'd been allowed into the dormitory, but I couldn't pretend that what'd happened with Emerald didn't affect them or that I hadn't felt a bond with her.

I didn't keep secrets. Well, *much.*

The hour before dawn was the best time to confess. The song of the sun wove my magic around me in a cocoon. Perhaps, it'd protect me…?

Radley kissed down Felix's neck, before stroking his hand casually along his sides, circling to tweak his nipples. After any time apart, we needed to connect through touch.

I wet my dry lips. "So, I had to play the Apple Game and bite the magic apple. I pretended that it'd taken me to an orgy beside the mermaids' lake…"

Felix sat up straighter. "Oh, I've always wanted to screw a mermaid."

I curled my wings around myself, avoiding Apollo's close scrutiny. "In fact, it took me to Hope Forest." Radley drew in a breath at the same time as Felix. I met their anguished gazes, and I could sense their homesickness because it thrummed through me as well. "It was… just how I remembered it but *more*. It was beautiful."

Radley sat up, pulling Felix with him and leaning against the wall. His hands were bunched into fists.

Felix cocked his head. "Were you hunted through the forest? Did the trees explode? How many fire salamanders burst out and…?"

"Emerald appeared in a wedding dress," I got out in a tumble of words.

I bit my lip, eying the shocked faces of my mates.

"*Ehm*, why?" Apollo crossed his arms.

Belenus protect me…

"It was a Pleasure Spell, and apparently *she* was what I desired. Hello, is anyone going to say something? Do you want to drive the gold from my wings?"

Radley studied me with an inscrutable expression. For the first time, I was glad that we were kept in the black.

Felix arched his brow. "Apollo has already said it: *why?*"

My temples throbbed. If I hurled, would that get me out of admitting the truth?

I closed my eyes. "I may…just a little bit…I'm not entirely certain but…*I think I have a bond with her.*"

Yeah, my declarations of love were every bit as romantic as Apollo's.

Silence.

So, that'd gone down even worse than I'd been imagining.

Say something…for the love of the forest…say something.

I gritted my teeth and opened my eyes.

I didn't expect the three wickedly amused expressions.

Apollo gripped me by the neck, dragging me against his hard chest. "Aye, of course you have."

"What?"

"The way that you talked and fantasized about her in the orchard was different, Quince. We could all sense it." Felix's smile was soft. "Don't look like we'll snap your wings over it. She must be something special, if she's the right bond for our leader. If you love her, then we'll love her too."

My eyes narrowed. "Right, nice to know. But also, I'm not buying it. We swore that we wouldn't take bonds."

Radley's gaze darkened. "We swore not to take bonds that were *forced* on us. Is this new counselor forcing you?"

"I'd have to say that so far, I'm the one who's feeling the love. She's more…"

"Feeding?" Felix crawled closer. "You haven't forgotten our plan? I spent the entire counseling session working on it. I think she can be convinced to help. I don't know how she's meant to be taming our emotions though. She was…" *Wait, why was Felix blushing?* He ducked his head, mouthing at my neck. "…Beautiful, intelligent, and powerful. She was fascinated by Shakespeare and… Wait, when did she turn up as your bride in Hope Forest?"

Felix sucked on my throat harder, marking me. I shivered at the intense sensation. I loved wearing his bruises.

"During your session." I stroked my hand through his tumble of hair.

Felix frowned. "She did appear to zone out, when I was explaining that Shakespeare shows not the ideal of love but rather the difficulties that must be overcome between lovers. I think I lost her to you, when I started quoting: Love looks not with the eyes, but with the mind. How was I to know that succubi aren't turned on by that?"

"More than just succubi," Radley muttered.

I tightened my hand in Felix's hair. "Didn't you feel us? Her kiss and mine, together on your lips...?"

Radley growled, yanking Felix back onto his lap. Felix yelped as his hair was torn from my grip. "Did you feel it?"

Felix glanced between us. "Don't panic, but we're in trouble. I don't want us to be love rivals but I *may* also be bonded to Emerald. How do you feel about us all sharing a harem?"

Apollo's concerned gaze met Radley's.

I'd expected to flare with jealous rage that Felix felt a bond to Emerald. I mean, I would if I was a Court Fae, and in the orchard, I'd hated the idea of him touching her. But now, when we were together like this, it felt natural that the fae I loved would also share in this new discovery.

Wasn't that the exact type of love that my brother had led the Love Rebellion for the freedom to cherish?

All of a sudden, I wasn't alone in something that was more frightening than the demon Dean, cyclops guardians who ate students, or the Paranormal Prefect Patrol (the dicks) combined. *Nothing* in this school was as terrifying because the risk was so huge. Yet it could also be the most amazing thing to happen to all of us, together.

Love and bonds had seemed impossible outside our brotherhood.

My magic flamed down my wings, lighting them like a call to the dawn. I grinned at my mates by their flickering light.

I'd thought that they'd reject me for the first time in my life, but instead they'd accepted my choice.

I loved them for that.

Apollo stretched out his legs, crossing his ankles. "Love, bonds, and your wildest dreams come true. I don't want to be the one to say it, but what if this is what Emerald was brought here to do?"

"Kiss us?" I asked.

Apollo looked like he wished he still had his beak so that he could peck my balls. "Right, like that's all she's doing. She's this bad bastard Emotions Counselor brought here to break *you*. Did she try and hurt you cute behind during the session?"

Felix shook his head.

Apollo's butterfly lashes fanned across his cheeks, as he looked down. "What if *that's* her method? You can't think that Wells would hire someone to talk about Shakespeare or offer you pleasure? Perhaps, she's able to read your emotions and then…"

"Offers us what we need," I whispered.

I was shaking. *Why was I shaking?*

Stop it, stop, stop…

Radley tightened his hold around Felix, who was shaking as much as me. "She tricks each student into loving her and then tames them." His gaze blazed. "No one hurts my brothers in the wing like that. Let's see how she likes it when I trick her into *loving* me. I'll shatter her heart into a million pieces and then devour them."

Wow, that was typical Radley romance. Except, I still only wanted to protect Emerald.

I wished that Apollo had never worked it out or that I could deny it. But Emerald had even been honest about it. She'd told me that she'd only been offering pleasure because we were under a spell. She'd said that it wasn't *real*.

Why hadn't I believed her?

Because it was real…and it was for Felix too.

We'd been sent away by our own people and treated as prisoners all our lives. Emerald was the first female who I'd risked loving.

I couldn't stop, even if it *was* only a fantasy. The bond was real on my side. I'd just have to prove it to her.

If Emerald thought that she could play with our emotions like that and walk away, then she didn't know the obsessive love of the Fae Three.

She was ours now, she simply didn't know it yet.

Apollo pointed at Felix. "By my wing, your scholarly self just wanted someone intelligent who—"

"Would respect me," Felix's voice was soft and heartbroken, "and who I could respect."

I clenched my jaw. "And I wanted someone who admired me and let me take the lead. She offered me choice…and I thought it was real. So, I'm an idiot, okay?"

Radley shrugged. "She's using our desires against us. She's a succubi; it's what they do."

This Emotions Counseling was worse than any punishment that'd been used before. It wouldn't simply tame me.

It could break me.

Yet I *was* the leader of the fae. It didn't matter how much this unrequited love hurt because what was real to me was only a fantasy to Emerald. She was still our best chance to escape before Saturday.

I tilted up my chin. "She doesn't know that we're onto her plan. That gives us the advantage to trick her back. I know it hurts like a wolf shifter bite, but even if she doesn't know it, we're still hers. I'd never abandon any of you."

Apollo pounced on me, pinning my wrists and kissing along my jaw. His hard-on pressed against my thigh.

"I'm sorry," Apollo murmured. "I've made you sad. Should I've kept secrets too, My Lord?"

I stiffened. Why hadn't I known *that* would come back to bite me in the ass?

I caught Apollo's lips with mine. He tasted of a spring day, and I wanted to fall into him and forget the damp forest and the heat of the succubus…

Only, I couldn't because she was what had filled the emptiness that'd always been inside me. I needed her, even if she didn't need me.

"You're my sacred, beautiful swan who hides nothing from me. Never change. Remind me." I arched against Apollo.

His eyes lit with excitement, and he nipped my bottom lip. "Aye, My Lord. I'll blow you this time, but you're doing me next time."

Sometimes, Apollo was more practical than romantic.

When Apollo slunk down me and his silky hair caressed my skin, however, I didn't care. I cared even less, when his cool mouth worshiped the head of my cock and his fingers played with my balls. I gasped; my skin tingled. My toes curled, as I tried to clutch against the smoothness of the floor. He licked along the length of my prick, before clasping its base loosely and pumping. I stroked my hand through Apollo's hair, more in encouragement than demand.

Radley pushed Felix towards his prick, however, in unmistakable order. Felix grinned up at him cockily. Then he swallowed him in the familiar way bred of long practice. Radley tangled his fingers in Felix's hair, pushing him up and down with a roughness that he saved only for Felix because it turned them both on.

I moaned, as Apollo circled his tongue in the way that I loved along the head of my cock, then he sucked. I flushed, and sweat dripped down my chest.

My magic danced along my wings; explosive joy prickled like static along every feather.

I pushed on Apollo's shoulder. *On Belenus, I couldn't hold it any longer…*

This moment of union was a bond of love. I was certain of that.

Apollo gave my prick a final lick, and I groaned. He caged me beneath him, as he kissed my wingtip, which was the most sensitive part of a fae's wing, and then sucked on it.

My eyes widened, and I came. I bit hard on my lip to hold back the holler. A pearly stream arced onto my stomach, marking me as surely as the bruises on my throat. Apollo traced his finger through it, drawing the picture of a swan. He shot me a smug smile.

I got the point: I'd always be his, no matter what happened with Emerald. It was just that if our plan worked, then we'd also belong to Emerald.

Let her love all of us…

Radley thrust into Felix's throat, holding him down as he came with a grunt. Radley had a thing about his lovers *swallowing*, and Felix took pride in having no gag reflex.

It was always the quiet ones.

I smirked, grabbing Apollo by the neck and settling his head onto my shoulder. Sometimes, as the leader, I could assert myself.

I watched as Felix raised himself to his knees with a glassy but satisfied expression. Instantly, Radley hauled him back onto his lap, smoothing down Felix's hair. He ran his hands down Felix's sides to calm him.

Radley always offered gentleness afterward. *What would it be like with Emerald?*

My still sensitive prick twitched in a valiant effort to get hard again.

Then Felix became ashen like all his post-orgasm calmness had been chased away. "Pluck my feathers, where's that Court Fae?"

He meant Beau...

My throat became dry, and I swallowed with difficulty.

"He was taken away by Wells and he never came back." *It sounded stark put like that.* Felix's eyes widened. "You know, it doesn't matter how many rules we try to follow, this whole place is set up for us to fail. If even Beau can't pass their tests, then we don't have any hope."

Felix's lips curled. "We may have to work on your motivational speaking."

"On my feathers, I'm making a point here." I stroked Apollo's hair, and he glanced up at me through his thick lashes. "Four days left and then on the fifth day… Well, most guys don't know the day that they'll die, but we do. So, why don't we at least have a bucket list."

"*Don't*," Apollo pleaded. "I won't let you die, and if you do, you're killing me too."

"I'm letting us *live*." At last, after centuries trapped at the Court and in the Wicked Reform School, I understood that. "Friday is Beltane Night, which marks the start of summer. Number One on our Wicked Bucket List is to celebrate the magical rituals of our god, Belenus, like we did as kids. Don't you remember how special the night was with our families before it was taken from us?"

Felix leaned towards me; his eyes were bright with both excitement and fear. "B-but it's b-banned. The C-court Fae don't allow such savagery."

I'd make the Countess suffer for both Felix's stutter and ever making him think that the Forest beliefs were *savagery*.

"It happens on Friday night." My grin was dark. "What will they do to us if they catch us? Threaten to execute us?"

Radley's grin was even darker than mine. "If we're going to die, then we die as Forest Fae. We do that through the rituals of the Beltane." I shivered at his intensity. "But that's Number Two because the top spot goes to experiencing a true bond."

More than anything, I craved to live. But the other paranormals had already given us odds of 200:1 against last time, and I believed that they'd be worse on Saturday. But at least we could all feel a true bond, before we died.

Then I noticed how Apollo had tensed in my arms and realized that he thought we weren't including him.

I gripped his chin. "So, what's Number Three?"

Apollo blinked. "I can choose, My Lord?"

I nodded.

To fly with the phoenixes (or break their wings, I was never sure how competitive the swan shifters were with them), go skinny dipping in the lake under the moonlight, eat his own weight in pizza...

Apollo bit his lip. "To free the cygnets."

Radley looked like Apollo had slapped him. Then Radley's gaze fell on the sleeping cygnets, as if he'd snatch them possessively to his chest.

Apollo ducked his head onto my shoulder. Yet I burned with pride. I knew that he'd suffered from being stolen as a kid and now he wanted to save our cygnets.

I entirely claimed the credit for his leadership qualities.

"Done." I kissed the warm crown of his head. "It appears that we'll have to break out."

Apollo twisted, bouncing onto his knees with a joy that made even our impending danger worth it.

Felix cast a fond glance at Odile, before his brow furrowed with concern. "You do know how your wild schemes always end up."

I shrugged. "Of course."

"That's okay, just needed to say it."

Radley simply grunted.

The fire, however, that lit Apollo's eyes made my own fire within me surge. I needed to make someone happy at least. I'd had enough of grief.

The fae had taken the cygnets, and now I was giving them back.

First, I had to risk breaking out of the House of Fae. The dawn sang to me, tempting me into its forbidden light. Yet what would happen if I was caught?

CHAPTER SEVEN

**Wicked Reform School, House of Fae Grounds
Tuesday 27th April**

Dawn's light crept around the House of Fae's tower, as *I* crept from shadow to shadow. My stomach fluttered with a mixture of fear and excitement as it always did when I broke the rules. Felix and Radley prowled at my shoulders. I shivered in the breeze.

I glanced in the thin light of the morning across the grounds. They looked different like this: *wilder and free*. The trees were sleeping. I clutched Apollo's feathery body closer to my chest. Felix had snapped on his collar, despite Apollo's protests, before we'd lowered the wards that trapped us inside at night.

If…okay, let's be honest, *when*…we were caught

on this escapade, there was no way on Belenus' cock that I'd allow Wells to also discover Apollo outside the turret in his human form.

I might not be a typical fae warrior, but even I knew that it wasn't brilliant strategy to free cygnets but lose your own swan shifter.

I hugged Apollo tighter at the thought, and he glanced at me questioningly.

I darted through the trees, humming the theme tune for *Mission Impossible*. Apollo hissed, pecking at my chest. I didn't know what he was complaining about. Radley had already vetoed me listening to the soundtrack on my iPod.

I scanned the area for movement, before peering up at the sun streaked sky, which sang to the magic inside me. The Paranormal Prefect Patrol were always lurking around the school at this time. They were the dick paranormals who worked for the staff just for the sake of extra privileges and proving that they'd *reformed*.

Really, I should throw them a doggy treat next time I saw them and pat them on the head. Although, Oscar, the pure blood vampire who led them was such a jerk, he'd probably self-combust with outrage.

I smirked; I'd just found Number Four on my Bucket List.

Outrage a vampire.

Although, that did sound kinkier than I meant it.

Oscar and I had *history* (again, not with the kinky), and I'd insulted him before, but this last time needed to be something extra special. I'd given them their nickname: *The Prick Patrol.*

How was I to know it'd spread throughout the entire school?

It *was* catchy.

Also, I had a habit of breaking out of the House of Fae because I had a reputation to uphold as one of the mythological *Rebel* tribe. Usually, leaving the dormitory at night would set off the wards in my pants, and you *never* wanted to be punished by your own pants. I was certain that the Countess had chosen the settings. They were like being wedgied at levels that included atomic, bouncing, and Bankok.

Wow, did I hate Bankok (because feeling like you were being kicked in the balls during a wedgie really added to the experience).

It'd been days before I'd walked normally.

No fae had even risked breaking the magical wards that surrounded the skies and stopped us flying to freedom because a Bankok at that height would lead to a seriously embarrassing crash to your death.

But then, I'd bargained with the witches for spells that confused our wedgie-happy pants, and my mates and me had been able to start our prank feuds with the rest of the school. My personal favorite had been leading the zombies in a flash mob of the House of

Necromancers with a dance rendition of the Cranberries' "Zombie".

The Duke of Wells should award marks for pranks like that because they took true genius and organization.

The House of Necromancers hadn't seen the funny side. After all, they did spend most of their time hanging out with the dead.

Of course, the witches *had* tricked me too. What had I expected? They *were* dark witches. The spell to let me out of the House of Fae at night failed to include the one to safely return me without notice. Every time that I escaped, I knew that it'd end with my punishment. But it was worth it because the call to unleash my pent-up wildness was too great.

Forest Fae were never meant to be imprisoned.

I dashed across the farm towards Swan Pond. I breathed in the fresh air that hinted at the onset of rain.

All of a sudden, there was movement across the sky.

Had I been discovered already? I hissed out a breath, as my heart beat against my ribcage.

I glanced back at the cygnets who were nestled in my mates' pockets.

Don't let me fail them…

My lungs were burning, and my knees were close to buckling, but I ignored the warning signs and pushed through the pain. I spun behind the shed, which was as neat as the rest of Wells' farm, pressing myself into its shadow.

Felix and Radley stalked either side of me.

Odile poked her head out of Felix's pocket. "*Are we nearly there yet?*"

Felix stroked her head. "You've asked that six times already. And almost."

Radley raised his eyebrow at me.

"I thought I saw something," I explained. Radley went days sometimes, talking only with the power of gestures and grunts. "This close to the Day of the Wicked, the Prick Patrol are sure to be keeping a close eye on us."

"*If that Night Slave causes you any trouble,*" Lil Swan's voice was disturbingly menacing, "*then you rip out his fangs, right?*"

I blinked. "She's sounding more like you every day, Rads."

Radley huffed, amused.

"I've always wondered," if I didn't ask now, then I'd never know, "why are you pretending to be a gangster?"

Odile snickered at her sister.

Lil Swan puffed up her feathers. "*You can't be brought up in the Big House and not earn respect. Fear me...?*"

The quiver of uncertainty now in her tone, made

my heart ache. Radley scooped Lil Swan onto his palm and gave me a hard glare.

I cleared my throat. "I am genuinely terrified. You have the Fae Three as—"

"*My bitches…?*" Lil Swan crowed.

Radley growled, but Lil Swan only flapped her wings.

"Your bitches," I agreed.

Lil Swan settled down, satisfied. "*Don't mess with the swan from the pond.*"

"Deluded," Radley mouthed at me.

"*Aye, you're all <u>my</u> bitches.*" Apollo fluttered his eyelashes at me.

He didn't pull off the innocent face.

I gaped at him, but Felix laughed, softly.

"*We're going home,*" Odile murmured in wonder. "*River, are you coming with me?*"

Felix froze. His gaze darted between Radley and me like we could help him.

But what could we say?

"I wish that I could, Odile, but I'm not a shifter," Felix replied. "We're taking you to your real parents. They've missed you so much and…I know because I'll miss *you* just as much. But this way, you'll be safe after…"

He couldn't tell her after he was *dead*.

Let Odile understand…

"*But I want <u>you</u>,*" Odile wailed. "*I'll miss <u>you</u>.*"

"Stop it," Lil Swan's voice was sharp but as raspy with tears as her sister's. *"Don't you get it? They're not abandoning us, sis, they're freeing us."*

"We love you." I hadn't thought that this would be so hard. Had it been like this for our families when they'd given us up as Hostage Lords? Had they hoped that the Court Fae would foster us and treat us kindly? *What if we weren't doing the right thing?* "I promise, your true family will love you too."

"If there was something watching us, it's not there now." Radley clasped Lil Swan to his chest. "We need to move."

I nodded. "It was probably nothing anyway."

I hoped.

Court Dictate 697 stated*: If you're paranoid, your enemy has already defeated you.*

Wait, that one actually made me feel *worse.*

I forced myself on towards the lake across a carpet of gillyflowers, which were just starting to unfurl into sun-burst yellow life. Their cinnamon aroma shocked me with its spiciness because it reminded me of Emerald.

Suddenly, I wished that Emerald was with me, sharing the heart thudding excitement of this moment. I stopped at the edge of the pond in the hushed silence. When I placed Apollo down, I missed the shape of Emerald's hand. I was certain that her fingers fitted perfectly between mine.

My boots crunched on the reeds. The pond was black and silent. Bats snatched insects off the water.

The sacred swans slept floating on the surface with their heads tucked underneath their wings or standing on one leg. Like this, you wouldn't know how deadly they were.

Carefully, Radley and Felix placed the cygnets on the edge of the pond but not in the water because they couldn't even swim.

Without their parents to teach them, they'd never learned. My hands balled at my sides. Perhaps, the other fae were right to sneer that I was the Court's tamed *fae*. I'd had no one to teach me the true ways of the forest.

But I'd learn.

Odile glanced back at Felix. "*I'm scared.*"

"Me too." Felix bit his trembling lip. "But you'll be fine. Trust me."

"How do we wake up the swans?" I asked. Apollo launched himself into the water with a *splash*. "That'll do it."

The swans startled awake.

Apollo was as brave in his own way as Radley because the way that the other swans' eyes glittered and they reared up, surrounding the intruder, I was certain that they'd peck him to death.

"One way to go is to murder the shifter who's helping you," I hissed. "Or you could turn your feathery asses around and see that we're here to return something precious to you."

The swans' necks swiveled, and Apollo shot me a grateful glance.

Odile and Lil Swan huddled together like they were being assessed and if they didn't pass, their parents wouldn't want them back. But I'd seen the despair on their mum and dad's faces when they'd only been able to look up at them through the net.

They loved them.

Two graceful swans swam away from the flock and to the edge of the pond. Felix and Radley's wings brushed against mine; they were trembling, and I knew that they needed to sense my touch, as much as I needed to feel them.

Just for a moment, the swans' necks entwined in a perfect love heart.

"*Ma?*" Odile whispered.

"*Da?*" Lil Swan shuffled closer to the water's edge.

The two swans bobbed their heads in thanks to us, and then turned, allowing Odile and Lil Swan to climb one onto each of their backs. When the cygnets settled into their feathers, I'd never been so sure that they were where they belonged.

"Take care of them," Felix called, as the swans glided back to join the circle of shifters, "and love them."

"We'll be checking," Radley warned.

I'd never seen anything as beautiful as the swan shifters reunited in the dawn's light.

Apollo swam back to us, shaking out his feathers. *That's Number Three on the Bucket List checked off, My Lord. The cygnets are free, and even if I plucked out a feather and laid it at your feet every day for the rest of my life, there wouldn't be enough to thank you.*"

"I could've done without the horrifying plucking image but that aside, you don't need to thank me. I only wish that I could also free you, but even though Wells is one of the few fae who takes the whole *swans are sacred* thing seriously, you're a white Forest swan and too close to me for him to let you go. The cygnets, on the other hand, are from the Court flock and will be guarded by their own now." I glanced at the swans who were circled protectively around the cygnets and their parents. "He'll have a swan rebellion on his hands if he tries to take them back."

We'd done it. In the name of the forest, maybe I *had* been paranoid.

Then I yelped, as something tugged on my ears.

I stumbled backwards, flailing my hands only to meet a handful of squirming fur. The creature tugged on my ears again.

"On my feathers, I am the Marquess of Spring," I snarled.

Felix stared at me. "I appreciate the announcement. It's possible that I may have developed amnesia in the last five minutes."

The skvader, a small half bunny, half bird creature that like the myrmidons lived in the territory, which the Wicked Reform School had been built on, and were…to put it diplomatically…*jerks*, yanked on my ears again.

I gritted my teeth. "My ears."

Radley huffed. "Only your ears are noble? As an attempt to pull rank that's feeble."

"There's an asshole skvader behind me." I thought that it was restrained of me not to punch my mates in the dick, so yeah, brownie points to me.

Yet skvaders often worked as scouts for the Paranormal Prefect Patrol. What if they were about to raid the House of Fae?

Radley gripped the skvader by his long ears (see how he liked to have them tugged), and hauled him away from me. The skvader squeaked and then hung defiantly between us, staring up from his black eyes.

I gestured towards the farm. Felix and Radley stalked after me away from the pond and back under the cover of the trees. If an attack was coming, I wanted to be as far away from the swans as possible.

When I nodded at Apollo, he reluctantly flew towards the turret. He couldn't enter it, but he'd be safer sheltering at the walls than with us.

"So, are the Prick Patrol on their way?" Radley demanded.

The skvader turned up his twitching nose, refusing to answer.

"Wow, really good chat." I glared at the skvader; he eyeballed me back. "Let him go. He won't talk."

"Leave the bunny bird with me and a single carrot, and I'll have him singing like a canary." Radley's grip tightened around the skvader.

How'd we become good cop, bad cop again?

When the skvader's eyes widened, and his white wings that were tipped with black beat frantically, I shook my head.

"Let him go. If that band of bootlickers are on there way, then it's too late, they're already—"

"Here," a creepily arrogant voice wound out of the shadows.

How did Oscar always seem to manage that? Could pure bloods truly materialize out of smoke, as Oscar always boasted (read *lied*), or was he just sneaky?

Oscar slunk closer, swinging his cape like he was auditioning for the role of villain. His hair was short and brunette and he was far too pretty to pull off threatening, even with his fangs extended.

I'd heard rumors that Oscar had got caught up in vampire politics and killed half his own family. Oh yeah, he deserved to be allowed out early on good behavior as reformed just because he led this patrol of pricks…*not*.

Speaking of…

"You're feeling brave today." I fixed on my patented sneer, and next to me, so did Felix and Radley. Oscar would never admit it but he was terrified of the Fae Lords like most of the students in the other Houses. Never underestimate the power of a cold sneer and a reputation as a rule-breaker. "Are you here on your lonesome?"

Radley dropped the skvader, who flew up to perch on a tree branch, quivering.

"You know that we're duty bound to slice you into pieces and leave them as a bloody gift in front of the House of Vampires now?" Radley slipped out his scimitar.

"Oh, they'll love that!" Felix beamed.

I drew my sword as well, at the same time as Felix. The magical runes along their blades glowed.

Oscar became ashen. "Why would I expect the Fae Lords to respect the sanctity of my Prefect status? I enjoyed the little play you put on yesterday, by the way, with you on your knees." I stiffened. *He'd better not say it…* His expression became dreamy. "It was better than every one of my fantasies. I'm quite giddy about Saturday. The whole school is betting on you dying, and I'm personally crossing my fingers for strangulation. It has a certain type of poetry to it."

When Radley growled, lunging forward, Oscar clicked his fingers. "And how foolish do you believe me? I didn't come alone."

A pack of seductive female vampires flitted out of the trees around us.

Brilliant. Oscar's backup dancers had arrived.

Except, I didn't make that quip because last time I had, the vampire with Barbie pink nails had kneed me in the balls.

When she leered at me, I cupped my groin protectively.

Then a Nephilim with milky-white skin and deep brown eyes slipped with an arrogance bred of his too *beautiful to be real* brilliance out of the trees to stand on one side of Oscar. He patted at his golden hair, as if to check that it was still perfect.

It was, the asshole.

A giant shambling man who seemed to be nothing but muscles and soulful eyes rambled to the other side of Oscar: one of the most feared bear shifters.

The gang was all here.

I cocked my head. "It's not like this isn't lovely — surprising me in the romantic setting under the dawn trees — but if this is your last-minute proposal, Oscar sweetheart, then you should truly get on with it."

Straight face…don't laugh…

The bear shifter growled, one of the vampires gagged, and Barbie nails looked anguished like she couldn't decide who she wanted to kick in the balls first.

"You brought us here to marry this…irredeemable fae?" The Nephilim arched his brow. Before, the glow around him had been peaceful, but now it'd darkened to something terrifying.

The Nephilim could throw a compulsion around others that made them obey. The staff punished any Nephilim who was caught, but the sneaky assholes were good at hiding their schemes. Any calm that they exuded was no more than a predator tricking their prey. But it didn't trick *me* because a fae's magic could see through it.

The Nephilim's posturing didn't scare me, *much*.

Oscar reddened, bouncing up and down on the spot and twirling his cape in his outrage.

I grinned. That was Wicked Bucket List Number Four (outrage a vampire), checked off.

"Never!" Oscar burst out. "I'd rather marry the Dean of Discipline in a huge open-air wedding on the training grounds with mutants as my bridesmaids."

Felix pointed his sword at Oscar. "So, you have a crush on the Dean as well?"

Oscar howled, storming towards us. "I'm offering you a single chance to come with us quietly. If you do, then I'll tell your Head of House that you didn't resist arrest. Perhaps, he won't punish you too harshly."

The Nephilim crossed his arms, pouting with disappointment.

Adrenalin flooded me. I'd forgotten how much fun these little chats with Oscar could be. He was an asshole, but at least that meant I had something to *fight*.

My smile was dangerous. "Have I ever agreed to that?"

"I wondered whether you'd been broken." Oscar's fangs glinted. "Being close to death often has that effect." My patented sneer darkened to something real in my rage. Oscar stumbled back a step. "It was just a thought…"

I raised my scimitar, before slashing it through the air. "Fight me."

Oscar swallowed, glancing around at his gang, who were watching avidly. "Students are banned from attacking the Paranormal Prefect Patrol."

"Well, look at that, I don't care."

Oscar shoved the bear shifter forward, although he was such a mass of muscle that he hardly moved. "I nominate Barley to be my champion."

My eyes narrowed. "Coward."

Oscar shrugged. "But just watch. I'll survive this week, and you won't."

When Barley rolled his shoulders and then shifted into a huge grizzly bear with brown fur that looked like it'd been torn out in places, I shivered.

After dragons, grizzly shifters were rumored to be the fiercest.

My hand was sweaty around the hilt of the sword, but my magic rushed through it, ready for the fight. Oscar hadn't been lying about the ban on fighting with Prefects, but I was already in enough trouble, what was a little bit more?

That was the type of philosophy that branded me *irredeemable* by the other Houses.

I'd have smirked, if Barley hadn't reared onto his back legs and roared.

Instantly, Radley stormed in front of me, in full-blown protective mode. I caught him by the shoulder, however, before he could launch himself on the bear.

"Wicked Bucket List Number Five." I grinned. "Fight a bear."

Radley bowed, sheathing his sword. "Be my guest."

Then he and Felix, along with the vampire gang leaned against the trees to watch the fight. I should've added *become a gladiator* to my list, but then, I was enough of a slave already.

I danced around Barley, as he slashed at me with his claws. He snarled, tossing his head, and spittle flew out of the corners of his mouth.

Yuck.

I slashed down one of his haunches, and a clump

of fur fell into the undergrowth, then I slashed the other side, and another clump went flying.

Barley roared again, launching himself at me. I stumbled back at his sheer weight. He caught me in his paws, pulling me off the ground. I became pallid, struggling to hold in the cry. His claws raked my side, and his mouth looked like a yawning cave this close.

Don't eat my face off... How would Emerald love me without a face...? Idiot brain, you're about to be eaten by a bear shifter, thoughts of sexy succubi won't help...

I raised my sword under the bear's chin; the runes flared. "Checkmate."

"Why don't you kill him?" The Nephilim asked, nonchalantly.

Did he mean me or the bear?

"I said fight a bear and not get myself a bearskin rug," I rasped. The shifter transformed back into his human form. I squirmed in his sweaty hold. "Do you mind letting me go now? This is rather intimate."

The shifter growled, dropping me.

Felix and Radley prowled forwards with their wings outstretched menacingly.

"Fighting a Prefect, using a weapon without permission, resisting being taken into our custody, and of course, being caught outside your dormitory." Oscar counted off each offense with great relish. "My, what trouble you're in."

"But at least we'll always have our secret love." I blew Oscar a kiss.

Oscar spluttered in disgust.

The Nephilim turned on his heel. "Lord Spring is more badass than I believed."

I gaped at him. *A compliment from Mr Arrogance?* "Thanks."

"And marginally less of a jerk than everyone says."

Ah, there it was…

I inclined my head. "Thanks again…I think."

The Nephilim glanced over his shoulder at Oscar. "He entertained me. Let them go."

"What?" Oscar snarled. "Nothing could compel me to do so, and that includes your compulsion party trick. If you even try to force me, then I'll rat on you. How severe do you think the punishment will be for a Prefect who's caught abusing his position?"

The Nephilim pulled the *do I look bothered? Face*, for which his kind were well known. "I said, we're letting him go."

Oscar nodded, mechanically.

There were many kinds of slavery and ways to turn someone into a doll like the siren's song that enthralled humans. The Court of Fae had theirs, and the Nephilim's power was just another version.

If it meant that we escaped at least some of those

charges, then just this once, I'd be happy that Nephilim were controlling assholes.

My shoulders relaxed, and I sheathed my scimitar. My chest burned, and my breathing was ragged. Tonight had been invigorating, but I'd pushed myself too hard. I needed to sleep. Perhaps then, I wouldn't feel so dizzy and light-headed.

"No one is letting the fae go." Wells stalked out of the trees; his eyes blazed with fury. I jumped. *No, no, no...* "This is *my* House, and these are my wicked boys, who are in more trouble than they can imagine."

I groaned, finally sinking to my knees with exhaustion.

It'd always been inevitable that Wells would catch us, but I'd at least hoped to catch a couple of hours break to recover and that he wouldn't know the worst of our offenses against the Prefects.

Instead, Wells had heard everything, and since I could imagine *a lot* of trouble, I shook with dread.

CHAPTER EIGHT

Wicked Reform School, House of Fae Grounds
Tuesday 27th April

I knelt on the stone step in front of the turret with my wings held outstretched. The sun was high in the sky. Other fae passed me with sneers that I knew *I'd* patented and taught them. My thighs burned, my wings quivered, and I swayed with exhaustion.

Yet this Kneel of Shame was familiar in a way that would've been comforting if my knees didn't feel like they were bruised to the bone, I could hardly gasp in each aching breath, and the rain wasn't drizzling down the back of my neck.

Then my stomach rumbled.

Brilliant. I'd also missed breakfast *and* lunch. How long did Wells plan to keep us kneeling here?

When Felix's stomach growled in sympathy, I couldn't hold back my smile. Felix and Radley kneeling either side of me was just as familiar.

My brothers in the wing had never allowed me to kneel in shame by myself.

Once, I'd been sentenced to kneel in the central courtyard of the Queen's Court as a teenager because the Countess had said that I'd failed **Dictate 77:** *Be as graceful as a swan.*

She'd obviously never seen a swan in a fight.

All morning, the Court Fae who were my age had gathered to hurl insults at me. Back then, when I'd still cared what they'd thought about me, their words had hurt more than my bruised knees.

Then Radley and Felix had quietly entered the courtyard and knelt either side of me.

Felix had stared ahead of him, opening his wings. "We'll be your kneeling partners."

"I'm not asking you to be," I'd hissed.

Radley had shrugged. "You'll never need to."

We'd glanced at each other with small smiles that had been shields against anything that the Court Fae could humiliate me with because it'd felt like we'd been merely *choosing* to kneel there, rather than being shamed.

By the time that I'd been allowed to stand up, I'd swayed and had to lean on both my mates. *But that was okay because I hadn't needed to ask.*

I struggled to hold onto that feeling now.

Except, why had Wells only dealt out this punishment, rather than handing us to the Dean of Discipline? Oscar had tried to *insist* that the Dean should deal with us, before he'd shrunk back from Wells' frosty anger.

I had the feeling that we'd only been put in timeout on this step, rather than this being the punishment itself.

Apollo squirmed next to Felix, *honking* sadly.

"What are you moaning about?" I muttered. "Swans can't kneel. You're just sunning yourself on your feathery ass."

Apollo shook his tail at me. "*It was a sympathetic honk, My Lord.*"

I attempted, no matter how tired I was, to snicker.

"Behind the daffodils," Felix motioned with a lift of his chin, "kicking up the dirt. The little rascal is trying to burrow under them. That's *seven* to me."

Radley groaned. "I think you're in league with the skvaders."

Felix grinned. "Just lucky, guys."

Strictly speaking, when put in the Kneel of Shame, a fae was meant to reflect on his wrongdoing and how he'd brought disgrace on the Court. By being a public punishment, other fae could witness the humiliation and attempt not to be so dishonored.

Strictly speaking, it was *not* the time to play Spot the Skvader.

Also, strictly speaking, I didn't care.

"The game's not over yet." I gritted my teeth, struggling to ease some of the pressure off my sorest kneecap. "Check out the student with the face that looks like he's sucking a lemon."

"He stopped to take a swig of coffee in front of us this morning," Radley growled. "He's going to be waking up drenched in the stuff tomorrow."

"Revenge aside, notice the bunny ears behind his head." Many skvaders were playful and liked to play tricks as much as me. This one was amusing himself by giving the asshole fae bunny ears or sprouting wings out of the top of his head. Felix chuckled. "And a point to me, pulls me up equal to Felix."

I looked down, even in my triumph. I'd had time this morning to think about Emerald. I didn't want to be like this skvader, playing tricks for the sake of it, and I couldn't become like the Court Fae who plotted schemes.

I needed any bond with Emerald to be real, and for her to help because saving my people was right. The Nephilim *compelled* people, but the Forest Fae didn't. If I lost the beliefs of my people in how I rescued them, then shouldn't I just reform now and let us become Court Fae?

We couldn't die for something that'd already become corrupted.

I shook, as the rain slid down my face. I wouldn't be the one who broke my own people.

Clack — clack — clack.

Wells' polished boots stepped in front of me, and his shadow swallowed me.

I sighed. *How many times must I look at his boots from kneel?*

Lincoln stood next to Wells, imperiously glaring at Apollo.

"I hope you've had time to reflect on your shameful actions, Lord Spring." Wells arched his brow.

"I've done nothing but reflect and wallow in shame, Your Grace." Sad, serious face should do it.

"Eight!" Felix yelled, pointing at the skvader who was gnawing at the scabbard of Wells' scimitar.

Wells twirled around in shock, before turning back to us with narrowed eyes.

"Do you know why I didn't hand you over to the Dean?" Wells demanded.

"Demon prejudice...?" Radley suggested.

"A romantic but troubled history between you two that didn't end well with hushed up conspiracies and broken hearts...?" Felix offered, looking hopeful.

"Because he's a bastard...?" I cocked my head.

Wells clenched his jaw. "Because *I'm* Head of this

House, and no demon shall control my wicked boys or murder them and call it *punishment*."

"Good for you. Except for on the Day of the Wicked, of course, and then you're just ecstatic to see us all killed, right?" My eyes blazed.

"My only joy will be if you survive. When will you understand that you're the one who has to fight for that?" Wells gripped my chin, wrenching up my head. I bit back a cry. "Have you heard the story of the *Ugly Duckling*?"

"It's f-from the human world. D-doesn't learning that break your precious Court Dictates?" Felix forced out.

Wow, go Felix.

"Like many fairy tales, it was from *our* world first," Wells replied. "When you were a child, Lord Spring, you reminded me of the ugly duckling."

"Thanks a lot."

"Everybody dismissed you as an uncouth, inelegant child, whereas Quinn and Prince Lysander were always beautiful, shining swans." *Why did that hurt?* I'd never craved Wells' approval, had I? "They thought that they were invincible because they were so perfect, swanning around, gaining all the attention and followers from the weak cygnets who followed in their wake to be *drowned*." His fingers tightened hard enough to bruise, and I winced. "But *I* saw your potential and beauty, duckling, even when others didn't. And look at you now. *You're the swan who survived.*"

My throat was suddenly too thick to swallow, and my eyes smarted with tears.

Wells was wrong, but I couldn't tell him. Surviving my parents and then those executed after the rebellion hadn't been anything to celebrate. And I hadn't escaped, he just thought that I had.

I tried to shake my head, but he held me still.

"It's true," Wells insisted. "Except, *I'm* a swan as well, just like you, and I *own* this pond."

When he gently stroked my hair, I flinched.

"Remove your hand from him," Radley growled, "or I'll…"

"Glare at me some more?" Wells' eyes were ice-cold. "After last night, Lord Spring, it's clear that you need one-to-one Emotions Counseling as a priority. Professor Emerald is already the most feared staff member on our books. Her therapy room is on the top floor of the tower. Don't keep her waiting."

I fought to hold in the grin that threatened to bloom across my face because at last, I'd meet Emerald and not in an apple induced spell or across an audience of thousands of bloodthirsty students.

My magic danced over my fluttering wings in anticipation. My prick thickened and hardened in my pants. *Would she want me as much as I wanted her?*

"I wouldn't dream of keeping an esteemed

member of staff waiting." I tried to jump to my feet, but my legs were too numb from all the kneeling, and I stumbled.

To my shock, Wells caught me in his arms. Why hadn't he let me crash onto my face? He'd batted Beau away, allowing him to collapse.

Where was Beau?

My heart twisted at the thought that Beau was still missing. I'd kept an eye out for him all morning, hoping that he'd pass us with his haughty nose in the air and a snide comment about how we'd deserved at least an atomic wedgie for the break out.

But there'd been no sign of him.

What had Wells done to Beau for daring to disgrace the name of Court Fae?

Radley and Felix staggered to their feet, flexing their limbs to regain circulation. Apollo flapped his wings. Then Radley stormed to Wells, snatching me from the Court Fae like his touch would contaminate me. My thighs ached, and my knees buckled again.

There was no way that I was walking to the top of the tower.

Yet it was Emerald on the top floor. Perhaps, she'd find it romantic if I crawled all the way up to her?

Then Radley swung me into a bridal carry, and I broke at least three Dictates by yelping and clutching onto his shoulders.

The Kneel of Shame hadn't humiliated me, but the

way that Radley marched with me held in is arms into the House of Fae past the milling students flushed my cheeks pink.

I squirmed, hiding my face on his shoulder.

"Stop worrying," Radley commanded. "You're the Marquess of Spring. You deserve to be carried."

Well, put like that...

I emerged from the safe wood and rich leather scent of Radley's coat and turned my head back to stare down the gawking students imperiously. "I'll imagine that I'm merely too lazy to walk, and you're my personal slave."

Radley huffed. "Imagine what you like. We both know that tonight, you'll be *my* slave."

I shivered. To be fair, that sounded more likely.

When Radley carried me up the spiral staircase that wound through the center of the turret like I was no heavier than a bag of feathers, I realized that I took his strength for granted.

At last, we emerged at the top floor, which was the most feared in the House of Fae: The Discipline Floor.

Only a single strip light illuminated the implements that were tied to the walls. Whips of various lengths were ranked next to canes of differing thicknesses. The paddles were decorated like they were works of art, rather than pain. Yet the room was dusty because despite the Countess' frequent attempts to get fae sentenced to the top floor, Wells had at least controlled her.

It was disturbing to be under a Head of House who was as complex as Wells. He didn't want us hurt, and yet if we couldn't be shaped and reformed as he wished, then he'd kill us. Other Heads of Houses were straightforward sadistic bastards. At least I could simply hate them, without the confusion of trying to understand them.

In some ways, I could've become Wells, if I'd been raised alone at Court, and that was an even more disturbing thought.

I flinched, as Radley carried me past the leather straps. Those were the Countess' favorite to use on my wings.

Yeah, that was the unfortunate thing. Wells had been able to protect the fae apart from *me* because if I was to be bonded to the Countess, then I needed to learn her discipline.

When Radley dropped me on an ivory couch that I knew hadn't been there the last time that I'd been dragged into the room, I noticed the new sign on the wall: **Emotions Counseling Waiting Area**.

I lifted my eyebrow, as my gaze rested on the curled bullwhip just beneath the sign. Either this was the worst possible placement of a waiting room for therapy, *or the best*.

It all depended on the true nature of the therapy.

I glanced at a door on the far side, which was black and didn't even have a door knob. I'd always assumed that it was a closet and I hadn't wanted to think about what could've been hidden inside. But now, it had **COUNSELOR EMERALD** in gleaming letters across it.

Why did my breath hitch at that?

I rubbed my sweating palms on my pants, before easing my legs to swing back and forth. This time, the kneeling truly had done a number on my knees.

"You'd better leave me now, Rads," I said. "By my wing, I haven't forgotten the plan. Bucket List Number One is experiencing a true bond, but my duty is to save our people. This might be my last week, but I won't let it be my people's."

Radley snatched me by the collar of my coat. "Stop talking like you're already dead."

Don't let him do this... Don't make me say it...

I grasped his strong hands between mine. "We have this week and we're going to *live* it, remember?"

Radley's eyes gleamed dangerously as if with tears. He let me go with a shove, before turning on his heel and clattering back down the stairs.

I missed him the moment that he was out of view.

I was alone.

I traced over the runes on my coat.

I *hated* being alone.

Then the black door clattered open, and I jumped.

My pulse raced, and it felt like my insides were vibrating alongside my magic.

Emerald was here…

Only, instead of a gorgeous succubus, the bear shifter who'd fought me last night, shambled out, slamming the door behind himself. He looked *wrecked*. Sweat dripped down his forehead, and he was ashen.

Shaking, his legs gave out, as he slumped onto the couch next to me and stared into space.

I straightened.

What in the name of the forest had Emerald done to him?

Wait, what was she going to do to *me*? In the forest of Hope, she hadn't been my counselor. Yet she'd been kind to Felix. Although, I thought that it was impossible *not* to be kind to Felix.

I peered at the shifter. "Barley, isn't it? Are you okay because I don't fancy being squashed if you collapse?"

At last, Barley appeared to notice that he wasn't alone and turned his huge bulk to stare at me.

"*You*," he snarled. "I was sentenced to this session because I fought with you. That bitch in there tore me apart over it. I hope that she eats you alive."

Emerald was angry because he'd fought with me…? I couldn't help the goofy smile, which probably looked freaky considering Barley wouldn't understand the twisted romance of Emerald's gesture.

At least, I was choosing to take it that way. It made me feel better about the *eats you alive* sentence because I had a feeling that he was right about that too.

I was way over my head with Emerald.

"I happen to have anger issues and low self-esteem." Barley clasped his hands in his lap. "How would you like to suffer from magical mange? It comes and goes. Even my ass is bald."

That explained the tufts of fur that'd been missing.

"*Ehm*, I wouldn't…?" I ventured.

"Damn straight." The bear shifter sniffled. "It was the Dean of Discipline's idea. No one likes me anymore. The others call me *baldy*. They even have a game, which is named Touch the Moon. Can you guess what it is?"

I cringed back in my seat. This was just what I needed.

Confessions of a Furless Bear Shifter…

I shook my head.

Barley lowered his voice, conspiratorially, "The game is to be the first one to touch my bald ass. The *moon*, get it?" *Belenus, rescue me…* The bear shifter leaned closer. "I bet you were staring at my ass too, during the fight. I told the counselor that."

"You did *what*?" I gasped.

Brilliant. Now Emerald thought that I went around getting into fights so that I could stare at my rivals' ass.

"She was extremely interested in that little fact. In fact, she made a lot of notes about you. You're going to be ripped apart in there." He smiled, satisfied.

"Did you ever wonder if you'd be liked more if you weren't a member of the Prick Patrol and such a *prick* yourself?" I hissed.

The bear shifter twisted, crushing me under him. I struggled for breath.

"I can't say as I have. But I am wondering what it'd feel like to rip off your nose." When he opened his mouth, his teeth shifted to fangs.

I struggled, and my eyes widened. Yet all those hours stuck kneeling in one position had weakened my muscles, and I couldn't break free.

This was why students from other Houses shouldn't be allowed into our one. They were psychopaths and killers. Why on earth had Emerald allowed in Barley? Surely, it couldn't just have been to gather information about *me*?

Barley's fangs grazed my skin.

Goodbye, fair nose...

Then there was a cough from the doorway, and Barley froze. Was he trembling...this shifter who'd attacked me like I was nothing but a doll? He carefully drew back, straightening my clothes and patting me on the head, as if he'd only been playing.

I twisted to the now open doorway of the Emotions Counseling Office. Candlelight flickered around its edges like it was the entryway to hell, when I knew that it was my escape to heaven. I bit back a smile, although I was breathless with a surge of excitement.

I'd never truly understood Apollo's grand declarations or the Shakespearean stanzas that spoke of love, which Felix read to me with a soft smile.

Yet now I did. Every single line swelled through me at the thought of *Emerald, Emerald, Emerald…*

Her outline was just beyond the shadow of the doorway.

I'd be with her at last, and I knew then, that it didn't matter if she wrecked me as she had Barley, because I'd still yearn for her all the same.

Love was a dangerous, burning thing.

"Having fun already?" Emerald's voice was low and amused. "It's time for your session. Enter my lair."

Emerald pushed the door wider.

I struggled onto my numb legs and staggered towards her. My heart beat wildly, as I followed her into the light.

CHAPTER NINE

**Wicked Reform School, House of Fae, Emotions
Counseling Office
Tuesday 27th April**

When I stepped inside, I was dazzled by the light of hundreds of scarlet candles. I threw my hand across my eyes, before gradually lowering it and squinting at the flames of the candles, which hovered magically around the edges of the office.

After the dimness of the waiting room, the brightness was shocking.

Even though there was no window in this room like the rest of the House of Fae (I'd bet that it *had* once been a closet), it was as light as day.

I glanced around at the sleek wooden desk that was shoved against the wall. Two leather chairs had been placed close together in the center more like they were set up for a romantic encounter than therapy.

Wait, had Emerald rearranged her room before my session? There was no way on Belenus' cock that the bear shifter had fitted his huge legs in the small space between those chairs…

I glowed, allowing just a little cockiness to sneak into my swagger.

Did Emerald feel the bond?

Emerald was wearing the feathered white dress again, but her hair was loose and tumbled in waves past her bronzed shoulders. She was gorgeous and predatory as she prowled to her chair.

So, I'd found my type.

All of a sudden, I caught a glimpse of something red and fluffy moving near her ass. I peered closer.

Emerald glanced over her shoulder at me, before settling into her seat. "Are you staring at my ass?"

The tips of my ears reddened. I rushed to throw myself down in the seat opposite hers. The chairs were so close that our knees touched. I thrummed at the contact.

"*Ehm*, more like the hairy part. These sessions aren't recorded, right? I admit that out of context that sounded wildly inappropriate." I squirmed in my seat.

The fiery scent of ginger wound from the candles. My mind became hazy; I was intoxicated. I shook my head to clear it.

Was this her trick?

The red…snake-like…fluffy thing twitched and wound around Emerald's waist. My eyes widened.

That wasn't what I thought it was, right? Did she truly have a tail?

"A certain student told me some interesting things about you." Emerald leaned forward, swiping her fingers like she was scanning through invisible notes. *Was she pranking me?* "Yep, here it is." She gave me a considering glance. "So, you have a thing about bears' asses?"

I snatched the hilt of my scimitar like I could cut out Barley's lying tongue.

Too late…

"Hilarious." I attempted to smile. "Those shifters are real comedians."

Just then, Emerald's tail crept out and edged between my legs like it had a mind of its own and its slinky naughtiness had nothing to do with the serious counselor sitting opposite and questioning me on my *ass kink.*

Had she deliberately kept her tail tucked away in the forest?

Emerald's tail was soft and scarlet. *Why didn't it match her hair?* I had the strange compulsion to cuddle it like it was a plushie and then lick it.

Was a succubus' tail as sensitive as a fae's wings?

Experimentally, I stroked my wingtip along the

fluffy end of the tail and it quivered. Emerald's breath caught. Then the tail wound higher between my legs, pushing them apart with disturbingly powerful nudges.

What would it feel like if it decided to whip, rather than stroke?

If this was a session in learning to trust, then surely, I'd passed

When Emerald's tail caressed over my balls, I fought to stay still and not arch into the maddeningly light touches.

Emerald cocked her head. "Is this thing with asses a childhood obsession of yours, or do you think that it results from a trauma with shifters here at the school?"

Her lips twitched. *She was playing with me…*in more ways than one.

Yet fae were renowned not for compelling other paranormals or ripping them to shreds with their strength but for outwitting them. It was one of the reasons that we were feared. I didn't want to trick Emerald into loving me, however, but I could meet her on equal stepping in any game that she was playing.

To her, that'd probably be a turn-on.

I gripped her tail, circling it tightly as it twitched. She gasped.

"It's not bears' asses that I'm interested in." I sucked on Emerald's tail, tonguing it into my mouth.

This time, it was Emerald who arched, gripping onto the chair's armrests. Her knuckles whitened.

"Huh, so it's just Barley that you're stalking?" She forced out.

I let her tail fall out of my mouth with a shocked *pop*.

The tip of her wet tail stroked along my cheek, and her gaze softened. It was more intimate than if she'd stroked her tail up and down my prick. Although, for the record, I'd be up for that too.

When her gaze met mine, it was too knowing.

Succubi couldn't read fae's minds...?

"I'm only stalking you," I insisted. That had sounded *so much* more romantic in my mind. *Apollo, where were you when I needed you*? He'd have known just the right line. "I only *want* you. Look, can't we just forget all this counseling nonsense and take up where we left off in Hope Forest with the kiss?"

Please...

Emerald's tail whipped away from me, curling around her like a rejection. I shrank back in my chair.

"How many times, sexy wings? That was a Pleasure Spell. It wasn't real." Her eyes narrowed dangerously.

It sounded rather like she was trying to convince herself.

"It was to me."

Then my stomach growled, and I wrapped my

arms around my middle. I was light-headed with hunger, my knees ached, and my pride smarted.

Brilliant. So far the plan had gone: be embarrassed, suck a tail, and beg for a kiss.

Except, Emerald's expression had changed to intent concern. When she leaned even closer, her eyes blazed with a fierce protectiveness that I'd only ever seen in Radley's gaze directed at me before…like she'd battle the world for hurting me.

But that was just the dizziness making me imagine things, right? I couldn't let myself hope that it meant she could love me like I loved her. I'd battle the world in the same way if anyone dared to even think about hurting her.

"You're being starved," she muttered.

Rage radiated from her like a living thing. I shivered; she was terrifying and *hot.*

I shrugged. "Dictate 852 states: *Complaining weakens the fae who moans and the one who listens.*"

"Uh-huh. Is that why you complain all the time?"

"Since when did I listen to Court Dictates?"

Emerald's hair hung across her face, as she ducked her head. "I hated how mom would starve my brothers and use dickish stuff like…all those implements hanging in the waiting room…to discipline them." I winced. "Do they hit you with them too?"

I weighed up whether to tell her the truth.

On the one hand, it was brilliant to discover that

Emerald wasn't the same as the Countess and wouldn't use a bond to enslave or hurt me. On the other hand, she looked about one wrong word away from exploding, and I didn't want her ending up sentenced as a *student* to the Wicked Reform School alongside me.

Yet wasn't this my chance? I didn't even need to lie to her. Weirdly, it was the truth that might set us free.

I tilted my head, assessing Emerald. She looked younger, talking about her family.

Where were they? Why wasn't she with them?

If she was only projecting what I *needed* to feed from my pleasure, then why hadn't she flattered me with admiration and allowed me to be dominant, as she had in the forest? Telling me about her family couldn't have been part of that.

If I'd molded a perfect woman for the day (as the Dean of Discipline had with his golem secretary), then Emerald wouldn't be her.

Yet…*she was.*

I had to tell Emerald, and my insides squirmed at the thought. But first, I had to tip her just the right way to the side of the fae.

I leaned forward, clasping Emerald's hand between mine; I wished that I never had to let go. In surprise, she raised her head to meet my gaze. "Professor Wells doesn't allow most fae to be marked, which means that he doesn't permit corporal punish-ment. For an uptight bastard, he at least attempts to protect us in his own way. But I'm excruciatingly familiar with the implements in the waiting room because Countess Pond is in charge of my discipline."

Emerald's grip on my hand almost crushed it. "Why?"

I eased my hands out of Emerald's grip. *She was powerful.* "The threat of bonding on the Day of the Wicked or death hasn't been her only attempt to force a bond with me. She's been trying for years, and the strap has been one of her favorite methods of persuasion."

Emerald shot to her feet. Her eyes glittered with sudden fire. Her hair wove like serpentine tails. The candles guttered.

My heart beat hard in my chest at the sudden danger in the room, which vibrated with an electric charge.

Emerald hid it well beneath the purity of her dress and her pretty smiles but she was a predator.

I loved that she was badass.

Then to my shock, the emotion of her rage made the magic that'd been holding a glamor around her shimmer — just for a single moment — and her golden hair shortened to a fiery red. Her face became more heart shaped, and her eyes larger.

Emerald was even more beautiful beneath the illusion.

I gaped. Why would she be hiding who she was? Was she in some sort of witness protection or fleeing someone violent? Is that why she'd taken up this job that she hated in a school that was in the mountains, cut off from the outside world?

Yet what had made her snap had been a threat to *me*.

"You know what'll happen on Saturday," I said. "Nobody here cares about the culling. Do you?"

I held my breath.

It took more courage to sit with my nails biting into my palms, waiting for her answer than it had to kneel under the ogre's blade.

On my feathers, let her say *yes…*

"It wrecked me to witness your mock execution," Emerald confessed. "And it wrecks me to know what Countess Pond is trying to do to you…and has done. There are succubi who are cruel bitches like her. I grew up with a friend who was a Duchess; she used her influence to abuse her bonded incubi. My brothers were always terrified…"

She broke off, hugging her arms around herself.

I understood what that must've been like for her brothers. I'd never had a sister. What had it been like for Emerald to grow up, favored but helpless to protect her brothers?

I'd imagined that none of the female fae cared about *our* fear. *Had I been wrong?*

"Whatever you're running from," I insisted, "we can work it out *together*. There are weaknesses in the school. Other students have escaped with outside help. Alliances are possible..."

Emerald's tail cracked down between my legs, dangerously close to my balls. I took the hint, snapping shut my mouth.

"Don't be dumb. I'm a staff member, and we're inside the House of Fae. You're lucky that I'm letting you off with a warning." Yet I read the double meaning gleaming in her eyes: *not here.*

She was right. I was dumb to talk about escape inside the House of Fae. If Emerald decided to take some wicked pleasure from her students, as long as she didn't go too far, then that would be seen as part of her method. But even Wells couldn't protect me from the Dean, if I was caught in a true escape attempt from the school, rather than a freeing of the cygnets.

When Emerald waved her hand through the air, a box of chocolates appeared on her palm. She sat down again, placing the box on my lap.

"Hey, you didn't think that I'd forget you were swaying from hunger? Open it." She gestured at the chocolates. I pulled on the ribbon that hugged the box, and magically the lid sprang open. The rich aroma of the truffles inside made my mouth water. Would it be rude if I stuffed two inside my mouth at once…*maybe* three? She appeared to read my expression. "Nah, hold on. Each one is as filling as the food that you imagine. I'll let you have one every time that I like one of your answers during the session. Let's call it an incentive, which helps you savor the pleasure."

She licked her lips like she was going to be the one devouring the meal. Then I realized that she *was*. She'd be feeding from my pleasure. Was it weird that I found that hot?

I picked up a heart shaped truffle that was flecked with dark chocolate. "Thank you. I'll have a Full English breakfast, please."

If I was polite, there was a better chance of the magic getting my order right (and not leaving out the fried mushrooms and *three* rashes of bacon).

When I placed the chocolate on my tongue and then bit into it, despite *hoping* that the breakfast I'd craved since my exile from England would truly be replicated, I was still shocked by the intense flavors of bacon, eggs, and sausages. I took another chew, and a burst of baked beans hit me. I squirmed in the chair, giving an orgasmic sigh. When I swallowed the chocolate, it gave off a final delicious taste of fried mushrooms.

"Do you and the chocolate need a minute?" Emerald asked. "Shall I book you a private room?"

I licked my lips with a satisfied smile; I wasn't

starving anymore like I truly had eaten a fry up. "I could ask you the same question."

Emerald blinked. Then she glanced down at her hands, which had been rubbing between her legs like she was a moment away from hiking up her dress and slipping her hand down her panties.

"Your pleasure is more erotic than I was expecting." She flushed. "But then, those chocolates are a special treat awarded to incubi bonded."

My muscles became rigid, and I tightened my grip on the ribbon until it was pulled taut.

Bonded...?

Was this part of *her* courting ritual? Did she wish a bond the same as me?

I wanted it so badly that every one of my feathers burned as if on fire.

I plucked at the ribbon. "I guess that you have a whole harem of those incubi bonded loyally waiting for you back at Court?"

"If I had any," my gaze shot to Emerald's at the sharpness in her tone, "then they'd be at my side."

I bit my lip. "Did you give Felix any of these special chocolates?"

When Emerald nodded, her tail whipped out. It tipped up my chin, as she in turned leaned closer. "I'll meet your second friend, Lord Brooke, soon. Then I'll offer him the chocolates as well. Do you think he'll eat one? You see, I sense that all three of you should—"

"Eat you…I mean your chocolate?" I inquired with my pious face fixed on.

It didn't convince Emerald, who now wore her stern face.

For the first time, I got role play tingles for bad student and strict professor.

"You're using humor to distract from your feelings. You do that a lot. Don't you want to be joined with your friends in love?"

"Really, is that what I do? Well, here's some honesty. The Forest Fae and my own brothers *died* to be allowed to choose who and how many people they loved. The idea that I could have a bond *with* my friends has seemed impossible, but it'd be everything I've ever dreamed. So, don't go dangling it in play or as a method to break me."

Please, don't…

Emerald's tail stroked my jawline, as she kissed me, just once. It was so light that I thought I could've imagined it.

"I'm not playing or trying to break you, sexy wings." Her breath was hot against my mouth. "If you feel…something…then I do as well. But I won't *take* anything from you like I'm no better than the Duchess, just like you wouldn't from me. We all have to choose this."

She meant it.

"I do," I murmured (on my wings, I'd never consented to anything so much in my life), "I swear what I feel is the will of the forest."

She glanced at the stiffness tenting my pants. "Uh-huh. That forest has some large trees."

"Fae are blessed."

Emerald laughed, settling back in her chair. Instantly, I missed the touch of her tail, which twitched between us in the air. "So modest as well. Relax, this session isn't over just because we've…you know…"

I couldn't help the hurt coiling through me. I'd broken sworn oaths to my mates and risked dangerous punishments by approaching a staff member. But now Emerald was continuing the therapy like nothing had changed?

I furrowed my brow. "Nice to know that declaring bonds isn't a big deal to succubi."

Emerald's lips pinched. "It's a *huge* deal. But you and I are only just starting on this journey, and I have to at least have something to falsify my notes with, or do you want the Duke of Wells to choose a different method of reforming you this week?"

"I couldn't take it if he kept us apart." I didn't mean to say it, but the words slipped out.

She had that effect on me. I'd bet she was a deadly counselor with the other students.

"I won't let him," Emerald insisted. "So, tell me why you ended up being attacked last night?"

I froze.

She'd made the question sound casual, but there'd been an edge to it like I'd provoked the fight.

Wait, I *had*.

Whoops.

I shrugged. "Brawling with bears isn't my biggest problem."

Emerald swiped her fingers through the air and across her magical notes again (I was beginning to really *hate* those). "Disobedience, defiance, refusal to reform, and last night a break out attempt. Care to explain?"

My role play was going into overdrive now.

I curled my wings around myself like I could hide how turned-on I was, but since Emerald could gain power off my pleasure, *she knew*. Her eyes sparkled with amusement, before she fixed on her stern face again.

"You're making me blush." I smirked. "Those aren't even in my Top Three Favorite Failings."

"And what are?"

"Is this your famous method?"

The corner of her mouth slipped into a smile, before she was able to control it. "Depends. Is it working?"

"Depends. Do you know why *I* did that long list of wickedness?"

Emerald studied me shrewdly. "I know that last night wasn't a true escape attempt. You'd have been sent to Dean Aero if it had been. You weren't being wicked; you were being the noble leader." My head jerked back, and all of a sudden, it felt swelteringly hot in the candlelight. No one apart from my two Hostage Lord mates had ever considered me a *true* leader, even though I'd spent the last decade trying. "Lord River was frantic about the safety of his shifter yesterday. Seriously, tell me: why did you decide to risk so much for a shifter?"

I raised my chin. "Because if I can't be free, then someone deserves to be."

"That kind of honesty deserves a chocolate."

Why were my hands shaking?

I selected a lemon-scented white chocolate, imagining my perfect lunch if I hadn't missed it: fish and chips. When I bit into its crisp outer layer it was like the first bite into crunchy batter, before the soft cod inside melted on my tongue. I wrapped my wings more tightly around myself and rolled side-to-side on the chair, as the next chew brought the taste of perfectly fried chips with just the perfect amount of salt and vinegar.

When Emerald opened her mouth to speak, I held up my finger. "Just give me a second."

In the feathered heavens, no wonder succubi used these chocolates like declarations of love and also doggy treats for their bonded. I'd sit up and beg for another box like these.

"Are you done making love to the chocolate?" Emerald's eyes were glazed, and she was panting. But this time, she'd managed to keep her hands to stroking her tail, rather than her pussy. "Because I need to ask you something serious. *You* could be free as well. All you have to do on Saturday is to say that you're reformed. Then you'll be freed into the Court's custody. At least you'll be alive. If you want to escape after that…then why not do it?"

Instantly, I sobered.

With reluctance, I placed the box of chocolates on the floor. "I'll never be free and neither will my people. The choices aren't between freedom and death: they're between slavery and death. Up there on the stage, it's a public *shaming*. To demand that one tribe of fae renounces their heritage and joins another forcibly will forever dishonor them. We wouldn't be equals with the Court Fae: we'd *belong* to them. On my wing, a life like that in a forced bond isn't worth living."

Emerald clenched her jaw. She took a careful breath. "Yet when you're back in England, couldn't another tribe help you escape?"

I snorted. "Wow, you really respect the bravery of

the fae. Do you think that after the example the Queen made out of the Forest Fae any of the others would have the courage to rise up against her? In her Court, we'd be alone and trapped in a worse prison than this one for the rest of our long lives. I wish that I'd simply been executed alongside my brothers. At least then we'd all have died together."

"Don't ever say that again." Emerald yanked me out of my seat, and I swayed on my stiff legs. "A succubus doesn't allow her bonded to die. I'll find a way to help you. I just…don't know how yet."

I gripped her arms; my pulse was beating too fast.

Did she really mean it?

Yet why had that haunted look crossed behind her eyes? Why was she so frightened?

Tremors ran through me. *This was the plan.* It was precisely what Felix, Radley, and I needed to work any rescue attempt. Yet it felt wrong. My role as leader was to save my people, yet my role as Emerald's lover was to protect her.

"It'll be dangerous," I warned. "I'd rather cut off my own wings than risk your life…"

Emerald stopped my words with a kiss.

I gasped at the intense heat of her lips. When she drew back, ruby sparkles passed from her mouth to mine. They tasted like fiery ginger. I snatched her closer, devouring her and the magic like I'd hungered to since the kiss in Hope Forest. The chocolates couldn't fill the hole in me that starved for *her*.

I twisted Emerald around, splaying her across the desk. I wrapped my hand in her hair, and her tail *thwapped* around my lower back, yanking me closer. Then my knees prickled, and I gasped.

Emerald's power was healing me.

Panting, I pulled back from her, and she smirked up at me. "How are the knees? I could feel your pain all through the session."

"You can do that?"

"Only for those I love." She nipped at my lower lip. I wished that she wasn't studying my face because I couldn't hide my intense joy. *She loved me.* "Perhaps, try to stop getting hurt so often, huh?"

"Brilliant idea. Why didn't I think of that? Oh yes, because this is the Wicked Reform school, and I was sentenced here to *be* punished."

"Not anymore: *now you're mine*." Emerald's tail curled possessively around me, tapping my ass. "I can sense desires and needs with my powers, and it's been like being trapped in the middle of a nightmare, since I stepped into this school. But Lord River and you don't fit." Her lips curled into a smile. "Lord Brooke has his dark moments, on the other hand, even from a distance. But his strongest desire is to protect *you*. I can relate."

"He'll love you because I do. We'll all love you."

When I traced my fingers down her throat, she arched. "I'll share you with my fae and shifter lovers because you're the woman who we've been waiting for." I lowered my head to lick across her peaked nub through her dress, and she moaned. "Now we have you, we'll never let you go."

I slid up her dress, caressing her thigh.

Emerald reached for my hand, teasing my fingers towards her silk panties. But then, she stilled. Shuddering, I met her gaze in confusion.

"I'm not trying to run." She pulled her hand away from mine, pillowing her head on her arms. "You're the most beautiful creature that I've ever seen and those Nephilim are hot, even if they're jerks."

I drew circles on Emerald's inner thigh, and her breath hitched. "Do you want to talk about jerks or…?"

I curled my tongue between my teeth.

"This is your first time with a woman, right? I'd rather that it wasn't over a desk."

My prick was so hard it hurt, and my balls felt like they'd burst. I forced myself to smile. "Dictate 852, remember? There are no complaints about over a desk from me. I'd be fine on the floor, against a wall, or pretty much anywhere right now."

Emerald patted me on the back consolingly with her tail. "*Aw*, but I'll manage so much better than a desk for our first time, I promise. Blue balls never killed anyone, you know."

"Says someone who doesn't even have balls," I grumbled.

"So much for Dictate 852." Emerald leaned forward, touching the rune on my belt buckle. "Have you ever found out how high this goes?"

I yipped, as a low-level wedgie made my underwear feel like it was riding up my ass and crushing my balls. Luckily, only at the uncomfortable level.

"What was that for? I'm not into that kink, and what happened to the *no punishing* the beautiful and noble Lord Spring rule?"

Emerald kissed the tip of my nose. "Sorry, sexy wings. Firstly, it'll help with your little situation down there." Less of the little and okay, my *prick* had definitely wilted in shock. "Secondly, along with my falsified notes, it'll trigger to the other staff that I'm doing more than snuggling you in these sessions."

Grudgingly, I nodded. "You're forgiven."

"How gracious, My Lord," Emerald said in possibly the worst impression of an English accent I'd yet heard since arriving in America.

And I'd heard a lot.

Could I take back the *forgiven*…?

"Just don't make a habit of it." I attempted a haughty arch of my brow as if I was Beau, but

Emerald only laughed. "And when will I see you again?"

She tapped her chin. "Honestly, you're the wickedest case I've ever seen. You need daily sessions at least. I'd suggest group ones as soon as possible with your friends so that we can root out the causes of your rebelliousness."

Emerald meant with our bonded mates, so that we could work out how to save the fae together...and hopefully screw.

Both the plan and Number One on the Wicked Bucket List was complete.

Emerald was smart, kind, and as special as I'd sensed when I'd first glimpsed her. Yet that just meant that I had more to lose because now the woman who loved me was also in danger.

CHAPTER TEN

**Wicked Reform School, House of Fae, Sports Pitch
Tuesday 27th April**

The last class of the day with thirty other students, just before it was time to be sealed into the dormitory with wards, Fae Ball. I trudged to the pitch, which was behind the orchard, where the brutal game was played. Rain drove from the stormy clouds, and I shivered.

I scanned the line of trees for a chalk-white smudge. When Apollo had tried to watch this class any closer than the tree-line, his wing had been broken by a stray ball. But it wasn't safe that he was so far from us now either. I shot another glance at him.

What if Wells decided that the key to breaking us was through Apollo? *He wouldn't be wrong.* I'd only been lucky so far that he treated his own shifter, Lincoln, more like a hissing fashion accessory.

The pitch was on higher ground than the rest of the House of Fae, and from up here, I could see beyond the House of Zombies' dark roof to the main campus buildings and the Trial Area. It felt like my death on Saturday was so close that I could reach out and catch it between my finger and thumb, in that tiny patch of gray land beneath me.

Yet first, I had to survive the final lesson today.

I hated Fae Ball for two reasons.

Number One: No Marquess who'd been trained in elegant sword skills should be reduced to throwing balls like this was High School, even if it was a magic ball that read your mind to find its target.

Number Two: the balls were covered in a light sheen of iron, which hurt like being branded if it even caught a fae's skin, despite the fact that fae healed rapidly.

There were no teams. It was simply a battlefield, where everyone fought for themselves. Once you were hit, you were out. The winner was the last fae standing.

Of course, Radley *loved* it.

"Let the slaughter commence." Radley rubbed his hands together.

Well, he had to get out his psycho energy somewhere.

I wiped the rain from my eyes. "This is really very exciting. Being burned before bedtime always helps me sleep better than warmed milk or being sucked off."

I eyed the glittering balls that hovered at the side of the pitch. Fae were eagerly selecting their one for the game. The balls would follow behind them like the worst ever familiar. I grimaced.

"I thought that *I* helped you sleep the best...?" Felix clasped my hand, dragging me closer. "You drop off as soon as we snuggle up, and I start reading to you."

I ran my hand through Felix's hair, loving the familiar feel of it, and the sparkle in his eyes that were such an unusual color. "That's only because you use books with all those long speeches about love."

Felix's fingers tightened around mine. "Or is it just that you've found *someone* you'd prefer to fall asleep with each night?"

I didn't understand the insecurity in his eyes.

Radley threw off his scabbard with his scimitar, before ripping off his coat and tossing it onto the ground as well (maybe I could just pretend that my muscles bulged in the same impressive way as his?). ""He means, short wings, did you unleash the kraken on Emerald?"

I'd been so caught up in wondering how I could make my own six-pack look as defined as Radley's (his abs were a genuine work of art), that my unimpressed eyebrow wasn't as convincing as it should've been.

Trust Radley to reduce long speeches of love to a single sexual line. It was a genuine talent.

"The kraken," I insisted, "stayed in my pants." A passing fae glanced at me, shocked. I blushed and then winked at him. *Quinn, whatever realm you're exiled in, I apologize for sullying the name of Spring.* "Wow, there'll be some weird rumors going around about me."

"Like there aren't already," Felix muttered.

Wait...what?

I blushed again.

Felix patted me on the cheek, before pulling away to prepare for the lesson.

My lips thinned, as my shaking fingers dropped to the buckles of my scabbard just like Felix.

Fae Ball was played without scimitars, which went against Court Dictate, as well as fae heritage that a fae was never parted from their weapon. Taking my weapon off now and gently placing it next to my mates' swords was being stripped of my manhood.

It was like standing on a hill in the rain with my prick out, waiting to be hit in the balls...with iron balls.

It wasn't a good feeling.

Felix's head was still ducked. I couldn't go into a

lesson as dangerous as this one, without him understanding what had happened in my counseling session.

"Emerald's my bond," I explained. "And it's the will of the forest that *she* chose me as her bond as well."

Radley merely grunted like he'd been certain of it all along.

Felix's head shot up, and he grinned. He bounced up and down, hyperactive in his joy. "*Of course* she loves you. How couldn't she? Anybody with a brain would."

I huffed. "Most of this school hates me."

"I said a brain." Felix brushed the wet strands of hair out of my eyes. "Now you'll have Emerald, and we'll be able to work on our plan."

I didn't miss the heartache in his tone, even though he tried to mask it. Did Felix think that he wasn't included in the bond? Yet he'd still been happy for *me*.

That was love.

"Did Emerald offer you a chocolate?" I asked, carefully.

Felix's eyes lit up. He gave a quiet laugh, scratching the back of his head. "Pancakes with lemon and sugar."

Radley blinked. "What's with your *about to come* face? Why are you making me jealous of a sweet?"

I glanced between them. *Here goes...* "Succubi

have this interesting courting ritual with chocolates. Emerald offered Felix *and* me one. She's also keen on *you* trying one, Rads." If Felix's grin became any wider, he'd hurt his mouth. Yet Radley's look hadn't changed. *Did he want to bond together with us and Emerald?* "In fact, she said that she'd bond with all my lovers and help us on…you know, *the important thing*." I glanced across at the hut, which was halfway down the pitch, where the Countess huddled from the rain, watching the lesson. Emerald was right that we had to be careful. "Beltane Night on Friday could be our opportunity to talk more freely outside. Until then, we can plan and… This is our only chance to be truly together in a bond. Don't you want that?"

Radley dragged me towards him by the collar of my coat, and my breath hitched. "We'll see." He kissed me hard enough to bruise. His hand clasped me around the neck. I melted into his claiming assault. When he broke away, his pupils were dilated, but his expression was hard. "I don't trust Emerald yet. If she hurts you or Lix, then I'll teach her why fae are feared as the most terrible enemy. If she tries to betray you, then I'll cut out her lying tongue. And if she ever dares to break your heart, then I'll rip hers still beating from her chest."

That was the longest threat he'd ever made and it was for me.

How romantic.

"She won't," I promised. "Really, you'll see."

Radley cocked his head. "She *is* hot. I bet that she has the sweetest smile when she's asleep."

Felix shivered. "You know that you're freaking me out right now…?"

"Don't I always?" Radley raised his eyebrow.

This wasn't the best time to bring up the glamor but…

"You know that I said you could trust her?" I licked my dry lips, and Radley's flat stare didn't leave mine. He wasn't going to make this easy on me. "She might be…just a little bit…hiding her appearance."

"Like you stuff socks down your pants?" Felix asked.

"That was *one* time," I hissed, "and we were teenagers. I was feeling insecure because Rads just has to have a monster dick."

Felix snickered.

"You mean that she's wearing some kind of glamor?" Radley demanded. "Well, that just inspires me to place my life in her hands."

"It slipped when she was, ironically I'll admit, riding high on emotion. It's only because of the strength of my own magic that I saw through." I avoided Radley's gaze.

"Belenus' cock, I've been wanking to fantasies of a hag, haven't I?" Felix gagged. "I knew that it was too perfect someone like that was interested in me. She's probably actually a zombie called Frank."

I rolled my eyes. "She's still a succubus, only her hair is red. Why would she want to hide that?"

"You mean, *who* is she hiding from?" Radley slipped my coat off my shoulders, puddling it at my feet. "There's crap going on that we don't know about, and we have to discover it, before we can plan. I won't let the woman you love be threatened....by anyone but me."

With unexpected gentleness, Radley bent like he was performing a service and folded my coat, placing it next to his. Ever since we were kids, he'd never allowed me to pull rank. Yet he'd also never allowed me to forget that I *was* the Marquess of Spring.

Heat flooded me, and my skin prickled. I ached to kiss over every inch of Radley's exposed skin in thanks.

I reached to run my hand down Radley's back but then I caught sight of the Countess, who'd raised her binoculars to watch me. Self-conscious, I crossed my arms over my chest. The Countess had introduced the rule about *No Coats*. It meant that we could fly without the runes woven into the lapels stopping us, although those could've been adjusted for the lesson. She'd pretended that it was in order that the balls would hit our skin and leave sear marks. It was certainly thoughtful of her that if we were hollering in pain with burn marks, there could be no disputes that we'd been hit.

It was just as likely that she'd wanted to ogle *me*.

Three balls whizzed to spin in front of my mates and me, as if eager for the game to begin.

I searched the gangs of fae in desperate hope that I'd see Beau's pale face amongst them. Yet he was still missing.

Why would the Duke of Wells take it so personally that a Court Fae lost a single game to us?

I hoped that Beau was okay. On the name of the forest, I'd never thought that I could care so much for a Court Fae.

I sighed. Exhaustion dragged at me. As Beltane approached, my magic was both growing and attacking itself inside me. I knew that my illness was progressing at a frightening speed. Doctors had examined me as a kid but had never been able to find the reason that I couldn't transform into fae form, and now, even fly at normal size.

I always sensed that there was something truly wrong…*different*…with me. Yet it'd been years since I'd trusted anyone in authority enough to be honest about how I felt.

All I wanted was to drop into a deep sleep (sexy dreams of Emerald would be a bonus). Dodging iron balls in the rainy twilight was more of a nightmare.

Unless, I could add my own fun into the mix…

"Cover me," I whispered to Felix.

Felix stretched out his wings to block me from the Countess' view. I crouched next to my coat, slipping out my iPod and clipping it onto my belt.

I'd rather have a dance workout, than a battle against my own tribe. But maybe I could combine the two...?

"Get ready!" The Countess bellowed.

The rest of the fae rose into the air with a fluttering of golden wings. Their balls spun next to them like rabid war dogs.

I alone was abandoned on the pitch. I should've simply had *target* daubed on my forehead. Yet Radley and Felix hovered above me. We didn't exactly follow the rules of the game. Instead, they remained as my bodyguards.

There'd never been a time when my mates hadn't protected me.

"Three...two...one... *Fae ball*!" The Countess dropped a swan feather to start the game.

Instantly, iron balls shot through the air like they were fired out of cannons by thoughts alone. Fae hollered, crashing to the ground.

"Boom!" Radley yelled in victory, as he clipped a fae's wing.

Seared fae sullenly limped to the side-lines to watch.

Yet I was too caught up in surviving to notice who

was in or out. I hissed, as a ball grazed my wing, close enough for me to feel the sting but not to count as a hit.

Too close.

I dived over a fallen fae, spinning around balls that were directed at me and hurling my own one upwards in a sneak attack.

Then I turned on my iPod.

Prodigy's "Warrior's Dance" exploded out. I grinned, caught in its rhythmic wave of serious bass and synth rhythms. If the Countess wanted to make this into a dangerous fight to the burned, then I'd transform it into a *rave,* until I was burned.

Ah, the happy memories of the illegal raves that I'd held here over the years...

One thing that I'd admit about the dwarfs: they knew how to headbang.

I lost myself in the music, from my wings to my hips. I breakdanced, even as my lungs gasped for breath. The fae falling from the sky and the spinning balls were nothing but the strobe lighting of my own party. I danced to my own beat.

Radley's ball slammed into a fae's guts.

"Another one bites the dust!" Radley's grin was devilish.

Felix's ball spun faster than any of the other fae's, shooting in accurate trajectories to pick off adversaries one by one, as they tried to sneak closer to me.

Felix was so smart that he'd worked out the best angles to hit as many as possible like potting pool.

"Sound trumpets! Let our bloody colors wave! And either victory, or else the grave." Felix looked dangerous as he spun his ball above his palm like he was a warlock.

Felix did realize that this wasn't a true battle, right? Although, caught up in his Shakespearean blood-lust, he was *hot*.

I glanced around the pitch. At least half of the fae were now defeated on the side-lines.

Why had it gone quiet all of a sudden?

Shocked, I realized that now I was breakdancing all by myself in the center of the pitch.

Flushing, I switched off the iPod and shuffled back underneath the shelter of Radley and Felix.

Why were the other fae huddled together at the other side like they were discussing team tactics and this was football, rather than Fae Ball?

The fae with the sour face, who'd taken his long swig of coffee in front of me, when I'd been in the Kneel of Shame this morning, glanced over his shoulder. His eyes narrowed.

I understood the look. It spoke of anger and hate. It was the look of bullies everywhere who didn't understand someone who was different. It was also the look of someone who was scared and going to die… and in his mind, it was *my* fault.

He wasn't wrong.

"I won't just drench him in coffee, I'll force him to drink so much of it that his stomach bursts," Radley hissed.

"He's stirring up the others against you." Felix was cool again; he cocked his head, assessing the situation like he always did. "Rads and I will spread our wings and take the hits."

"Oh, really? Because what's actually going to happen is that we'll *all* stand side by side and take them." *Why would they think that I wanted them to sacrifice themselves for me?* The Hostage Lords suffered together. "Brothers in wings," I murmured, unable to hide how raspy my voice was.

Radley landed next to me. "Brothers in wings."

His wings stretched to touch mine. They meant love, home, and protection.

Felix landed on my other side. "Brothers in wings."

Felix's feathers brushing mine tugged my mouth into a wicked grin, despite the fact that the other fae had spread themselves out opposite us like a firing squad.

The Countess stood up in shock. "What's going on? Stop at once…"

"Three…" Radley counted.

"Two…" Felix continued.

"*One…*" I finished.

My mates and I hurled our iron balls at the collected fae, at the same time as they let off their barrage directly at us.

"We live for our brothers," I roared.

Then the wall of balls hit.

I screamed, as I was seared by iron, over and over. My sensitive wings and chest were burned. Next to me, I felt Felix go down.

Breathe…come on…in and out, in and out…

I dropped to my knees.

Radley attempted to drag me back up, but the opposing fae were hurling balls at us again, even though we were out of the game.

There was a sudden flurry of white feathers and hissing, as a swan landed in front of me, shielding me with his wings.

Not Apollo…they'd break his wings again…he'd be killed…

"Stop," I gasped.

Then Apollo was lost underneath a sea of iron.

I choked on a wail, trying to struggle onto my feet.

When a ball hit me square in the back, my skin scorched. I gritted my teeth, but it shoved me face first onto the muddy grass.

I was going to die today.

Emerald…somehow…hear me…know that I love you…

All of a sudden, my lips heated and I tasted fiery ginger. I tugged back on the bond in desperation.

"Emerald…?" I murmured.

Finally, my vision faded, and the battlefield went black.

CHAPTER ELEVEN

Wicked Reform School, House of Fae, Dungeon
Tuesday 27th April

I awoke from the black into the black.

I gasped like I'd been brought back from the dead (and having witnessed how kinky the Necromancers were, I didn't want to think about having been under their control). I cupped my balls just to check that they hadn't been sliced off to become bauble trophies on another Houses' wall.

Then I slid my hand along my prick to be certain that *it* hadn't been claimed by the fae who'd defeated me as a battlefield trophy.

Thank Belenus, I was still alive and hadn't been castrated, which really showed how a decade spent in the Wicked Reform School lowered your expectations.

I was, however, naked, cold, and in the dark.

In the name of the forest, where was I?

I should've been in agony. Yet when I ran my hand along my skin, I couldn't feel a single burn. I flapped my wings experimentally.

No pain.

Sure, I should've been happy that I'd been healed. But mysterious luck was only good if it came from Felix's Fortune Magic, and he wouldn't have cured me and then abandoned me alone in a secret dungeon.

I clasped my wings around myself. I'd bet that this hidden room was based on the cells beneath the Queen's Court. I had to give Wells kudos for how dedicated he was in his recreation of Court life.

I didn't know if it freaked me out more that I didn't know that this room existed or that I'd finally broken Wells' composure enough to send me here now.

I shivered in the dank air, as my nose wrinkled at the stuffiness. I blinked up at the shadows. Then I ran my hand over the smooth metallic wall, before pushing myself to my feet.

Where were my mates and Apollo? Were they even alive?

I gritted my teeth.

Don't think it…mustn't think it.

"We live for our brothers," I whispered, but it sounded more like a plea.

My words were swallowed by the black.

I was alone, and I was trapped.

My pulse pounding in my temples, I clawed at the wall.

What if Wells kept me down here until Saturday…*when it was too late?*

"Emerald!" I yelled.

I knew that she couldn't hear me. Yet her name and the bond lit hope through me, making the dark less oppressive because there'd always be my love for her.

I edged along the sides of the room, testing out every surface that I could feel.

Yeah, this fae wouldn't be escaping through solid gold.

In frustration, I kicked the wall. Then I howled, clutching my toes. Kicking walls hurt *so much more* without my boots on.

"Can't you control your emotions at all? Calm down, it doesn't do any good," Beau's cool drawl wound from the shadows behind me.

I jumped and then twisted around with a grin so wide that my mouth ached.

A light flared, hovering above Beau and casting the cell in a soft glow like moonlight.

He had some serious magical skills.

I'd been right: I was shut in a dungeon. The circular room must be below even the dormitories, and there was nothing in it, except Beau.

Had he been imprisoned in here ever since he lost the Apple Game?

Beau was a pale beauty. He sprawled on top of a pile of rags with an affected nonchalance, as if I'd invaded his bedroom. Wait, what if Wells shut him up here so often at night that it *was*? I'd barely noticed where he slept before.

Was that another reason why Beau was so touch starved?

I ached to massage his shoulders and wings to stop their twitching. He must be in pain.

"Fancy meeting you in a place like this." I leaned against the wall. "And I'll get right on that calming down. I mean, it's not like I've been worrying about you for days now after you disappeared."

Beau's haughty mask dropped, and a blush spread across his cheeks. "You worried about...*me*? But I'm a Court Fae."

"I'd noticed."

Beau swallowed. "I'm surprised that Your Lordship would even note the absence of a peasant like me."

I frowned "You don't have to keep calling me that. Quince will do."

Beau arched his brow to hide the way that he'd

mouthed *Quince* like it was something precious that he was frightened to dirty. "Your friends may disagree. They were forceful in their insistence that I show the proper deference. I know how harsh Lord Brooke is to those who don't respect you."

Radley's justice against those who hadn't *respected* me flashed through my mind, including hiding shrimp all around the House of Demons, so that it'd smelled like a corpse for months, chucking an elf into the Fountain of Woe, and my personal favorite, making a Nephilim kiss my ass, after he'd mooned me with his.

Good times.

"I can't spin that Radley's hot on creating a fierce image for us because it's what we've needed to survive, but you're," ...*special*... "my mate now as well. Look, you deliberately failed the game to save my shifter, and you've been suffering for it since. Only someone..." *Why couldn't I get myself to say special?* "just as loyal and brave as Radley or Felix would do that for me. Perhaps, we should call ourselves the Fae Four now...?"

Beau's intake of breath was sharp. His wide gaze was both broken and hopeful in a way that tore at me. He pulled the rags around himself in jerky motions.

What had I said?

I studied the way that Beau's face was even paler

than before. "*Ehm*, maybe you're the one who needs to calm down?"

"You say it so casually," Beau muttered, blinking rapidly. "As if it wasn't what I'd waited for my whole life."

His wings twitched: the advanced stages of touch starvation. *Had it driven him crazy?*

"Well, thanks for the chat, but we need to get out of here. Do you know where the others are?" I turned back to the wall, banging on the metal with a *clang*.

"The Duke of Wells shan't let you out," Beau's voice sounded hollow. "He's forbidden me to tell the Forest Fae the truth because it'd endanger me, but I believe that it's more likely that he's ashamed of me. You see, I'm his only son, and he locks me in here whenever I disappoint him. If he's decided that he wishes you to spend the night in here, then there's no escape."

Beau was Wells' son...?

I ought to hate him now on principle alone.

Yet I didn't because I finally understood why a Court Fae was risked here at the reform school: he was visiting his father.

Beau was subjected to the same lessons as the other students like he'd been sentenced to a crime.

Beau was innocent.

My hands balled into fists.

I knew that Wells wielded power as Head of

House but not that he could treat his own son in this way.

All of a sudden, it was clear to me that the division between Court or Forest Fae didn't matter when it came to brotherhood. Whatever happened, Beau's fate was entwined with mine. But how could I convince Emerald that she needed to save Beau as well? He wasn't part of my tribe or the Day of the Wicked. Yet there had to be some way to take him away from the cruel Court.

If I survived, I couldn't leave him behind.

Wait, how long had this silence dragged on? Did that mean it'd been my turn to respond?

A resigned look had settled on Beau's face. He'd expected me to reject him. He was, after all, the son of the man who I'd been rebelling against ever since I was a kid.

Beau's expression became shuttered, as he deliberately plumped the rags like they were feathered pillows and settled down with his back to me. "Keep it down," his slim shoulders were tight, "some of us need our sleep."

At last, I smiled because for the first night since he'd arrived at the reform school, Beau wouldn't sleep alone. Instead, he'd experience what it was to sleep like a Forest Fae.

I longed to stroke him, until his wings stopped

twitching. When I dropped to my knees and crawled behind him, he froze.

"What are you doing?" Beau demanded in a panicked whisper.

"*Shh*, sleeping." I sighed with contentment, wrapping my wings around Beau's middle.

"You're a strange fae." Beau glanced over his shoulder at me, although I noticed that unlike the last time that I'd hugged him, there was no demand that I *not touch him*.

"It has been said." I snuggled closer, sniffing his hair that smelled deliciously of peaches.

I sucked a strand just to see if it tasted as sweet. I sighed dreamily when it did.

Beau yelped. "*Liberties*."

My eyes widened. "If you're the Duke of Wells' son, then that makes *you*…"

Beau twisted in my arms; his face was so close to mine that I could see each delicate eyelash and feel every gust of his breath across my lips.

Beau's smile was smug. "The Marquess of Wells, which interestingly enough as a Court Fae means that *I* outrank *you*."

I groaned. *Karma bites me in the ass again.*

Amusement danced in his eyes. "Perhaps, you should try calling me *Your Lordship*…?"

Why was it so sexy the way that he blushed, even as he tried for commanding?

"Of course, *Your Lordship*," I whispered against Beau's lips. I had no problem with someone who was either higher rank than me or who was, like Emerald, more powerful. In fact, it was a turn-on. By the way that Beau moaned and his prick pressed against my thigh, having someone finally acknowledging his status was a turn-on for Beau. He was a Court Fae, color me surprised. "As you're now the leader," Beau moaned again, wrapping his arms around my neck, "how about telling me why I've been trapped down here with you?"

Beau licked his lips, and his wings fluttered. "My father is allowing you to take the blame for the fight. Your friends look set to be apportioned some of the blame too. When they carried you here, the Countess and he had a terrible argument over it. The Countess said that you provoked the battle, even though the other fae are remorseful and have confessed. They almost killed you; I don't believe that they meant to."

I snorted. "That's funny because it certainly felt like they were trying."

Beau nipped my lip, and my eyes widened in surprise. "Surely you don't blame your own people for being angry and scared? They lost control of their emotions and should be punished for it, but you of all fae should understand them. They have no control over their own deaths. They look at you and see someone who doesn't belong, just like when they look at me. But yet they know that their suffering is because of *you*."

"Don't pull any punches."

Tentatively, Beau raised his hand to stroke the back of my cheek; I wondered if he'd ever done that to another fae before. The gesture meant everything to me because I knew how hard it was for him.

"They don't know the Court, or what you've suffered. They're not as strong as you, *Your Lordship*," Beau breathed.

Beau's magic entwined with my own. He was pledging to follow me, even though he outranked me. In fae tradition that bound us closer than a bond.

I buried my fingers in Beau's feathers, and he shook at the sudden touch. He was more sensitive than any fae I'd known because of the touch starvation. I massaged along his feathers, tracing each one individually, as he panted.

"And *you* survived the Court, Wicked Reform School, and your own father." I remembered with horrified disgust the way that Wells had dunked Beau in the grimy water. "They're not as strong as *you* either."

"You still don't remember me, do you?"

I blinked. *Remember him...?*

Why were my guts roiling like I'd forgotten Felix's birthday and his cute face was about to crumple only much worse?

"I don't remember why I'm not covered in burns," I answered with my classic distraction technique.

By Beau's narrowed eyes, it hadn't worked. "The counselor healed all of you, even Apollo. She's truly the most powerful succubi that I've ever known."

"You've known many?" My bond sang at the thought of Emerald after the intense way that she'd visited me through our connection on the pitch.

Yet why was I surging with jealousy?

On the other hand, the idea of Beau and Emerald together was hot.

Beau waved his hand airily. "The Countess is friends with the Succubi Court. Father has allowed me to dine with Emerald and him since she was hired by the Dean. I like her because she notices me."

"The Dean hired her?" I wanted to ask just precisely what *liking Emerald* meant, but first, I needed to know why our Emotions Counselor hadn't been directly hired by Wells.

Beau bit his lip. "I just know that the Dean hired her into the school, and then Wells gave her the post as counselor."

Was that normal?

This time, I needed to distract *myself* from the troubling thoughts. I tightened my fingers in Beau's feathers, and he arched like I'd squeezed his prick.

Interesting.

"Too much," Beau gasped. "It's like this...

swelling of pleasure inside me and it's cresting but just…not quite. Plus, we're breaking three Dictates right now." He humped against my leg; his prick was hard and pulsing. "All this pleasure beneath my skin, and I need…"

He broke off with a sob.

"I'll give you what you need." I swept my hand across the nape of his neck, squeezing. "Just hold on a little more. I promise, it'll be worth it."

I rubbed my prick against his, and sparks of pleasure shot through me. My balls were full and aching. Desire coursed through me, driving me closer and closer to the edge, but I held myself back with a struggle.

Beau needed touch and intimacy. He needed to *feel* this.

I caught his lips with mine; they were sweet and soft. Yet the way that he pushed back, meeting every thrust of my tongue, was passionate and spoke of a desperate yearning that I didn't understand. When he sucked on my lower lip, biting it, I clutched him by the neck, dragging him onto his back, and caging him underneath me.

Beau's prick was hard, but his eyes were wild. He lay beneath me with his wings outstretched like he was my sacrifice or *craved* to be.

What was I missing?

Beau's alabaster chest rose and fell too rapidly. I

caressed along the path of his muscles, and they jumped.

"How could any father keep their son from touch?" I watched the way that Beau both arched into and then immediately away from every caress.

"You don't have a father." Beau's voice was suddenly low and dangerous. "You wouldn't understand. My father lost his wife who he idolized, and I can never live up to her ghost."

"I'm sorry." I kissed Beau's pink nipple in apology, and he gasped. "But I have a brother. I thought for a long time that he'd simply abandoned me as a Hostage Lord to the Court. Of course, I know now that the Queen had him by the balls. If he hadn't handed us over, she'd have murdered the entire tribe. I wish that Quinn hadn't rebelled for my sake. But at least I know now that he never stopped standing with me wing by wing."

"I'm thrilled for you." Beau's mouth twisted like he was holding back tears.

Why was he using *my* sarcasm?

I tenderly kissed Beau's chest, before resting my head against it and wrapping my wings around him. "Go on then. Why should I remember you?"

Beau stiffened. "I don't know. Why should you remember a child who played with you at Court? I imagine that you hated all Court Fae back then, and I was only too stupid and lonely not to realize that you merely tolerated my presence. Father allowed me so few play hours that those I spent with the Hostage Lords, who always appeared so full of joy despite being apart from their families, were the best of my life. I didn't exactly know *how* to play, so I mainly hung around on the edges watching…"

Oh no, please no, how could I've forgotten…?

"You were the cute kid who always asked shyly to play chase," I said.

I remembered now.

Beau had been the only Court Fae to treat Felix, Radley, and I with kindness. He'd never jeered at us, when we'd been in the Kneel of Shame and sometimes, had sneaked us water. Yet even back then, I hadn't known his name because in my mind, he'd merely been another enemy Court Fae.

I'd been an idiot because in fact, he'd been a *Marquess,* who'd been as lonely as us and had only wanted our friendship.

Beau's heart was *thudding* too hard in his chest. I could hear its rapid drumbeat, and it was matched by my own against his.

I wished that I could go back and change things. Our companionship had meant so much to Beau, and yet I'd forgotten it entirely.

Beau nodded. "I'd seen you play chase once, so I knew how to play it. I longed to break into the closeness that you three had. I knew that I never would. For years, I'd dream that you'd invite me to join you as one of the *Fae Four*."

My breath hitched. I'd offered that so casually earlier.

Beau should punch me in the dick.

Instead, Beau stroked his hand through my hair like he was touching a god. "When I became older and father stopped me playing with you, they became my happiest memories. I had to hide my excitement when I was first ordered to accompany father to the Wicked Reform School because I'd see you again. Let me guess, you don't remember our first meeting here, either?"

It was strange to have been important to someone, and yet to have barely noticed them.

I flushed with shame.

Radley, Felix, and Apollo had been my family and world for so long, maybe I'd forgotten that other people existed, loved, and hurt as well. If I could be open to Emerald's bond uniting us, then I could be open to finally seeing Beau.

"Was I a jerk?" I entangled Beau's legs with mine, so that every inch of our skin was touching.

"Of course you weren't, Your Lordship, you were perfectly kind. You were never anything *but* kind to me like you'd be to a stray kitten that'd wandered over to join in the fun." I winced: *ouch*. "That morning, I'd had a terrifying meeting with the Dean, been intimidated by a gang of Forest Fae, and shown this cell if I misbehaved by father. I was frightened, but then I saw *you*, hanging around underneath an apple tree. I'd rushed to you, thinking that I'd have a group of friends at least. You'd been laughing at something Lord River had said, then you'd turned to me coldly like I was a stranger and asked, "Are you lost?" You had no idea who I was."

"I didn't even know that I'd spoken to you."

Beau wrenched back my head. "I was so devastated that I just stood there in silence like…you'd broken me…and Lord Brooke muttered something about *kicking haughty Court Fae's asses, if they were crazy enough to bother the Marquess again…* So, I didn't."

"I've spent the last days and nights doing nothing but thinking about you, as well as searching for you in every face." I wrapped my hands around Beau's cheeks hard, even as he gripped my hair like we both needed the pain and connection. His olive-green eyes were pooled with tears, and when one fell, I licked it from his cheek. "Even when I was kneeling in pain or having iron balls thrown at me, *you* were what I was remembering: the Marquess of bloody Wells." I pressed my lips against his in a kiss that willed him to both believe me and to force myself to imprint the feel of them. I couldn't bear the thought that I'd ever forget him again. "You're mine now. I can't take back the years that I wasted without your friendship; I wish that I could. But your silent loyalty and love is a gift. I swear on the forest that you shall never be forgotten again."

I moved up and down against Beau like it was a dance, never letting go of him, as he never let go of me. Our pricks rubbed against each other, pushing us both towards that crest of blinding pleasure.

Beau trembled, and his wings curled around me, pulling my body even closer against his.

"Not yet," I murmured, "together."

Beau's eyelashes fluttered against mine, and I trapped his moan with a hard kiss, as we both hit the crest together and came.

I shuddered at the sensation of my prick pulsing against Beau's, sticky with a mixture of both my own cum and Beau's.

We didn't always recognize what was precious the first time, or even the second.

I was blessed by Belenus that Beau had offered me a third chance.

Beau vibrated with bliss, yet his smile was shy. I loved that he no longer hid his emotions behind an expressionless mask, as the Dictates taught.

"We're *truly* together now?" Beau asked.

I traced my name on Beau's stomach through the pearly liquid. "Look, I'm even marking you as my official property."

When Beau laughed, I was shocked at the beauty of the sound.

By the surprised way that he clamped his hand over his mouth, I guessed that it was a long time since he'd broken Dictate 987: *Laugh quietly.*

Then Beau lowered his hand, and all of a sudden, he was serious again. "I'm afraid that I've been rather selfish. I didn't want to spoil my first night alone with you by admitting that you're to be punished further tomorrow morning."

I stiffened, and my pulse raced.

Sorry, Emerald, but I just didn't appear capable of avoiding punishment.

"What's it to be this time? Prostrate of Disgrace? Dunk in the Pond? Or…"

"You're being sent with your friends for a session with Professor Emerald."

I grinned, kissing the tip of Beau's nose. "I'm failing to see the downside."

"Only, the Countess argued that first you're to be sent to the Dean of Discipline's office."

Ah, that actually *was* scary.

Had Beau only admitted who he was and such crushingly sad memories to me because he thought…*what*? That tonight could be our last night together…*ever*? That it didn't matter if he finally flayed himself before me and risked rejection because it was his final chance, since tomorrow I could be eaten by flesh eaters, weighted and sunk to the bottom of the ocean, or *literally* flayed?

I wondered if he'd kick his haughty self if I *survived*.

I raised my eyebrow. "And your father just decided to throw his *wicked boys* onto the Dean's non-existent mercy?"

"That was why they argued. The Countess said that they could blame the Hostage Lords as the troublemakers who'd caused the fight. My father is desperate not to lose face, and you're the scapegoat."

When Beau settled his wings around me, tugging me to nestle facing him on the rags, I spooned him.

Despite all my pranks and rebellious behavior, I'd never been summoned to the Dean's office before. Wells had always dealt with discipline within the House of Fae, which is how he ran things.

I kissed Beau on the forehead, before closing my eyes. But how could I sleep? Tomorrow, for the first time since I'd been sentenced, I'd meet the demon Dean.

CHAPTER TWELVE

**Wicked Reform School, Dean of Discipline's Office
Wednesday 28th April**

I perched on the edge of the soft green couch in the small waiting room to the Dean's office, shifting anxiously. My fingers clawed into the fabric. Everything smelled fresh in a fake way like it'd been sprayed out of a can. I wrinkled my nose, as I squinted at the morning's light that streamed through the window. After a night in the dungeon, I couldn't look away from the sun, even though it burned.

Where were Felix, Radley, and Apollo?

I hadn't expected to face the Dean alone. I'd always had my mates by my side before. Now I'd have to walk in to be punished by the actual Dean without them.

I ducked my head, and my hair shielded my face. My wings curled around me.

Earlier, when the dungeon's door had *clanged* open, I'd fought the guards who'd dragged me out to the Dean of Discipline's office in the main campus but not because I was frightened of my punishment (although on Benelus' prick, *I was*.)

Most of all, I hadn't wanted to leave Beau behind in the dark.

I'd promised Beau that he was *mine* now.

Yet in the end, Beau had called, "Control yourself. You mustn't hurt these guards because the Dean's sent golems, can't you tell? They can't fight their orders. Please, Quince, for me."

It'd been the *Quince* that'd done it.

I'd stilled, no longer resisting. If I'd realized how hard Beau could make me just by saying my name, then I'd have dropped my title from the start.

As the identical guards in their gray uniforms had first shoved my clothes at me, allowing me to dress, and then marched me away from the House of Fae, I'd understood what Beau had been telling me. Golems were molded from clay by the Dean to become staff. They *had* to do as they were told.

If there were any true innocents within this school then it was them.

Why could the supernatural world condemn us students and then use golems? It made me shiver because the Court Fae wanted to mold the Forest Fae just like the golems into a clay army of warrior lovers.

I couldn't let that happen.

"Do you want a cookie?" Natalia, the Dean's secretary, beamed at me as she held out a chocolate chip cookie like a distraction from the painful injection, which she knew that I was about to receive.

When I smiled back, her brown eyes lit up with surprise and delight like most students didn't show her the same kindness. "Sure, thanks."

I dragged my nails out of the couch with difficulty, forcing myself to swagger over to her desk.

Natalia was a pretty blond but everything about her was just a little bit too perfect like a doll…because she also was a golem. I sometimes saw her around the main campus running errands for the Dean.

The Dean had created her as his ideal secretary in tight pencil skirt and pink high-heeled stilettos. So, obviously demons hadn't yet discovered the concept of sexism or misogyny.

Personally, I thought that the Wicked Reform School would be better run if Natalia was in charge, even if she'd spent the last hour trying to figure out whether she needed to water the artificial orchid on her desk.

Clearly, intelligence hadn't figured highly on the Dean's list of ideal requirements for his perfect secretary.

But then, the Dean was a jerk.

I took the cookie from Natalia, balancing on the edge of her desk.

When I took a bite, I moaned. Okay, maybe indecently. "By my wing, this is delicious."

Natalia bounced in her seat, giggling. "You're the first to try them! Dean Aero growled that I'd probably poisoned them, so I should offer them to students."

I choked, swallowing with difficulty. I carefully placed down the cookie. "Brilliant. So, have you poisoned them?"

Natalia leaned across the desk, slapping me playfully on the arm. "Of course not, silly! Why'd I do that?"

I was having second thoughts on her running the school.

When something furry rubbed against my arm, I jumped and glanced down.

A skvader was curled beside Natalia's phone. His long ears pricked up, as he smirked. Then he snuggled down again, never taking his dark gaze from mine.

"I don't want to startle you, but there's a skvader on your desk," I warned.

Whatever the jerk was up to, he was certain to be taking advantage of the golem's sweet nature.

Natalia stroked along the skvader's wings. "Do you like my new pet?" The skvader shot me a smug look. "He just flew in my window this morning. I've decided to call him…" She tapped her chin in deep thought. "Treasure."

The skvader looked horrified.

I rubbed his head. "That sounds *exactly* the right name. Such a *treasure*." I leaned closer to the skvader, and by the way his eyes widened, I knew that my grin must be at its malevolent best. "Make sure that you cuddle, snuggle, and *never* let him go."

Treasure squeaked.

Ah, sweet karma.

The skvader would flee out of the window again as soon as the secretary's back was turned.

"I wouldn't cuddle Dean Aero today," Natalia whispered, conspiratorially. I glanced at the door on the far wall that led through to the Dean of Discipline's office. It'd been closed since I'd arrived. "He was muttering about *bears* and has been grumpy *as* a bear. There's another student in with him now."

Well, I hadn't heard any screaming, so that was a plus.

"At least that gives me some warning if he starts yelling," I joked.

Yeah, I wasn't joking.

Natalia broke up a cookie, feeding it to the squirming skvader. "He sets up…what do you call it if you don't want other people to hear?"

"Magical soundproofing."

The Discipline Floor was surrounded in it, and the Countess put it up whenever she wanted *privacy*.

Privacy was never good.

"You're smart." Natalia beamed at me again. "Just like Dean Aero."

"For once, that's a compliment that I can't accept." I caught Natalia's surprised gaze. "Plus, you're smart too, just at different things, right? And if you want to keep a pet or…by my wing, *do anything*…then go for it. I believe that you can."

Natalia flushed. "Really?"

I nodded.

All of a sudden, the door to the Dean's office opened, and Oscar stormed through, before slamming the door shut behind him.

I straightened off Natalia's desk, and my eyes widened.

Was Oscar crying…?

When Oscar saw me, he froze, and his fangs shot out. His hand flew to his head like he could cover the fact that his hair had been shaved into a buzz cut.

For a pure blood vampire who was arrogantly *obsessed* with his hair, it was like being bald.

Oscar's pretty face was streaked with tears at the humiliation of having his head shaved.

In other circumstances, I'd have laughed. Oscar had been the pain in my fae ass for nearly a decade. Yet there was a difference between battling him as equals and an authority above us humiliating him like this.

No one had a right to do that.

For a long moment, none of us spoke. Even the skvader stilled.

"What are you waiting for, Fae Lord?" Oscar's voice was raspy, but he still managed a snooty tilt of his head, which was impressive. "Haven't I sneered enough times about your punishments for you to know how it's done? How about starting with a jibe about whether I'm broken and then move onto a description of how my House will wreck me now that I'm shamed? I'm certain that you know many hilarious bald jokes."

I huffed. "You're an asshole."

He blinked. "That was weak."

"Nope, I meant that you're an asshole if you think I'd do any of that or maybe…I would've once…but I won't now." Oscar eyed me warily; I wasn't surprised that he didn't believe me. "I thought that you worked for the Dean with all that *Prefect* business. Why'd he cut off your hair?"

Oscar hugged his cape around himself. "That crazy bear shifter on the Paranormal Prefect Patrol reported me. He put in a complaint of harassment, saying that I was staring at his *bald ass*, so the Dean said I deserved everybody to stare at my *bald head*."

I gaped at him. The Dean had to know that

Barley's report was *false*, right? Hadn't he listened to Oscar's side of it?

Wait, Barley had reported *me* as well during his counseling session with Emerald. *Was I going to get the same treatment?*

I ran my fingers through my hair like that could protect it. "We could all have told the Dean that wasn't true. If you stare at anybody's cute ass, it's mine, right?"

Oscar reddened. "You've been summoned to the Dean yourself, yet you can still make light of such things?"

I shrugged. "It's a gift."

The way that Oscar's eyes gleamed with shame and distress, however, made my guts roil. I'd never thought that I could feel sorry for a vampire from the Prick Patrol. But the Dean was *playing* with him. He'd been the one to give Barley the magical mange, and he must've known that Oscar was innocent. Did it turn him on to toy with the students under his control, even though they were ones who were working with him towards becoming reformed?

Wells truly believed that he was saving us. I had a feeling that the Dean was doing this for kicks.

I clenched my jaw. It didn't matter what crimes the students had or hadn't committed. None of them could deserve to end up in a place like this, and every last one should be fighting to escape.

The offer of reforming was an excuse to cull the majority.

How could that ever be right?

When I sauntered closer to Oscar, he stiffened.

"*Don't.*" Oscar shook.

I slid the hood of Oscar's cape over his head to cover him; he stared at me in shock at my gentleness. "Pretend you've taken a vow for the next month never to lower your hood. You're good at pompous speeches; invent some pure blood nonsense. Get the witches to cast a spell so that your hood can't be lowered, even by professors."

For the first time since he'd staggered out of the Dean's office, Oscar's eyes sparkled with life. "For a fae, that's not an entirely foolish plan."

My lips twitched. "Stop it, you're making me blush."

When Oscar snarled, it was brilliant to see the return of his asshole self. He stalked to the door out to the corridor, banging on it like he was a prince about to step into his throne room, rather than a prisoner about to be led away by guards.

"Dean Aero probably won't cut your beautiful hair." Natalie offered me an encouraging smile. I tried not to shudder at the thought. "If he does, I'll keep it as my second pet and call it... Fairy."

Treasure snickered.

Oscar glanced over his shoulder at me; his face was lost in shadow. "Why would you help me?"

Good question.

I threw myself down on the couch, hugging my knees to my chest.

I was next in to see the Dean.

"We don't belong trapped in this school," I looked up, meeting Oscar's scrutiny, "and they don't have the right to change our bodies or steal our identities. They can call that reforming if they like, but it isn't. Perhaps, you should reconsider your membership of the Prick Patrol. It only betrays the other students, and if you haven't worked it out yet, it won't save you from being culled." I pointed my wing at him. "If you want to survive, every House needs to save themselves. Spread the word."

By the way that his eyes widened, I knew that he understood me.

I didn't know if it'd work, or whether every paranormal would continue in their own selfish attempts to reform or save only themselves.

But rebellions started from small flames. It was a start.

Oscar nodded.

Then the door to the corridor swung open, and a guard yanked Oscar out, before in a tumble of feathers and nervous joy, Radley and Felix with Apollo clasped between them were shoved inside. They descended on me like I'd spent a month in the dungeon, and they'd forgotten the sight, feel, and scent of me. Their relief was electric. After all, I guessed that they hadn't known what had happened, only that I was missing.

I'd been terrified for them, after all.

The breath was knocked out of me. Warm lips kissed mine. I gasped, panting.

My hard-on pressed uncomfortably against my tight pants.

"No sexy times in the waiting room," Natalia chirped. "I've just cleaned that couch."

I flushed, allowing Radley to manhandle me up onto his lap, just as Felix settled with Apollo on his. Radley needed to feel me close to him, as one of his hands circled my chest and the other clutched my neck like I'd disappear if he let go.

"Don't go off by yourself again, short wings," Radley growled, as if I'd simply been out partying with the Almost Humans House. "Do I need to get a leash?"

"Only if you're into that kink." When Radley's eyes glinted, I regretted my reply.

"*Enough of that.*" Apollo pushed his head against my leg, and I stroked down the curve of his neck. "*My Lord would never willingly leave behind his sacred swan. He knows that I'd fly into the sun for him. Did they hurt you?*"

"Number One, no cremating yourself in the sun." I tapped Apollo on the beak. "And Number Two: I wasn't hurt. In fact, even though I don't remember it, I was healed by Emerald." I stroked the back of my hand down Felix's smooth cheek. "Like you, right?"

Felix smiled. "By my wing, she's a goddess."

I glanced at Radley. "Do you sense that she's our bond?"

Radley flushed (okay, that was unlike him, but then Emerald had that effect). "She's a hot succubus, who I bet would look even hotter around my prick, *and* she's our bond."

Felix chuckled. "Shakespeare missed a trick not writing a sonnet that starts like that."

Radley bumped him with his shoulder. "Bite me."

Felix's pupils dilated. "I'd love to, but the receptionist banned sexy times."

"Number Six on the Wicked Bucket List," I said, urgently. *"Bond with all my fae and shifter lovers.* I've experienced a true bond with Emerald, but it's not enough unless you're wing by wing loving her with me."

Felix looked hopeful. "I want that one too."

"Good try." Radley's expression remained stern. "Where were you all night?"

Again with sounding like I'd been out after curfew partying.

"I was locked in a secret dungeon."

"Bullshit," Radley snarled.

"A *hidden* secret dungeon that we've never discovered because…" I glanced at Natalia who was busy combing the struggling skvader's fur and pinning it with glittery clips, "it's where the Duke of Wells punishes his *secret* son."

So, I liked the dramatic too.

I hadn't been able to shock my mates properly in years because we were always together and so knew the same things. It was fun just for once to know something that they didn't.

Perhaps, like Beau had wanted last night, I craved to hold him to myself for a little longer.

My mates were staring at me with the same shocked expressions that I must've worn yesterday.

"*The rascally bastard.*" Apollo's fury vibrated through him, as he flapped his wings. "*He steals the cygnets, and calls the fae his flock of one hundred but he locks away his own son?*"

"On my feathers, we have to free this boy," Felix declared.

"He's a Court Fae." I glanced between them.

Did this mean that they'd accept Beau?

Radley shrugged. "He's a prisoner. If you want us to save him, then we will."

I caught Radley's braid between my fingers, kissing it with a reverence that made his prick thicken; I could feel his excitement pressing against me through his pants. "Your loyalty honors both the forest and me. I'll tell you more later when it's safe. That's if we don't die now because of those backstabbing fae in our own House."

I glanced at Natalia, who'd finished with Treasure. The skvader looked like he'd had the *cute* makeover from hell.

When I turned back, Felix and Radley were exchanging a glance.

My brow furrowed. "What?"

"*They're trying to work out how to tell you that for the first time in a decade, they slept cuddled up with the entire tribe last night, including those backstabbing fae,*" Apollo explained.

I bit my lip.

Dictate 766: *Tears in the face of betrayal, simply prove the enemy right to have betrayed you.*

"So, it was only *me* who they've been shunning all this time. Great to know. I guess that I owe you an apology. If you hadn't been hanging around with me, then you wouldn't have been rejected." I ached inside like something had been torn.

"Don't be an idiot." Felix flicked me on the forehead. "They only let us sleep beside them because they were feeling guilty."

"I thought that I'd have to slice off some fae wings, since they almost killed you." Radley's arms tightened around me to the point of pain. *He meant it.*

"But the moment that the professors left, the fae knelt for forgiveness. They'd already confessed to Wells and begged that they alone be punished. It put me off my revenge stride."

"Wells has them in the Kneel of Shame for the whole of today," Felix added.

"But by the Shining God, why'd they say that they did it?" I demanded.

"One of the daft fae put them up to it. It turns out that he lost his twin brother in the Love Rebellion," Apollo replied.

It must be the sour faced fae…

I'd lost brothers, and Quinn was exiled. But what would it be like to lose a twin who was like your other half?

I wound my arms around Radley's neck. "All revenge is called off, right? We were kids when we left the tribe, and Wells has tried his hardest to keep us separate and marked as *different* to the others. They just want to live, and I don't blame them because they don't know that to join the Court would be like a slow death. To them, *we're* the Hostage Lord outsiders."

Radley pushed me back to scrutinize my face. "Who are you, and where's the real Lord Spring?"

Wait, he was serious…

By the reddening of Radley's neck and the way that his arm muscles were bulging, I'd say that I had about a minute to convince him that it was really me and not a golem spy or another fae under a glamor, before I'd end up tipped over his lap for some spanking interrogation, regardless that this was the Dean's office.

"Hold up…" I licked across his lips like somehow that would persuade him. *It didn't.* "Okay, okay, it's *me*."

My earnest face didn't work either.

Radley looked at me stonily. "Prove it."

I thought for a moment, then my grin became wicked. "You pretend that nothing scares you, but as a child you spent an entire month terrified that you were pregnant because a female fae brushed against you in the courtyard. It took the Countess explaining that male fae didn't have the correct *bits* to give birth to calm you down."

Natalia giggled.

Radley blushed and then looked murderous.

A little too far…?

I pointed my wing at Felix, and he shrank back. Actually, this was fun. "And *you* tell everybody that you admire Oberon the King of the Faeries in *A Midsummer's Night Dream*, but secretly you admit that you wish you could be Titania, the Queen."

Felix covered his face.

When I arched my brow at Apollo, he *thwapped* his wing across my mouth to silence me.

"*No need to convince me,*" Apollo said, struggling

to hide his laughter. *"You're the same blue-blooded rascal that you ever were. But how did you become all thoughtful and forgiving?"*

I ducked my head to escape his feathery gag, stroking the nape of Radley's neck, as I thought of Beau in the dungeon. He should've been part of our childhood memories, only I'd chosen not to treat the ones of him as precious.

"It was Wells' son." My grip tightened on Radley. "By my feathers, he helped me to realize that I don't...*we don't*...see everybody as they are or at least, we see them like we want to. We knew him."

Radley shook his head, but I looked hard into his eyes.

"We did. Only, he wasn't important enough for us to remember, and so we wrecked him. I refuse to do that to the other fae. I regret that I've allowed myself to stay safe wrapped in your brotherhood alone. I haven't made the effort to get to know the other students but I do know that no one will ever again be forgettable or unimportant."

All of a sudden, the phone rang shrilly, and I jumped.

The skvader startled as well, snatching the chance to fly into the air, as Natalia picked up the receiver. Treasure flapped his wings at me in parting, before diving for the window.

Thunk.

He smashed against the *closed* window, crashing to the ground with a groan.

"Just an idea, but maybe you should make sure that the window's open for your next escape attempt," I called, helpfully.

"Yes, sir. Thank you, sir. Okay, I'll remember to hang up this time." Natalia beamed at us, even though I flinched on each *sir*. The Dean had truly wanted a polite doll. "Bye, bye, bye…"

Natalia merrily sang *goodbyes* into the receiver, before placing it down like she'd arranged a date out for dinner, rather than for our discipline.

"You can go in now to see the Dean." Natalia smiled. "Oh, and he still sounds cranky. Remember, if he cuts off your hair, can you ask him to save it for me? My other pet doesn't look too well, and I think Fairy will be so silky to stroke."

I straightened my swan clip in my hair, sweeping it back like that'd protect it.

"Fairy?" Felix mouthed at me.

I ignored him, pushing myself to my feet. Then I led Radley and Felix to the door of the Dean's office. Apollo walked elegantly behind us with his head held high; he looked like Lincoln. Clearly, he wanted to impress the Dean.

The Dean was smart and dangerous. Yet I didn't know him and that was frightening. I had no idea how he'd react.

I knocked on the door.

"Just get your asses in here," a gruff voice called out.

Okay, cranky about summed it up.

I shoved open the door and stepped inside, expecting an office dyed blood-red with slaughtered students or decorated with medieval torture devices. Instead, the room was bright with black and white furniture like an office designed for the upwardly mobile executive. Big windows looked out at the courtyard below and a fountain.

It could've been peaceful. Except for the demon sitting in a plastic chair behind the desk.

The Dean didn't even look up, as my mates and I swaggered into the room to stand in front of his desk because there was only a single white seat, and I wasn't sitting if my mates had to stand.

The Dean's blue suit and tie were neat, just like his goatee and mustache. His hair was so short, I wondered whether he'd shaved Oscar's hair just because he'd wanted buzz cut twinsies.

Yet the Dean's expression was stormy like he was considering a hard puzzle and if he couldn't work it out, then he'd eat each puzzle piece slowly.

I swallowed. *Really, this would be fun.*

When I fidgeted, Radley wrapped his wing around me.

At last, the Dean looked up from the stack of papers that he'd been studying.

"I've read all your files." When he slowly slid his gaze across us, I felt weirdly dirty. *So much for small talk.* "Lord Brooke, you're a psychopath."

Radley raised his eyebrow. "I prefer *violently possessive*."

The Dean's brow darkened further; he glared at Felix. "And you're—"

Felix bounced on his toes like he was about to be awarded a gold star. "A budding playwright? Lover of the arts? Lucky?"

The Dean pinched his nose and sighed. "Don't even get me started on the swan."

"*Aye, you'd better not start.*" Apollo ruffled up his feathers.

"Swan soup," the Dean muttered.

Us Hostage Lords growled in unison.

"Then we have Lord Spring himself." The Dean pulled at his tie, loosening it. "Do you know that you've played more pranks than any student who's ever attended this school?" Mentally, I high-fived myself. "Here's where I'm confused. Your math, English, History, hell, even your Fighting classes have received top marks. But when I look at your special lessons run by Professor Pond, which are marked in number of Court Dictates broken, you score higher than any other fae as well. Interestingly, that ranks you *bottom*. Do you see the problem here?"

"There's a serious issue with the House of Fae's marking system…?" I ventured.

To my surprise, the Dean broke into a smile. "I don't like being played, either by students or professors. I'm the one who pulls the strings around here, and Professor Pond is trying to pull mine."

I sneaked a glance at Radley. He curled his wing further around me.

"How?" I asked.

The Dean sprawled back in his chair. "Do I think (with all my years of experience), that three fae *and a swan shifter who wasn't even playing* are somehow responsible for a mass Fae Ball fight, especially when my spies' report that at least fifteen fae openly targeted you? *Hell, no." Why was it not a surprise that he had spies in the school?* "Do I think that Professor Pond lost control of the lesson and decided to try and trick me by blaming her most difficult students? *Damn straight.*" He steepled his hands. "I'll defend each House's right to punish their problem students with my last breath, but her mistake was to try to make a fool out of me."

It was nice to see that he had his priorities straight.

"So, I imagine that you expect to be sent to the Detention Center for some horrific punishment now?"

When the Dean leaned forward in his chair, it squeaked.

Was that rhetorical…?

The Dean's smile crept across his face. "You're all sentenced to see the counselor like Wells wants, but before that…" *Here it came: Belenus preserve us.* I shivered, snuggling into Radley's warmth. The Dean casually reached into his pocket and pulled out three tiny iron balls, dropping them onto the table. "Let the punishment fit the crime."

"*Woah*, scary," Felix deadpanned.

"Shut up, Lix," I hissed.

Nothing with iron was ever good for a fae.

The Dean's smile faded, and his expression became stormy again. "Pick one up one each and drop it into your right boot. Don't take it out all day or you'll have ten to drop into your boots tomorrow. The swan is excused because (how sad for the Countess), he doesn't wear boots."

I stared at the Dean.

This was the punishment…?

I pulled off my boot, flinching at the way that the tiny ball burned my thumb and finger simply to pick it up and drop it into my boot. It'd sear the sole of my foot or force me to hop for the day but it wasn't deadly.

Plus, the Dean had been sure to devise it in a way to save the shifter.

This was his revenge on the Countess, as well as proving what happened when anyone attempted to *play* with him.

The Dean was a jerk, but he was a smart one. That made him powerful.

I grimaced as I eased my foot back into my boot. Already, the iron was uncomfortable through my sock. I didn't want to think about how it'd feel by the end of the day.

Yet now I had my counseling session with Emerald. I'd been desperate to be together as a group with her, longing to hold Emerald again. I couldn't wait to see if the bond could truly unite all my lovers.

Yet I was equally terrified that when she offered the chocolates to Radley or Apollo, they wouldn't accept…or she wouldn't accept them.

Would it break the bond if they were rejected?

CHAPTER THIRTEEN

**Wicked Reform School, House of Fae, Discipline
Floor
Wednesday 28th April**

I stared around the Discipline Floor in shock. Where was the ivory couch, coiled whips, and leather straps? Instead, there was a circular white bed, which was large enough to take up most of the room. A chandelier of cascading rubies cast lights across the ceiling.

Radley grunted. "Fancy."

I took a limping step forward, and the tiny iron ball dug through my sock. Had we been so keen to see Emerald for our session that we'd stepped off on the wrong floor?

Then I noticed the sign on the wall: **Emotions Counseling Waiting Area**.

"On my wing, someone's been busy," I muttered.

My heartbeat was suddenly too loud, and I was dizzy with desperation to see Emerald again. It was agony to be separated from her and unable to protect her, when I knew the dangers of this school.

Yet why did something tell me that she could protect herself?

Apollo flew over my head in a familiar flurry of feathers that made me grin, before settling with a contented *honk* on a nest of the silk pillows. "*If this is how Emerald welcomes her bonded, then she knows your value. Perhaps, I don't need to break her arm in your defense.*"

I pointed at him. "Swear on the pond that you'll do no such thing!"

Apollo bobbed his head smugly. "*Nay, of course I shan't hurt the woman you love. But to save you, I could, right?*"

Apollo allowed butterflies to ride around on his back, rather than disturb their sleep. He'd stand in the way of a battering that could kill him, like he had in the Fae Ball game, but he wasn't a warrior like Radley. *And I didn't expect him to transform into one for me.* I wasn't a Court Fae who needed my lovers to mold themselves to fit me. I loved them just as they were.

Still, I put on my serious face and nodded. "To save me, you'd be formidable, as well as beautiful, of course."

Apollo preened, before lying down.

"Couldn't I just try a little of my...?" Felix waggled his fingers.

When Radley shook his head, Apollo hissed sadly.

Felix had managed to hide just how powerful his Fortune Magic was for over a decade. Wells didn't bother to monitor the dormitories, which is how I'd eventually known that it was safe to change Apollo back into his human form there. But no matter how much Felix cast me his *just think how mind blowing the sex will be if you say yes* eyes, it was too dangerous for him to risk taking off Apollo's collar now.

Then Felix sniffed, and his eyes lit with delight. He grasped my hand, pulling me close. "Where does it smell like to you, Quince?"

I breathed in deeply the scent of damp moss and wet tree trunks. The air was fresh; even the fire in my lungs eased. My eyes smarted because it was like I was back home beneath the shadowy coolness of the trees, and I'd never been sent away to be a Court that'd become my prison.

"Hope Forest," I gasped.

How had Emerald managed it? And *why* had she put so much thought and effort into today? Love coiled through me that she'd *remembered* the Pleasure Spell and recreated the forest, knowing that it was the most special place in the world for me.

It was like a slice of my exiled home here in America. This wasn't simply feeding from pleasure or a fantasy. Emerald was trying to get to know, understand, and accept all of us Hostage Lords.

This was real.

Radley's gaze darted to the black door, which didn't have a door knob. The words **COUNSELOR EMERALD** gleamed across it.

"I want my bond now," Radley growled. I shivered: *it sounded like he was about to devour Emerald.* If it'd been me, I'd have been okay with that. "This woman who cares enough to bring the forest of our homeland to us is mine."

When he hammered on the door, I jumped.

Bang — bang — bang.

Well, that broke **Dictate 912**: *Only knock once. More than this is unseemly and won't make them answer any faster.*

Except, it did.

When Emerald swung open the door, the ruby light from the chandelier sparkled across her.

Every time that I saw Emerald, she looked more beautiful. It was as if I could see through her glamor just a touch more. I wished that I could kiss her without the mask on at all.

I was desperate to ask her about the glamor, but if she wasn't ready, then I wouldn't rush her. Her identity was her own.

When Emerald smiled at Radley, I realized that her hair was pinned up with swan clips just like the ones in my hair. Had she copied my style on purpose to connect us or remind herself of me when we were apart?

My breath caught at the thought.

"You knocked?" Emerald's smile grew.

Radley blinked, before he jerked his thumb over his shoulder at me. "He's having an angst fit that we won't bond."

Wait...what?

When I flushed, Felix squeezed my hand.

Emerald arched her brow. "That's interesting because I could've sworn that I promised to offer to bond today. I mean, I'd have thought that the *bed* was a giveaway..."

Felix let go of my hand to run his fingers lovingly along the cover. "How'd you justify a bed, when we're meant to be kept pure? Not that I preferred the S & M theme that this room had going on before."

Emerald's expression became troubled. "The only advantage to having a screwed-up bitch like Professor Pond in charge is that she believes every twisted method you suggest. She doesn't think that I'm touching you. Use your imaginations about the other creative games that she imagines I'm having you play."

Really, I'd rather not.

"Enough talk." Radley held out his hand like it was a sword. "I demand a chocolate."

"*Aye, me too.*" Apollo waddled across the bed, before holding out his wing.

Emerald studied them with cool amusement. "Huh, students don't usually *demand* treats when they're here for *punishment* counseling sessions. You know," she narrowed her eyes at me, "I've only just had to heal you because you almost got yourselves killed. What happened to limiting the hurt?"

*Ah, that stern voice I so loved…*even if her lips pinched with concern.

I shot Emerald a sheepish look, before striding towards her. "*Ehm*, sorry…?"

"Are you *limping* now?" She winced.

I winced as well; the iron had wedged itself between my toes and no matter how much I wiggled them, I couldn't free it. "Maybe…?" I hopped on one foot to take the pressure off. "All better."

Emerald rolled her eyes.

"Chocolate." Radley shook his hand, and Apollo flapped his wing. "Then we can get to the good stuff."

When Emerald stroked her hand down Radley's chest, my skin prickled that it wasn't *my* chest that she was touching. "Lord Brooke, I see that you're the romantic of the group."

Felix chuckled, sprawling on the bed. "Quince has made this Wicked Bucket List of things that we wish to do before Saturday, when we..." He trailed off, and Emerald's expression darkened. "Number Six is *bond with all my lovers*. By my wing, we'd do anything to make that happen for him, and he's worried it won't." He glanced down, shyly. "I want it too."

When Emerald's gaze met mine, it was soft and loving. "If you haven't guessed it yet, I'd do anything for him too."

I didn't know if I liked being discussed like this.

Wait, I did. Because it felt like I'd known Emerald for years, and she just fitted into our familiar banter like she'd been the missing piece that we'd needed all along.

"Hey, that's...true," I weakly protested. "But I was a good fae. I didn't even complain."

"*Will Emerald offer my gorgeous lovers a chocolate? What if they don't accept the chocolate? What if there are* no *chocolates...?*" Apollo mimicked me with a faux English accent that was so posh I refused to accept it was me. *Okay, it did sound like me.* Felix snickered. "*Your frown on the way over here, My Lord, although dominant and sexy, was giving me a headache.*"

When my frown deepened, Felix snickered again.

I forced myself to smile instead. That'd teach them to know me so well.

"I did have a big romantic build up, which you'd have loved by the way, on how to offer these… But how can I leave Lord Spring to suffer?" Emerald waved her hand through the air, and a box of chocolates appeared on her palm. She pulled on the ribbon, and the lid sprang open. I hopped closer, sighing at the delicious aroma of the truffles. Radley appeared mesmerized. "Why doesn't the swan pick first?"

Apollo hissed, *"Is she mocking me?"*

"His name is Apollo," I said. "He's my sacred swan shifter, who's only trapped in his swan form by that bloody collar. He's loyal and devoted, *and I love him.*"

"You don't need poetry," Apollo sounded like he was holding back tears, *"and I don't need anything else on the Wicked Bucket List. You've fulfilled my every wish, My Lord."*

Emerald caught Apollo's head between her hands and gently kissed his beak. "I'm sorry, Apollo. I can't wait to meet you properly. I know that it sucks not to show your true face to the world. You're a beautiful swan, so I bet you're the most beautiful man in this place, and wow, you have some competition with these Fae Three."

Apollo ruffled his feathers up with pride; Emerald was good at reading people. *"I am beautiful. All is forgiven, and I'd like strawberries, please. We came across wild ones in the gardens at Court once. They tasted like freedom."*

Emerald glanced at me; it was easy to forget that she couldn't hear Apollo. Would that change after the bond?

I nodded. "He forgives you, and would like wild strawberries and a stroke."

Always upsell.

Emerald shot me a sly look as if she knew what I'd done, but she still stroked Apollo's feathers, as he pecked at a truffle delicately.

"Aye, that's the taste of freedom," Apollo sighed, dreamily.

Apollo wasn't allowed to experience the same foods as the other students. I was desperate for him to live in his human form. How many other experiences had he missed out on?

When Radley let go of him, Apollo flew to the end of the bed, just as Felix crawled further onto it, resting against the headboard.

Radley snatched a mint truffle. "Beef Sunday roast with five roast potatoes, three Yorkshire puddings, and lashings of gravy."

My mouth watered. I didn't know whether I was more jealous of Radley or the truffle, when Radley tongued the truffle and moaned, rubbing his hand across his clothed prick.

Emerald groaned in turn, sliding her own hand down her stomach, before inching up her dress. Now I was most jealous of Emerald's fingers, which circled across her inner thigh and then her panties.

Feeding from Radley's pleasure must've been erotic then. *Everything* about him was erotic.

Radley licked his lips with a contented grin. "I'm full now but I'm still hungry for *you*." He grabbed Emerald around the waist, and she vanished the chocolates before they could tumble to the floor.

Radley twisted her, spinning her towards the bed.

Emerald's tail coiled out, twitching to stroke Radley's thigh.

"You didn't think to mention that she has a *tail*?" Radley's glare at Felix and me was murderous.

Felix hugged his knees. "Then you wouldn't have had the same surprise as us. Aren't you just imagining what it'd be like to sleep with it wrapped around you?"

Well, I was now. *Bliss.*

Apollo shook his own tail feathers. *"If you ask me, it's her best part."*

Radley gripped Emerald's tail, stroking along it with a technique that my own prick could write a testimonial for and it'd read: *ah, ah, ah, please let me cum, cum, cum…*

My prick was such a talented wordsmith.

"It's lucky that I'm not assessing you, right?"

Emerald's voice shook, as she wound her arms around Radley's neck.

"What would you write?" Radley kissed up her throat.

Emerald shivered. "Alpha, forceful, and passionate…"

Radley snorted. "That sounds more like my dating profile. Where's the *psychopath who's a danger to society* part?"

"It seems to be missing," Emerald replied. "Although, have you forgotten that this is a punishment session?"

I swaggered (okay, hopped…but there was a swagger in my hop), to Emerald, kissing her like I'd thought about ever since my last session. Caught between Radley and me, she melted. Her eyelids fluttered under the intense pleasure coursing through her and feeding her power.

"*Punish* us then," I murmured.

Emerald's breath hitched. Then her lips curled back in a devilish way that made my stomach flutter with sudden nerves.

Had I just played with fire?

"Oh, you'll enjoy the way that I punish." When she nipped my lips, it was as gentle as the brush of a feather. She glanced at Radley, whipping her tail out of his grip. "Didn't you order the good stuff now? Get naked."

Felix's eyes widened.

Radley didn't need telling twice. He lifted Emerald onto the bed next to Felix and then dragged off his coat, hurling it into the corner of the room like a fighter daring another before a battle. My tongue darted out to wet my lips. Then Radley's hands moved to the buckle of his belt.

"Wait, don't take off your pants," I called out. Radley raised his eyebrow in his *you're an idiot* look, which was usually reserved for me. "The Dean will know if we remove the iron in our boots, which means…"

Felix tilted his head. "Bare chested and pricks out looks sexy…" He stroked his hand down Emerald's cheek, and she kissed him tenderly. "You have witchcraft in your lips."

"And you in yours because I'm under your spell." Emerald pushed the coat from Felix's shoulders, pooling its green against the white of the sheets.

Radley grunted. "No more pretty words."

He snatched me around the neck, before stripping my coat from me like a squire serving his king. My skin warmed at every brush of his fingers across my skin. Then he lay my coat across the bottom of the bed, and I lifted Apollo onto it, so that even if he wasn't able to join us in human form, he'd still be cocooned in the warmth of my scent.

"*I love you, My Lord.*" Apollo's gentle words

made me shake. "*I love all you blue-blooded rascals. And I'm honored to be bonded to the woman who'll unite us.*"

"I said *no pretty words*." Radley clutched me by the neck, throwing me onto the bed next to Emerald.

"Aren't you the leader? Does he always manhandle you like that?" Emerald asked.

Felix patted my shoulder. "Quince loves it."

Emerald twisted on her back between us, as Radley watched from the end of the bed, looking even taller and more powerful as he loomed over us.

Alpha, forceful, and passionate…

Emerald sure had that right.

I shrugged. "The despotic leadership style is overrated."

Emerald's eyes glittered, as she scrutinized me. *Why was she so intense all of a sudden?* "I knew that you were beautiful and my bond but not that we had so much in common. Let's just say that I agree." Then she waved at the room. "This is better than the dickish stuff that they had in here before, right? I told you that your first time wouldn't be over a desk."

Felix's wings stiffened in shock. "Why, you naughty fae! I was in there discussing Shakespeare, but you used your session to… I thought you told us that you didn't unleash the kraken?"

Radley laughed.

Emerald straddled me, palming me through my pants, and I arched. "The kraken?"

"She said that my first time wouldn't be…and I told them that I *didn't*…" I choked, confused.

Then they all burst into laughter, and I realized that they were playing with me.

Wow, my pranking status was being really challenged here.

I *loved* that.

"Does the fact that I'm a Marquess count for so little?" I demanded.

Emerald licked over my nipple, and I gasped. "Since you're not a *despot*, I'd go with *yeah*. So, this Wicked Bucket List, what number is: *Screw my lovers, until I see stars…*? Because that's what's about to happen, sexy wings."

I squirmed to try and encourage her tongue to my other nipple, but she appeared to be waiting for a response. "I'm onboard with that but I'd rather we made Number Seven: *Make love underneath the stars.* We've always been prisoners and trapped inside. Forest Fae should claim each other outside. What if we risk that on Friday?"

"*Risk.*" Radley leaned his fists on the bed. "Everything about the Night of the Beltane will be a risk."

"Tell me," Emerald demanded.

"It's the most important night to us, when the veils are lowered between worlds, and our own magic is at its strongest. We celebrate our god, Belenus, or we would, if the school would allow it," I explained.

"It's the welcoming in of summer." Felix unpinned Emerald's hair, and it fell in a golden waterfall to her shoulders. Then he slowly unzipped her dress, kissing over the creamy curve of her shoulders in worship. "The ritual means growth, rebirth, and transformation. It's the night when every element shifts and changes. It's our last chance to worship our traditions and to be alone together."

Emerald's eyes were as bright as mine at Felix's description.

"I'll swear that you'll get to celebrate it this year," Emerald breathed. "We'll welcome in the summer together. How'd you know where to hold the ritual?"

Radley's wings beat. "The wild-fire leads you."

I reached up to slip Emerald's dress from her shoulders. As each inch of skin was revealed, I licked and kissed like she became more closely bound to me with each touch.

Radley watched, hungrily, as if I was unwrapping her just for him.

Emerald wriggled completely out of the dress, before allowing Felix to turn her onto her back. Then she wound her tail around my waist, and I shivered at the combination of its softness and power, as she yanked me over her. My dick was hard, and I ached to push down my pants and free it.

"Kiss me," she commanded.

When I leaned down to kiss Emerald, however, her lips curled into that wicked smile of hers, and she caught me by the hair. "Did I say on the lips?"

When I looked into her eyes, I caught the challenge, as well as the question. I could choose where I took this, but I *always* rose to a challenge.

"Lix, kiss this beautiful bonded of ours on the lips. I'll be busy." When I untangled her tail from around me, she shivered.

"I'd be honored." Felix caressed his wing down Emerald's cheek, before tipping up her chin and kissing her.

I loved when he kissed like that: as if the world would end if you didn't love him back.

Then I slithered down Emerald, caressing her stomach and edging my fingers around the silky edges of her panties. I teased her, as her muscles tensed, before sliding down her panties, following them with my mouth and tracing the path with my tongue.

I sucked, marked, and licked, wanting to wreck her at the same time as protect her from every danger, as much as she did me. I longed to kiss her, until she couldn't think of anything but me and the way that Felix tasted.

Until she could never forget or leave us.

Emerald quivered, as my tongue danced lower

towards her clit. I clasped my hands on her hips, circling patterns with my thumbs on her inner thighs.

My prick was even harder than before, but only Emerald's pleasure mattered.

All of a sudden, I heard a snarl behind me, and Radley launched himself onto the bed. He caught me by the belt, hauling me to the side, although Emerald's tail whipped out to catch and drag me close again. Felix broke away from his own kiss to look up in shock.

Radley straddled Emerald. His wings were outstretched like he could hold all of us on the bed under his power. "I'll share you with my lovers. But right now, they'll watch, because *you're mine.*"

I understood. Radley had only just gone through the courtship ritual with the chocolate; I'd felt the same in my first counseling session.

When Radley flashed his sharp white teeth at me, I clasped Emerald's hand, instead. Felix clasped her hand on the other side. We were still connected.

Radley and Emerald deserved their moment.

Still, when Radley caught Emerald in his intense gaze, slipping his fingers into her pussy, and pushing her rhythmically towards one shuddering orgasm, before slipping on a condom from the stash he'd bartered from the Almost Humans, thrusting into her to spiral her back towards a second, I ached worse than my balls.

Felix and I were caught in Radley's bondage as much as Emerald. Yet it was hot to be forced to watch, and I wasn't jealous of either of them.

I loved them both.

Emerald trembled, but her eyes burned with a fiercer fire than I'd ever seen. The pleasure had fed her power; my magic could sense it blazing within her.

Radley sat up, with his knees on either side of Emerald. He folded his wings, before slipping off her. He tossed the condom into the corner and tucked his prick away with a reluctance that made my still hard one bitter.

Emerald turned her head towards me, pulling me closer by her tail to kiss me. Then she drew back.

"Lord River," she whispered.

Felix leaned down eagerly, and she sucked on his lower lip.

"Aye, forget the sacred swan shifter again." Apollo swooped over the bed, crashing against the chandelier with a *tinkle* of crystal and then nesting on the pillow next to Emerald's head. "That *la di da, aren't I the princess* light wasn't expensive, right?"

Emerald sat upright in shock. "Hey, rude…but I can hear you."

I laughed. "It *is* a bond. Better watch what you say, Apollo, or she'll be profiling you."

"Enough of your cheek, My Lord." Apollo snug-

gled down, wrapping his wings around the naked Emerald, who laughed. *"You're talking about my bonded, and I'd die an infinity of deaths for the woman who's connected us in love."*

Suddenly, a ruby flame lit above Apollo's head. I shouted, expecting him to catch on fire, but Emerald only clutched tighter to him, pulling him away from me, before I could roll him in the covers to put out the blaze.

"Stop," she commanded. "It's the bond."

Apollo didn't burn. Instead, the flame leaped to Radley's head, then Felix's, and finally to mine. I could feel its heat, yet it didn't hurt.

A hush fell over us.

I expected the fire to vanish, but instead, it moved to hover in the air in front of Emerald.

"Why's it doing that?" I asked.

"Because there's someone missing," Emerald said, quietly. "I haven't found all my bonded yet."

Radley exchanged a glance with me. *That wasn't good.*

At last, the magic flame faded.

"Honestly, to see the flame with your bonded is seriously rare." Emerald wrapped her tail around herself as she ducked her head. "We're fated."

Fated...?

Why did Emerald look excited and yet terrified at the same time?

"What's fated mean?" Radley demanded.

"Time's up. This session is over." Emerald looked away; her fingers trembled, as she stroked Apollo's feathers. "Just believe me when I say that being fated means that I'll do anything to save you."

Perhaps, that's what frightened me the most because *I'd* do anything to save *her*.

Why was she in danger?

CHAPTER FOURTEEN

Wicked Reform School, Library
Thursday 29th April

Morning class was Magical Research in the dark freeze of the Wicked Reform School library that stank of ancient enchantments.

I scrunched up my nose at the musty scent of books, which silently ranked the shelves. A single light flickered on the ceiling. Apollo shifted his wings in his sleep. He'd shoved a pile of dusty (okay *priceless*), magical books into a heap so that he could nest in a corner of the bookcase with his head tucked underneath his wing.

To be fair, last night when Felix had slipped off Apollo's collar with his Fortune Magic, we'd taken turns until dawn wearing out Apollo. It hadn't felt fair that he'd missed out on all the sexy fun with Emerald.

Apollo had warned that since *we were such rascals to make him sore all over, he'd expect carrying around like a prince tomorrow.*

I'd never wanted to let Apollo go. But then, of course, he'd found himself a nest and fallen asleep.

Now, I danced with my bare feet sliding along the marble floor between the bookshelves, humming Pharrell William's joyful "Happy".

Radley leaned against the far bookcase with his arms crossed. His gaze looked hungry enough to both devour me at the same time as the amused curl of his lips told me that *he'd* never take off his boots and socks to dance.

"Do you have a problem with my happy feet?" I spun around him, wiggling my toes in the air. "They're celebrating their freedom from the iron tyranny."

After yesterday stuck wincing on every step, I'd take this small victory. After all, every hour closer to the Day of the Wicked became more dangerous.

Radley snorted.

Wells should've been watching the lesson but he'd shut himself away in the office down the corridor with the banshee librarian, Ms. Farah. Either they had a thing for each other (*yuck* and also, *unlikely* since Court Fae claimed to have a single mate who could never be replaced), or Ms. Farah spied on the rest of the school for Wells.

Either way, it was an opportunity for Felix to do what he did best…sneaky research.

It should be his personal superpower, just as Radley's was inventive threats, and mine was leading my tribe to their deaths.

Perhaps, mine was actually battling to *save* my tribe, despite walking in the shadow of death. Either way, this morning my feet were still happy.

I twirled to Felix who'd made himself a nest out of books just like Apollo. Felix's was on the floor, however, wedged into the corner of the magical section.

I could've watched Felix like this all day. I shuddered with desire at how smart he was. The library was his kingdom, and I'd have worshiped at his feet if he'd noticed me. Except, Felix would've probably only used me as a handy prop to hold up his book.

I had a feeling that the scent of old books was like a drug to Felix. His eyes blazed, as he flicked between three opened books at the same time, scanning pages faster than I'd ever hope to be able to keep up.

Did he know how much I admired him?

The lesson plan today was to look up essential facts that we Forest Fae would need once we entered the Court like how to use cutlery correctly at feasts and why all fae were inferior to Court Fae (*list three examples*).

Instead, Radley, Felix and I had slipped away from the rest of the fae and down to the lowest, darkest, and most magical section of the library, instead.

Today's topic for us was the meaning of the word *fated*.

I rested against the bookcase next to Felix, attempting to peer over his shoulder.

When Felix slammed shut a book with a *bang* that shook dust from its pages into my eyes in a stinging cloud, I jumped. Then I choked, coughing.

Radley hid his chuckle behind his hand.

"We're legends," Felix exclaimed.

"Oh, really?" I spluttered. "And here I was thinking that we were prisoners."

"I'm always legendary in bed," Radley smirked.

Felix smacked his hand down on the book. "The *bond*." I stiffened, as the fiery bond snaked around me. "None of the books mention anything about succubi being *fated* mates."

"Our burning hair moment and Emerald would disagree," I pointed out.

When Felix ran his fingers through his hair, he looked so adorably nervous that I longed to drag him up into the embrace of my wings. Yet that would mean trying to take the special book, which he was now clutching, away from him. I knew Felix well enough to know that the adorable fae would be just as likely to whack me with the book as return the snuggle.

Never take a book out of Felix's hands. If there was one rule that I lived by, it was that.

"Let me guess…none of the books mention it, apart from the one that looks like it's been bound with dragon hide?" Radley grimaced.

Felix ran his hand over the cover of the book. "It's more ancient than the others. It talks of legends, including one from the Succubi Court. Once there was a succubus princess who bonded with five incubi. Flames hovered over them but didn't burn them. They were fated and became legendary. It says that maybe one day, it'll happen again."

He stopped, looking up at me. His eyes were wide and excited.

Breathless, I was hit by a sudden cold. The hair on the back of my nape rose; I was too aware of even my own heartbeat. I scrambled at the books behind me like they could hold me up.

Princess…? Legends…?

I was a leader of my own tribe. I was struggling to save them. How could I be *fated* to become part of some ancient prophecy?

I let out a shaky laugh. "This is very exciting. The forest has a funny sense of timing, throwing us into a fated bond with a princess, which is pretty much my biggest wank fantasy, just before we die. Apart from that, this is good news."

Radley strode to me, slamming his lips to mine to quiet me. His strong wings caged me. I pressed back against him, desperate for the touch.

Why had Emerald hidden who she was from me? I shook at the thought that she'd been playing me all along.

My heart was hers. She could shatter me with a look. *My secret princess.*

When Radley pulled back from the kiss, he gripped my chin hard to force me to look at him. "I don't know who Emerald is underneath that glamor. Maybe she's a princess and maybe she's simply the woman we love. What I do know? She's hiding, frightened, and *ours*. It doesn't matter if she's royalty or a poor orphan. We'll protect her."

Wow, for Radley that was like a speech.

I nodded, touching my wing to Radley's in agreement. "On my feathers, it'd be easier if we knew *why* a princess lives in fear. It was the Dean who hired her, and I'd bet that he's the one who's hiding her, unless he *kidnapped* her."

Felix tapped his fingers on top of the book. "Why don't we go and ask him? Ah yes, because of the threat of iron."

He glanced significantly at my bare feet, and my

toes curled at the phantom sensation of iron searing them.

So, no storming the Dean's office.

"Why don't we just ask Emerald?" Felix asked, softly.

I glanced down. "I tried, but she doesn't want us to know. It's my suspicion that she believes she's protecting *us*."

It was a strange, warm sensation: being loved by a woman. No one apart from my brotherhood had ever tried to protect me before.

Radley snorted. "Protecting is my job."

"We need to follow Emerald." I glanced between my mates. "She's working on saving us, but we can work on saving *her* at the same time."

Felix's elegant fingers caressed the spine of the book, and I wished that he was caressing me. "How? We have Fighting Class after lunch with the dwarfs."

"*Dicks*," I mumbled.

Felix's lips twitched. "Hey, sorry. I meant that we have to practice fighting with the dwarven *dicks*. I also passed on coded messages to the other Houses this morning about that…*other thing*." He didn't dare say *escape*. "The library is a great place to pass members of the other Houses and crazy as it seems, they're not quite as intimidated by me as they are by Rads." Radley shot Felix a patented sneer that even made him quail. He cleared his throat. "A-anyway, some thought it was a prank and others said they already had too much money riding on us dying. The mermaids are hoping for a drowning." He wrinkled his nose. "I think I may have gone off screwing one now."

Suddenly, light footsteps echoed down the corridor.

Radley twisted in front of me, stretching out his wings. Felix slid the book behind him like he was protecting a baby. I only just managed not to snicker.

Just.

"You're breaking **Dictate 555**: *Be as silent in libraries as the books*," Beau's cool drawl wound from the shadows.

When Radley prowled towards Beau, I stiffened.

Beau was pale. He clutched his arms around himself, and even though his chin was tilted up, I could read the insecurity in his eyes like he didn't believe that he'd be accepted in my group.

He never had been before.

Would Radley throw him out to protect me, just like he had when Beau had first tried to approach us?

It'd break Beau if he did.

I pushed away from the wall to stop Radley, but Radley had already reached Beau. I bit my lip…*don't hurt him*…but Radley only wrapped his wings around Beau and pulled him into a tight hug.

"You're not allowed to frighten me like that." Radley said.

Beau's large eyes widened. He flinched at Radley's fierce embrace, staring over his shoulder at me in confusion. "Why would you care what happens to a Court Fae?"

To my shock, Radley shook Beau. "You saved my shifter and sacrificed yourself. You're mine now."

Beau blushed in his pretty way that reminded me of how he'd blushed when I'd called him *Your Lordship* on our night together in the dungeon and how even his hair had tasted sweetly of peaches.

I only just held back the moan.

Just.

Beau had flayed himself before me that night, laying his past humiliations at my feet because he'd thought that we'd never see each other again. Would he still be brave enough to face me in the light of day?

Felix shoved himself to his feet and sauntered to Beau, stroking his wingtip down his cheek. "Where have you been all this time? We've been worried about you. You should've heard this one…" He rolled his eyes at me. "…having an angst fit. He's prone to those."

"*You* were worried?" Beau glanced between Felix and Radley like his dream had come true, yet he'd been tricked too many times to believe it.

I needed him to believe it.

"Fae Four, remember?" I insisted.

"You meant that? And you didn't tell them?" Beau ducked his head.

I smiled. "I can keep a secret. See, even without them knowing, you're our mate now. I meant everything that I promised."

Radley glanced over his shoulder at me, warningly. "What secrets? You're begging for a spanking."

I cocked my head. "Would I ever beg for a spanking? I admit that you've made me beg for a lot of sexy things but…"

"Promises whispered in the dark and kisses on the last night before death. No one expects you to mean them," Beau said.

I wished to stroke the tremors from Beau's wings, and kiss once again the anguish out of him. After a lifetime spent unnoticed, why was I surprised that he didn't believe me?

I spun down the corridor, thrilling as my magic spiraled on my dance. Even though my lungs burned, I ignored the pain because right now, I had a lover to free from his past.

Radley let go of Beau, dragging Felix into his arms and leaning against a bookcase to watch.

When I dropped to my knees in front of Beau, he gasped. Yet his pupils dilated, and his tongue darted out to wet his lips.

Yeah, he liked the commanding position.

When I reached forward to work off his boots, Beau pulled back.

"What in the name of the Queen are you doing?" Beau hissed.

"Let me show you how to *feel* like a Forest Fae. Let me love you, Your Lordship."

I sensed the way that both Radley and Felix tensed with shock and outrage at the title. To humble myself as their leader in front of another fae went against everything that we'd been taught at Court.

Yet I wasn't humbling myself, I was serving my lover.

It was time for less rules and more love.

Beau's eyelashes fluttered, as I slipped off one boot and then the other, before pulling off his socks. His feet were delicate and beautiful. I stroked along the sensitive arch of his foot, and he panted.

Then I pressed both of the soles of his feet to the cold marble, and he moaned.

I rose, gripping Beau's hands. When his gaze met mine, it danced with joy.

I ached to kiss away every year that I'd ignored and forgotten him.

"He's the Duke of Wells' son who was locked away in the hidden dungeon, isn't he?" Radley's expression was shuttered.

Beau raised an accusing eyebrow.

I shrugged. "Okay, I can keep a secret but not well."

Beau peeked at Radley. "I imagine that you hate me now."

Felix grinned. "Oh no, we just have far more banter opportunities, Y*our Lordship*. Do you expect us to kneel as well?"

Beau clutched me tighter but then the tension in his shoulders eased. His lips curled into a mischievous smile. "A bow will suffice. I save kneeling for when you blow me."

Felix gaped at him, before he burst into laughter. "We're keeping him."

Radley scowled. "As long as he knows that *I* don't bottom."

"I do," Felix added, breezily.

"Did Emerald…?" Beau hesitated. "I mean to say, *of course* she wanted all of you in a bond. Who wouldn't? Congratulations are in order." His smile was suffused with such heartbreak that I couldn't help trying to kiss it away. When I drew back, however, his jaw clenched with determination. "I want to help you."

"How?" Radley demanded.

Beau glanced between us. "Any way that I can."

"Right, so your dad sends you to a dungeon simply for failing a game." When I gripped Beau's chin, I was shocked again by how beautiful he was.

"Don't you think he'd more than send you to the corner for betraying him?"

"If you stand with us, you'll die with us," Radley added.

"Brothers in wings," Beau declared with a soft hope.

He held up his trembling wing.

How could I leave Beau hanging?

He'd just offered his life for ours, to betray his own dad and Court, and to help save my tribe. As romantic gestures went, it was epic.

Yet he'd carefully blanked his expression like he expected us to reject his offer.

"Brothers in wings." My sensitive wingtip brushed against Beau's, and he quivered.

Felix and Radley joined us in the circle, each raising their wing to touch like a vow.

"Brothers in wings," Felix and Radley pledged at the same time.

I could hear how fast each of us was breathing and feel the tremors running through Beau's feathers. I flushed with warmth that we were united. Like something that'd always been lost, had finally been found.

At last, Beau squirmed away. "What do you need?"

Radley clutched Felix by the neck, pulling him back to slouch against the bookcase. "To celebrate the Beltane Night."

Beau gaped at him. *I knew how he felt.* "Father hates Belenus. He'll never allow it."

"Welcome our optimist." I grinned.

Beau's brow furrowed in thought, then his eyes became filled with a steeliness, which made me realize for the first time that he truly *was* a Marquess, just like me. "Smaller steps. What do you need first?"

"A way to move around the school unseen," Felix answered like Beau's forcefulness was just what he needed.

"You mean invisibly?" Beau persisted.

"Is that possible? We need to talk openly and follow Emerald."

I expected Beau to question that but instead, as if he'd been commanding battles for centuries, he only asked, "When?"

"After lunch." Felix's eyes gleamed with excitement.

What was Beau planning? We had Fighting Class then.

Beau nodded. "It's my greatest wish to prove that a Court Fae is capable of helping, rather than hurting, a Forest Fae."

I pulled Beau to me. "You don't need to make up for the other Court Fae. They're not you."

"But when we were children...I couldn't save you."

I shuddered at the same time as Beau, knowing

that we were both remembering the same humiliations and abuses. What had it been like for him to witness them, rather than suffer them? Had it been like Emerald with her brothers?

"And there I was expecting another kid to take on his own dad, Queen, and entire Court for me…" I licked up a tear, as it trickled down Beau's cheek.

"I dreamed so many times that I could. Then they sentenced you here, and I thought…"

"Don't think. Just feel for once." I spun Beau around the dusty corridor. His surprised laughter was beautiful and better than any reward. "Do you *feel* the cold beneath your feet?" Then I glanced at my mates. "I've already marked him."

I loved that Beau flushed a deeper red and snuggled closer, rather than struggled to move away.

He'd spent his life invisible or publicly renounced. *Well, not anymore.*

"Ah, the signing his name in cum method," Felix said. Beau tried to hide his face on my shoulder. "By my wing, Quince *is* serious about you. We'll all have to repeat the ceremony with you tonight to add our names."

"We can't have a Court Fae running around unlabeled." Radley's smile was dangerous. "You may get lost or stolen, and no one takes what's ours."

Okay, possessive alert.

On the other hand, Beau shook like my hold, as I

danced him around, was the only thing holding him up. His smile shone radiantly enough to tell me that this was his fantasy come true.

Could he be our final bond? *Fair Shining One, please...*

All of a sudden, an eerie banshee wail rang down the corridor like an air raid siren.

I broke apart from Beau to cover my ears, gritting my teeth at the stabbing pain. I covered Beau's ears with my own wings, as he bent over.

Feathery hell, I hated it when the librarian did that.

Apollo woke up in a flap of terrified hissing. He circled the bookcase, crashing books off the shelves.

Ms. Farah stormed down the corridor towards us. Her dark hair flowed to her smooth shoulders, but her harsh expression was enough to make my balls wave the white flag. She was a petite whirlwind.

Thank the forest, she broke off her banshee scream in favor of a glare that was equally terrifying.

Clack — clack — clack.

My bare toes curled on the marble at the sound of Wells' boots marching towards us.

I lowered my hands from my ears, and reluctantly my wings from Beau's. Yet I was surprised that he didn't try to move away from me.

Apollo landed, huddling on my feet. *"I didn't order a bastard alarm to wake me up."*

"I'm astonished." Wells' gaze swept across us all, lingering on Beau in a way that made my wings tingle to sweep around him protectively. *Wells appeared to have caught sarcasm from me.* "It's clear how ineffective it was to send you to the sadist Dean, as I suspected. Do you understand how lucky you are that I, rather than Countess Pond, witnessed…this? I leave you alone for an hour, and already you're breaking any number of Dictates: studying Ancient Magic, dancing, going barefoot…"

"We're truly hardened criminals." My eyes narrowed. "Don't you see that the Dictates stop fae from being ourselves?"

"I don't care about the bloody Dictates!" Wells roared. "I'm trying to reform you, wicked boy."

"Good thing, since you just broke Dictate 555," Radley muttered.

I stumbled back a step at Wells' rage, and Apollo flew to shelter in Radley's arms.

Wells had never lost it like that before. Had *I* broken *him*?

Brilliant.

Yet next to me, Beau was shivering. Perhaps, he'd always seen this side to his father. Defiantly, I wrapped my wing around Beau's shoulder and pulled him closer to me.

Wells' gaze darted between us and then he yelped, as Ms. Farah smacked him on the ass.

"No shouting in the library," Ms. Farah admonished.

Felix chuckled.

Bad move.

"You've just made the discipline simple for me," Wells drawled. "No reading for the remainder of the week."

Felix became ashen like Wells had threatened to send us to the Rebel Academy to join Prince Lysander.

"*Enough of that,*" Apollo comforted. "*You have us; you don't need to escape into stories.*"

"S-s-sorry." *Why did Wells always know the way to hurt Felix until he stuttered?* "D-don't take b-books away f-from me."

"Thank you for reminding me." *That didn't sound good.* Wells' eyes glinted. "Your shameful Shakespeare book shall be burned before bed."

"*N-no,*" Felix wailed.

"I'll burn your wings first," Radley growled.

Ms. Farah smacked Wells even more sharply across the ass, and he jumped. "Sacrilege! How dare you talk about damaging books in front of me? Nobody shall touch a single precious printed leaf."

"I apologize for my dishonorable behavior." Beau shrugged off my wing, straightening his shoulders. He stepped in front of Wells. *What was he doing drawing his attention? Did he want to be burned instead of the book?* "I'm disappointed in myself. I know that I deserve punishment but I don't think that I can handle the heat today under the sun without shaming you further. I'd willingly take discipline, but chores with Tom is too humiliating."

Wells' gaze became frosty, before sweeping across all of us. "If you can't behave like a Court Fae, then chores like a servant is precisely what you deserve. In fact, it's the perfect choice for you all. The rest of the school can see the Marquess of Spring and his lords on their knees weeding."

Why had Beau manipulated Wells into this punishment? I was sure that he had. Beau was a Court Fae who'd learned their scheming talents and he knew how to play his dad.

When Radley snarled, Wells' smile widened.

"Humility under the sun may teach you where I've failed." Wells straightened his cuffs. "You're on Chores Duties for the rest of the day with Tom. He'll be working outside the dining hall right now, but don't even think about stopping for lunch." He narrowed his eyes at Beau. "I know all your excuses for laziness."

"Like breaks for eating, breathing, or collapsing from exhaustion," I muttered.

Wait, rest of the day...?

That meant Beau had managed to get us out of Fighting Class. I peeked at Beau from underneath my eyelashes, but his expression was shuttered like it always was around his dad.

I'd have to show Beau later how hot I found it that one of my lovers was clever at plotting. My prick thickened appreciatively.

"Who's Tom?" I demanded.

Wells spun on his heel, striding away down the corridor. His voice echoed back to us, "Tom's a ghost."

CHAPTER FIFTEEN

**Wicked Reform School, Main Campus
Thursday 29th April**

I trudged down the library's steps, squinting in the bright light after the dark. Apollo swooped overhead: a shadow across the sun. The air was fresh and like life after the stink of ancient magic inside the bowels of the library. When my mates jostled behind me, I wondered if I was the only one freaked out that ghosts were real.

Oh, and that there'd been one at the school all this time, but I'd never known.

How blind was I?

Imprisoned in the Court, I'd known little about other supernaturals until I'd come to this school, and now I knew far more than I wanted to know. But if ghosts existed, did that mean one could've been watching me sleep, screw, or shower?

I shivered. *Were ghosts dangerous, rather than pervy?*

I followed my mates across the immaculate lawns and around the clusters of buildings. Not a blade of grass was out of place.

I furrowed my brow. "So, ghosts are a thing then. You're all remarkably calm about that secret, almost like I'm the only one who didn't know about Tom." Radley stared at me, and Felix blinked in confusion. "I'm the only one, right?"

"Secrets are hidden." Felix snatched my hands, twirling me around a fountain and scattering a band of lounging elves who threw a flurry of cusses at him that he merrily ignored. "Tom's just the gardener."

"If you knew him," Beau drawled, "you wouldn't dare say that he was *just* anything."

"But I don't know him." I wrenched away from Felix, staring around at the shrubs and flowerbeds. "By Belenus, is he hovering above the daffodils or haunting the rose patch?"

"He's weeding outside the dining hall." Radley crossed his arms. "You say that you don't give a crap about status but then you've never noticed Tom."

Was this Gang up on the Posh Marquess Day?

When Radley clutched me by the neck in an act of both possession and warning, I swallowed.

"Why are ghosts good at telling lies?" I asked.

Felix fought hard not to smile…and lost. "Go on, why are ghosts good at telling lies?"

"Because you can see right through them."

Felix burst out laughing. "Truly awful."

"I'm here all week and even better, on the last night, the audience gets to execute me."

Felix stopped smiling, and Radley shoved me away.

Okay, that could've veered too much into gallows humor.

"Not funny, Quince," Felix muttered.

Beau slipped his hands into his pockets in a way that made me want to slip my own hands in there and start something much kinkier. "You've never seen anything apart from the other Hostage Lords and Apollo." My breath quickened at the sharpness of Beau's glance. I craved the way that he'd looked at me in the dungeon like I was his *world*. I hadn't known his love before, but now I had it, I couldn't bear to lose it. "If you didn't notice me, then why would you notice a gardener, even one who was cursed to work here forever after death?"

I gaped at him.

For the first time in a long time, I couldn't think of a single thing to say.

Then Felix's soft feathers brushed against my

cheeks, grounding me, and his wings wrapped around me. I snuggled into their warmth and touch.

Beau was right.

I'd needed the safety of the brotherhood to survive the Court but I couldn't cling to it any longer.

We weren't alone now.

"Still, *weeding*…?" I ventured. "What kind of life after death is that? Is chores a regular play date?"

Beau gave a moue of distaste. "I've spent hours on my hands and knees getting dirty…"

Radley smirked. "Sounds promising."

"…With *mud*." Beau marched faster down the path. Unlike me, he wouldn't walk on the grass. *But then, I was a rebel.* "Such manual labor is dishonorable and excruciating in the heat. I'm atrocious at gardening, but Tom is excellent. How do you think it's kept looking like a top academy?"

"Magic?" I ventured.

Radley snorted.

"Such a smart ploy to get us out of Fighting Class. Plus, you have something else planned, right? So, who's a sneaky fae?" Felix teased, stalking closer to Beau.

Felix's cheeks were flushed. He'd always been turned-on by cleverness.

Beau's eyes widened in adorable confusion. "Me…?"

Radley caught Felix's eye, before he nodded like he'd caught onto the game.

Did Beau realize that he'd just become the prey?

"The first one to catch the Court Fae," Radley said, casually, "gets to claim him first tonight."

Beau leaped back in shock, as Radley pounced. Then he grinned, vibrating with delight. Radley and Felix may be predators, but so was Beau.

Felix's eyes glinted with delicious malevolence. He darted around Beau on the other side to Radley. Beau was faster than I'd expected, however, as he dived between them both and sprinted towards the dining hall.

Radley and Felix glanced at each other, allowing Beau a moment's head start. It wouldn't be fun if they didn't allow him to *think* that he had a chance to escape. I knew, because they'd played this game with me. My prick was hard against my thigh at the memory of the wicked fun that we'd had when I'd been caught.

Well, Beau had always wanted to play chase with us when he was a kid.

"Play with us, Quince," Felix called.

Wow, was it tempting.

The game thrilled with a joy, life, and love. In the midst of danger, my bonded mates and I would always have each other.

Yet I still shook my head.

Radley and Felix shot after Beau with growls that made the hairs on the back of my nape rise up.

I couldn't play because I was too distracted by the incessant *banging* from the Trial Area. I edged past the stage on the way to the dining hall. Above me, a gleaming iron guillotine was being constructed by an identical team of golems.

Did the golems care that the guillotine, which was large enough to chop off ten heads at once, would massacre my tribe? Were they *able* to care? Did they have any freewill over what they did?

I struggled not to hurl, as I hurried past the stage. Instead, I concentrated on the struggling pile of fae up ahead, and suddenly, all I wanted to do was laugh.

Felix and Radley both pinned Beau to the grass in front of the dining hall. Beau squirmed underneath them like someone who desperately *wanted* to be caught.

"He's mine," Radley snarled.

"I touched his wing first." Felix clung onto Beau with as much possessiveness as if he was a book.

I shook my head, leaning against the side of the building. The rich aromas of lunch being prepared drifted out of the open windows and made my stomach growl: garlic meatballs and greasy burgers. Apollo had already landed in a patch of sunlight and settled back to sleep, despite the battle.

Then I noticed the gardener who was pruning the

ruffled yellow roses and watching the fae with a quirked eyebrow.

If there was an opposite to Wells' regimented elegance then this ghost was it. Tom's beard was bushy and wild; his eyes were dark and hidden in shadow by a baseball cap. His flannel shirt was rumpled over stained jeans. But then, how did ghosts launder?

Okay, I'd been staring at his legs for far too long.

Tom rolled his eyes. "What's got into you today? Do fae go into heats?"

We all reddened enough to look like we *might* do.

Radley and Felix scrambled off Beau, pulling him to his feet but still wrapping him in his wings as if to be clear that they weren't relinquishing their claims.

Beau was in for some fun tonight, if we survived the rest of today.

"My apologies, sir." Beau's politeness hurt me like a slap. *I hated it.* His back was stiff, and his face returned to its formal mask. "Professor Wells sent us here for a day of punishment chores."

I didn't expect the way that Tom pulled the petals off a rose in frustration. "Oh hell, boy, *not again.* What did you do this time to get your idiot self sentenced to work with me? It's not right."

Beau stiffened even further.

"He decided to hang around with wicked fae." I shot Tom a grin.

"He'll get himself killed, that's what." Tom scrutinized us, before holding up his gloved hand.

A glowing green light spiraled from his palm, before burning into all of our chests. I gritted my teeth at the searing pain, doubling over. Panting, I scrabbled at my skin, but it wasn't branded.

There was no mark.

Radley stalked towards Tom, who didn't even flinch. "You have three words to tell me what you did, or I'll find out whether a ghost bleeds ectoplasm."

"I only need two: Chores Pass." Tom jerked his head at Beau. "This one is too smart to have been sentenced to punishment with me, when the whole school knows the House of Fae are being judged on Saturday. So, I'm thinking that you're here for something else. I've spelled you all with a Chores Pass. It grants you access to the grounds equipment, allows you to move around the school between classes, and of course, to borrow my power of invisibility."

"That sounds good…wait, did you say…*invisibility*?" When I glanced at Tom, he nodded.

"Small steps," Felix whispered. "We can move around unseen."

Beau had planned this so that we could safely follow Emerald.

He was a smart and sneaky fae.

I didn't care that I hadn't caught him. I was claiming him again tonight.

Tom stomped out of the rose bed, shaking the mud off his boots in a dark spray. He made a lot of noise for a ghost. "When the Dean brings dignitaries to visit, he doesn't want them to see lowly staff or dirty students. In fact, *he* loathes seeing them too. So, that's when you and I go invisible. Understand?"

My wings beat in excitement. "How?"

"Click your heels three times," Tom instructed.

I blinked at Tom, confused. "Really?"

"No, not really. Just believe yourself not there, you idiot. Fading away is easier than you think."

When Tom turned away to leave, I grabbed him by the arm. It was a shock to feel him solid and warm.

"I've been imagining myself not here for years. Why should we trust you?"

"Because Beau does." Tom shook me off with surprising strength. "I don't help anyone that I don't want to. But for a decade now, he's been working alongside me because of his bastard of a dad." Beau recoiled, and Radley wrapped his wings more tightly around him. "Yeah, I know who that son of a bitch is. I'd do anything to kick his ass for hurting you all this time. So, I figure that you boys need something unseen…?"

Beau nodded.

Tom pulled his cap lower over his eyes. "Then I trust you to work on…what you need…without me overseeing you. Look, I'm forever trapped in this damn place, but I'd free every last one of you students if I could. Just remember that the spelled cyclops who guard the boundaries here will eat you up if you decide to try and walk out, whether you're invisible or not. But I hope you survive the culling." He was troubled as he studied Beau. He looked more like a dad than Wells. "You're one of the good ones."

"Thank you." Beau extricated himself from Radley's hold to rest his wingtips on Tom's shoulders.

It was an intimate gesture from a Court Fae that spoke of deep gratitude.

Tom's neck reddened. "Just don't get yourself killed, idiot, or I'll still find a way to haunt you."

Beau's lips twitched. "I shall do my best not to die."

For a moment, the sunlight glittered off Tom, then he grew transparent and vanished.

"My turn." I closed my eyes.

Thinking angsty Goth ghostly thoughts...I do believe in ghosts... I do believe in ghosts... I do believe...

I sighed. This wasn't working.

Wouldn't it be easier if I simply didn't exist…? If I could fade right now, freeing my tribe? They'd have choice, and I'd have quiet?

Peace at last...no struggle, just fade into peace...

When I cracked open my eyes, my mates were doing the same, blinking back at me.

"Not that it wasn't fun to make myself sink into an Emo depression," I rubbed my palms down my pants, "but it didn't work."

"It did." Beau slipped his hand into mine, tugging me to the corner of the dining hall and peering around to the entrance. "Those who turn invisible together can see each other."

"Convenient. But also, how do I know we truly *are* invisible?"

Beau pulled away from me before I could stop him. He marched in front of a warlock with dangerous eyes and flowing black hair. The warlock towered over Beau; he could snap Beau's wings in a heartbeat or burn them off.

A warlock had options.

Beau boldly crossed his arms. "What's the difference between a witch and a warlock?"

Oh, he wasn't going there…

"Nothing."

He went there.

I leapt forward at the same time as Radley and Felix. My heart pounded, and my pulse raced. I expected to drag an enraged, fire wielding warlock off Beau, but instead, the warlock just continued to stand, moodily clutching his backpack.

I grabbed Beau's arm, dragging him to the side of the building. "Hello, Mr Deathwish, what was that?"

"When we're invisible, they can't hear us either.

And I'm here all week too." Beau looked more uncertain now.

He met my gaze questioningly, like he was asking if it was okay that he'd made a joke.

Despite the danger, I had to taste his sweetness to prove to him that in the name of Belenus, it was *perfect*.

I kissed Beau, caging him against the rough brick, and he sighed against my mouth.

Radley settled amongst the fragrant sweet peas that grew beneath the dining hall's entrance, and Felix flopped into his lap.

"We need to watch Emerald to keep her safe. She's new here and won't know how dangerous it truly is. She eats here every lunch." Radley tightened his arms around Felix's waist. "Do you think that I wouldn't know her schedule? What's wrong with some stalker love? We only have to wait for her."

"We only have to enjoy being invisible." I raised my eyebrow.

It was a couple of hours until lunch. I was going to enjoy the prankster's wet dream.

It turned out that Beau enjoyed it almost more than me. After I'd resettled Apollo as lookout for Emerald underneath the window, Felix, Beau and I took turns singling out a student and then playing a prank.

Radley scored us out of ten.

So far, I was winning but only by a point. The winner got to top tonight.

I was going to win...

If I wasn't so hungry that I could eat a dwarf, I'd be enjoying myself.

Then the sour faced student who'd orchestrated the attack against us in Fae Ball sauntered out of the dining hall, clutching a cup of coffee.

"Don't do anything daft, but a bad bastard is swaggering your way," Apollo called.

When I froze midway in lowering the pants of a Nephilim who was casting a compulsion on a phoenix (let's see how commanding he looked in his underwear), Radley nudged Felix off his knee and prowled to his feet.

"Don't hurt him," I insisted. I remembered the agony and fear as the iron balls had rained down. The way that Apollo's wings had been broken protecting me. How I'd almost died... Then I remembered Beau's quiet words to me in the dungeon. This fae's twin had been killed in the Love Rebellion. There didn't need to be any more death because of me. "Rads, listen to my leader voice."

Radley only snarled.

"He's not hearing your leader voice," Apollo warned.

Radley paused in front of the other fae who looked smaller than I remembered. Then he knocked his coffee, spilling the hot contents down the front of the fae's pants.

The fae howled, hopping up and down. When a gang of vampires laughed, the fae hurried away across the campus.

"I told you that I'd drench him in coffee," Radley said with a self-satisfied smile. "What? *You said don't hurt him.* Since when did a snarl mean *I swear on my prick to obey you*?"

Felix pushed himself up, brushing the dirt off his pants. "And that's one fae who won't be touching his burned prick for a while."

We all winced.

Beau glanced between us. "Correct me if I'm wrong, but the first steps are in place. We have the run of the school and we're unseen. So, what do you need next?"

Felix's brow furrowed in the way that always meant he was thinking more intently about things than I'd ever managed. "To celebrate the Night of the Beltane because it's both on the Wicked Bucket List and a distraction."

I admired the way that Beau trusted us enough not to even question the plan, but rather simply said, "What you're asking for is a way to convince my father who hates Belenus to allow you to hold an ancient tradition that he's banned."

"Hey, you didn't see our longer list, which

involved dancing pink hippos and the Dean in a dress." Felix winked.

That image wouldn't be going away without serious therapy. *As long as it was with Emerald, I could live with that.*

Beau grimaced like he was as equally disgusted by Felix's suggestion. "You're essentially saying that you want father to reward you."

I cocked my head. "You make it sound so simple. Except from, oh yes, he's *never* rewarded us."

Beau wrapped his wings around himself. "Please, he spends his life finding ways that he can reward you. He always has. You force his hand to discipline you, but he never wants to."

I shook my head. "He just sobs into Lincoln's feathery wing every time that he orders us into the Kneel of Shame."

When Beau marched up to me like onto a battle-field, gripping me by the lapels, I froze. "Just because Court Fae don't dance in bare feet doesn't mean that inside he doesn't *feel*. Father punishes me because I can never be the woman who he loved and lost. But you...?" He broke off, stroking my crumpled coat in apology. "All I ever heard about was the progress and talent of the Hostage Lords and his duty to foster you. He did *everything* to save you from the Queen's wrath after the Love Rebellion. Your brothers' deaths broke him. Father isn't cruel because he hates you but because he *loves* you."

I stroked down Beau's cheek, but it was me shaking. I was back in the tiny room that'd been my cell, but I also remembered all the times that Wells had saved me from the Countess' discipline as a kid.

How could Wells bond me to her now?

"Would he truly kill us on Saturday?" I asked.

Beau's anguished gaze met mine. "Don't you see that he'd have no choice? He's exiled here just the same as you."

My breath caught. Why had I never realized it before? How could Wells have hidden it?

"Was it his punishment for standing wing by wing with us and begging the Queen for another punishment apart from execution?" Radley asked.

Beau nodded. "If you don't reform and return to be bonded to Court Fae, then father can never return either...or me. He made the bargain to save all the young fae of your tribe." Beau's gaze darted between all of us. "I no longer fantasize that father is noble or that I shall ever become the son that he wishes. Yet whatever plan we devise, I shan't hurt him."

At last, I understood why our Head of House was so complex because nothing was as simple as Forest fae vs Court or professors vs students.

Real life wasn't like that.

"So, how'd I get him to reward me with something as major as a Beltane Dance?"

Beau shot me a sly smile. "That's simple. Give him what he wants: let him think that he's won."

Suddenly, Apollo flapped his wings and wailed worse than Ms. Farah's banshee scream. *"This is your swan alarm system, Your Lordship. The Countess is arriving from the east and Emerald from the west. I may have those mixed up because for a bird, I have a terrible sense of direction."*

I spun on the spot.

On one side of the dining hall entrance, Emerald strolled, clutching a bundle of files. I smiled at the sinuous way that she moved, even as she appeared lost in thought. My magic flared at the sight of her.

On the other side, however, the Countess stormed *towards* Emerald. I called out, but of course, I was muffled by Tom's spell. The Countess' hand closed around Emerald's arm, yanking her away from the dining hall. Emerald's files tumbled to the ground.

Startled, Emerald stiffened. The Countess' grip tightened. Even at a distance, I knew that it'd bruise; I'd been held in her claws often enough. Emerald gave a smile that was forced and frightened and nothing like the beautiful ones that lit me up inside.

The Countess frogmarched Emerald towards a line of trees.

Why hadn't I guessed that the Countess had been

behind Emerald's fear? She'd been the reason for my every childhood terror. But I wouldn't let her wreck the woman that I loved.

Instantly, my mates and I prowled towards them. No one hurt our bonded. Apollo flew above our heads with a determined beat of his wings.

Yet just then, a gang of vampires rushed for their lunch in an excited crowd. Unable to see us, they tripped and stumbled, flailing and snapping with their fangs at their unseen assailants.

Beau howled as a vampire ripped through his wing. Radley snatched Beau to his chest to protect him. Felix rolled to the floor to avoid the blows.

I shoved one startled vampire to the floor, but another caught me in the mouth with a wild punch. I gasped, as blood coated my tongue, and I was also knocked to the ground. I panted at each heavy boot to my body.

Yet I never took my gaze off Emerald and the Countess, until they were swallowed by the darkness of the wood.

I had to follow them.

Why had Emerald been kidnapped?

CHAPTER SIXTEEN

Wicked Reform School, Main Campus
Thursday 29th April

I crashed through the wood, stumbling over fallen logs and catching my wings on low hanging branches. My tutor would be disgusted at my lack of grace in the pursuit of Emerald. Yet all I could think about was the bond that burned my lungs, which drove me to save her…save her…*save her*.

Ah yes, and my tutor was the bitch who'd kidnapped Emerald.

My swollen lip throbbed, and my pulse thudded in my temples. Why hadn't I pushed harder to find out what was troubling Emerald? I'd known that she was frightened and hiding behind her glamor.

What if she truly was a prisoner here as much as I was?

I shuddered at the memory of the Countess' hand biting into Emerald's arm.

I'd kiss over every bruise.

Behind me, my mates darted between the trees with greater agility than me, although Radley hadn't stopped growling from the moment that he'd helped us all out of the vampire scrum. Beau was an emerald blur, speeding beneath the cool shadows.

Beau had skills.

All of a sudden, I stumbled into the edge of a glade. I pulled up short in the startling sunlight, resting my hand against a trunk to catch my breath.

I could hide it from the others but not myself. It was close to the Beltane now, and my magical illness had become many times worse.

Great Shining One, I ask only that I survive until the Day of the Wicked. Let me free my people before... Allow me to complete what my brothers started.

My mates barreled into my back, and then Radley's arms were hauling me upright and steadying me.

He never let me fall.

Apollo landed on the branch above my head.

In the center of the glade, the Countess circled Emerald in silence. The women appeared to be weighing each other up.

I paled. "Do you want to drive the gold from my wings? Let's get in there and kick the Countess' scrawny ass, until she never lays a hand on our bonded again."

"That should be *my* line." Radley's arm tightened around me.

I struggled. "Let go. I bite, you know."

"I bite harder," Radley warned.

"*I* bite even harder." Felix tugged Beau by the hand into the glade, and I gasped. "We're invisible, remember?"

Okay, right *that*.

Radley led me after Felix, and in turn, we circled the Countess. If she intended to hurt Emerald, then she'd find that ghosts were brilliant fighters, and even better, couldn't be identified for punishment. Because kidnapper of counselors or not, the Countess was still a member of staff, and injuring a staff member meant twenty-four hours in the Detention Center with flesh eaters.

After meeting the Dean, I now believed that rumor.

"You wanted to find out the truth," Beau said, coolly. "This is your chance."

Why did it feel wrong to violate Emerald's privacy like this? We were meant to be watching her to keep her safe, as well as to find out her secrets, but this was eavesdropping, rather than rescuing.

"I should've just asked Emerald why she wore a glamor," I admitted.

Beau's expression softened. "I assure you that it's hardest to remove your mask to the ones you love."

When the Countess wove closer to Emerald, I stiffened. "Why does the hostage boy love you?" The Countess stroked over her swan badge. "At first, it was fascinating to see the way that he fell so quickly under your spell, but now it seems I must remind you that he belongs to *me*."

The Countess' face was hidden behind her veil of black swan feathers; I could only catch flashes of her eyes, but they blazed with a fire that I'd never seen before.

It terrified me.

Emerald didn't back down. Her eyes glittered with equal fire. "Trust me, Lord Spring doesn't belong to anyone. You're the guys who hired me to mesmerize the Hostage Lords and bring them to heel." *She hadn't done that, had she?* Radley outstretched his wings in fury, and Felix sheltered underneath them. "Didn't you want me to wreck them? Emotions training, right?"

The Countess' scarlet lips thinned. "I've known those wicked boys since they were children at Court. Do you think I'm a fool?"

Emerald cocked her head. "I think you're a bitch. Is that the same?"

Despite the way that my heart ached like she'd squeezed it along with my balls, I still laughed.

The Countess shook, before stroking her lace gloved hand down Emerald's cheek; Emerald flinched. "Then he'll reform on the Day of the Wicked, and *you'll* delight in watching me bond with him. I hope you'll visit us often because I wish to show you what he'll look like when he's *truly* wrecked."

Beau let out a cry, wrapping his arms around my neck like that could stop the Countess.

Yet I'd always known what bonding with her would mean. I guessed that Emerald hadn't by the way that she hissed, transformed in the instant from prey into predator.

Emerald wrenched back from the Countess so quickly that the Countess stumbled. Emerald's tail ripped out of her dress like a whip, snapping across the Countess' back with a *crack* that was startlingly loud in the glade.

I twirled with a grace that would've *impressed* the Countess, spinning Beau in my arms, so that the Countess didn't fall into me.

The Countess yelped, smacking into the hard earth. Then Emerald was on top of her, pinning her down and smashing her face into the mud.

Wow, was that a satisfying sight.

"And though she be but little, she is fierce," Felix breathed.

Apollo flew across the glade to watch from the air. *"She's a warrior, My Lord. At least, when she's protecting you. I'm honored to be bonded to a princess who fights like a devil for those she loves."*

Emerald whipped her tail across the Countess' ass, and the Countess hissed. "I've decided that I've had enough of this school's games. I've assessed a bunch of the fae now and not one of them should be in this dickish place. They don't need reforming; the professors do."

"You've forgotten why you're really here," the Countess gasped. "Don't forget that I know why the Dean is hiding you. You're lucky to have friends in such high places. But interestingly, so do I."

When Emerald's tail became limp with fear, I longed to stroke it.

Had the Countess been blackmailing Emerald?

"Drop the threats." Emerald raised her chin, defiantly. "I want the fae to be freed on Saturday, and that means being allowed to return to Hope Forest and not imprisoned in your Court. Reformed should mean that their sentence is over and not that another one begins."

I exchanged a glance with Radley.

Emerald *was* helping us like we'd planned. It

didn't matter that she'd been hired to entrap us. She loved us enough to risk everything to free us.

Yet that placed her in danger.

"How sweet that hostage boy told you about Hope Forest." The Countess spat a leaf out of her mouth with a grimace. "You must've got under his skin. What you don't understand, *Princess Laurel*, is that I chose him as my bonded the moment that he became a Hostage Lord. I *exiled* myself willingly to ensure that I didn't lose him to this ridiculous school. If you try and intervene further, then I'll reveal who you are. Then you'll be returned to your own Court and forced to bond with incubi. I don't understand why you're against it because from what I hear, your mother selected a delectable harem."

My breath hitched, and my hands balled into fists. The Queen of the Succubi had been forcing Emerald...okay, not Emerald anymore, *Princess Laurel*... into a bond, just as I was being forced into one.

Was that why she'd run away to hide in this school that was cut-off from the rest of the supernatural world? Why she wore a glamor to mask who she was?

It was a smart choice. Almost no one escaped this prison once they were inside, and it was as warded as a fortress.

Laurel's shoulders slumped. "I'm not the same as you. I don't want a harem who have no choice but to be mine. I'm not that kind of asshole. I'd do anything to stop myself becoming like my mom, and that's why you can just go ahead and screw-up my life if you want, but I'll tell the Dean what you've been doing. He already hates you or didn't you know? With you gone, I'm betting that the Duke of Wells will risk helping the fae because deep down, he cares about them just the same as me."

The Countess stilled, and her lips pulled back to reveal her razor-sharp teeth. "Do you know who my friend is at your Court?"

Laurel pushed herself to her feet. "A dick?"

The Countess swayed to her knees, brushing down her uniform. "*The Duchess.*"

Beau edged around me; his hand slipped to the hilt of his scimitar. "The Duchess has dined with father and me. She's cruel, controlling, and treats her bonded worse than pets."

"Ah, the perfect guest." Felix's eyes narrowed.

The Countess wiped mud off one hand and then the other. "She had to send one of her bonded incubi to Rebel Academy because he broke...or she broke him. So, she's looking to bond with another. *Hmm*, perhaps I'll suggest one of your pretty brothers...?"

"*Don't*," Laurel said, horrified.

When Laurel shook, I'd taken a step forward before I caught myself. Invisible wings stroking her would've been more of a shock than a comfort.

The Countess slunk to her feet. "Keep to our agreement, and I won't."

I couldn't look at Laurel.

I knew what she'd say but I couldn't watch as she abandoned my mates and me. Yet I understood. I didn't want her to reject her brothers. She loved them.

"I won't betray the fae." Laurel's tail whipped side to side "But seriously, you've no idea how much I'm going to kick your ass, if you go after my brothers."

She was still going to help us…?

Despite the threat from the Countess, joy thrilled through me.

The Countess' eyes flashed. "And *you* have no idea how much danger you're in now, silly girl."

All of a sudden, a buzzing like a swarm of bees grew from the trees.

Nope, it wasn't bees, it was *myrmidons*. But they weren't meant to come into the woods this close to the main campus. The Dean could be a dick to the creatures who lived on the grounds. Why would they risk it, unless they were hunting…?

Had they been following my mates and me, Emerald, or the Countess?

I squinted between the shafts of sunlight. Wings glittered and the tips of spears.

If the myrmidons were hunting, then this would be a fierce battle.

The Countess' eyes narrowed, and she stumbled

against a tree. "What have you done? How are you controlling these killers?"

Laurel arched her brow. "Hey, I have no problem with the myrmidons. I think the question is: what have *you* done to turn them against you?"

The Countess raised her hands to cover her head, as a purple and orange wave burst from the branches of trees. The myrmidons' transparent wings glistened.

I stepped forward at the same time as Radley because who knew if the warriors decided to attack Laurel as well, but to my surprise, the myrmidon who was leading the swarm, swiveled his head like he could see me.

When the myrmidon leader pointed at me and then looked like he was waiting for an answer, I realized that he truly *could* see through our invisibility spell. Could all the paranormals who lived on these lands, before the Dean had stolen them to build the school?

After all, they were more magical than we were.

When the myrmidon nodded his head, and his floppy ears wagged, I got it. He was waiting on my blessing: The Countess had stomped on the Chief Myrmidon, and this was their perfect chance for payback.

I did an enthusiastic thumbs up. "Go for it. Just make it interesting. But only her, or you'll be next squished under *my* boot, bug-face."

The bug shook his spear at me defiantly. A

moment later, however, he turned to the Countess. Then she was lost under a sea of warrior insects.

The Countess screamed, flailing and dragging at her hair. The myrmidons, however, bit and struck at her with their spears. They pricked her skin with their poisonous tips. Instantly, the drug made her stagger and rip at her clothes. She gazed around like she was surrounded by the fears that she'd threatened me with as a kid.

"Don't just stand there," the Countess wailed, "help me!"

Laurel leaned against a tree, examining her nails. "Why would you need my help? I'm only a *silly girl*. I don't risk my life for folks who threaten the men she loves or her brothers."

"I take it back," the Countess gasped, staggering to the edge of the glade like flesh eaters were after her.

Perhaps, in her poisoned haze, they were.

"Too late," Laurel singsonged.

The Countess howled in outrage, spinning in a circle and swiping at the myrmidons. Then she tore into the wood with a screech that was worse than the librarian's, chased by the vengeful cloud of insects, who she'd thought that she could step on.

Felix let out a yell of glee, and Radley beat his wings in victory. My own grin was at its malicious best. We'd all spent years wishing to show the

Countess what it felt like when the little guy turned around and bit back.

Still, I couldn't look away from Laurel. Now that the Countess had fled, Laurel crumpled. She collapsed at the base of a tree trunk with her tail wrapped around her knees.

In the name of the forest, if her shoulders were shaking with silent sobs, then my heart would shatter again...

I rushed forward at the same time as Beau, and we dropped to our knees on either side of her.

Apollo honked, dropping from the sky to rub his head in comfort against her knees.

Laurel's eyes widened in shock. "Where did you come from?"

Apollo swallowed. "*No fair, you caught me out. I'm probably in for a spanking now.*"

Laurel arched her brow. "From me or the naughty fae who are hiding somewhere around here spying on me?"

"*Both...?*" Apollo ventured.

Beau bit his lip, and his gaze darted to mine.

I shrugged. "I rather think that it's time we unveiled ourselves."

This was going to be fun...

I furrowed my brow. How did I make myself fade *back* into existence? Emerald the stern counselor had been a fun roleplay but *Princess Laurel* pissed off for real was something that I didn't know whether I wanted to face.

I'd enjoyed being invisible rather too much. If I'd had the chance to hide my title and start somewhere new, would I've taken it as well?

Then I saw the warm way that Laurel lowered her knees to pull Apollo onto her lap, however, and I knew that no matter what happened, I'd always want to be with her…Emerald or Laurel, counselor or princess…and it was easy.

Take me back to my love…

And just like that, I was visible again.

Laurel gasped, glancing around at my mates and I, as we reappeared in a tight circle around her.

Laurel clenched her jaw. "Well, the gang's all here and listening in on private conversations."

"Let's forget all that because you're *safe*." I rested my forehead against Laurel's.

My heartbeat thudded too loudly in my ears; my skin flushed with warmth even at such simple touch. It didn't matter what happened next, only that in this moment we were together in the sunlight, and the Countess was gone.

"So, you're a princess." Radley leaned against the tree.

"I'm also allergic to strawberries." Laurel's lips quirked. "Strange but true."

"You were *also* hired to mesmerize the Fae

Lords," Beau said. "Father ordered you to hurt them through their emotions."

I drew back from Laurel, studying her.

Laurel's tail twitched. "Honestly, I think the Duke of Wells wanted to give you guys something to love and live for because at the start of the week, you were just lining up for that guillotine. I was meant to play with your emotions but not to break you. He told me to make you crave to *live*."

I blinked. "I don't understand."

Laurel's smile was as crushingly sad, as when she'd watched me walking to my execution. "I know and that's the problem, don't you get it? Even now, you don't long to live, not really. Your willingness to die is frightening." My fingers clawed into the glade's floor. "The Court Fae have trained you to accept death as your due. They ripped you from family. Kept you from your culture and beliefs. Raised you to hate yourselves. Taught you that everything about your-selves must be changed, before you can be accepted or loved. They treat you like property and try to force you into bonds." Her voice hardened. "It's everything that I want to escape in my own Court and long to change there. And the worst of it...? When at last, your families come to rescue you, the Court capture and slaughter them in front of you."

I bit hard on my lip to keep back the sob. I forced myself to smile, instead. "That does sound bleak."

"Humor again. It can't hide everything."

"It hides enough."

Why had I thought that revealing the truth was a good thing?

Beau clasped my hand, and Apollo ran his wing down my leg. I wasn't alone. My bonded saw me, and they loved me still.

"Do you want to die?" Laurel demanded.

"The moment I saw you," I said, "I *longed* to live. But I can't do that if my tribe are enslaved. They don't have a clue what the predators are like at Court."

"But we do," Felix added.

"Then we live, we fight to save your tribe, and we become free together." Laurel dragged me into a kiss that was all fierce warrior spirit. She sucked on my lower lip, sliding her hand to stroke across my hardening prick in my pants, and I groaned. Then her tongue explored my split lip, and the spark of pain mixed with the pleasure. "What did I tell you about getting hurt?"

"My apologies." I licked across the seam of her lips.

She tongued ruby sparkles from her mouth to mine. I shivered, as the swelling went down, at the same time as the cut healed.

Laurel pushed me back with a slinky wriggle. "There you go. It's lucky that you're just so pleasurable to kiss." Then she turned to Beau. "Now it's time that I claim the final member of our fated bond." Beau ducked his head, and she chuckled. "You need to watch for this part."

When Beau peeked from underneath his long eyelashes, she waved her hand through the air and the box of chocolates appeared on her palm.

"Boom!" Radley fist pumped.

When Laurel raised her eyebrow, Felix grinned.

"We were all hoping that Beau would be the final bond." Felix nudged me with his foot. "Especially this one. Don't pretend that you didn't get up to delicious kinkiness on your night together."

Beau blushed, and I smirked. "A gentleman never tells."

"*Ignore these daft rascals, and choose your favorite food*," Apollo urged.

Beau wet his lips. "Peaches."

Well, what a surprise.

Laurel nuzzled along Beau's neck, before selecting a single dark truffle and tossing the remainder of the chocolates into a patch of nettles.

Radley straightened. "Hey..."

"I don't need them. I've selected the only bonded who I'll ever want." Laurel's smile was like bathing in the hot sunshine after too many harsh cold winters.

It was addictive.

Laurel placed the chocolate between her own plush lips, before clutching Beau by the back of the head and tonguing the truffle from her mouth into his. He groaned, as the truffle melted between them in the kiss.

She swiped the melted chocolate from his lips. "Sweet as I thought you'd taste."

It was no wonder that Beau was tenting his pants. I'd almost come from the sensual sight of the two of them together. It was even hotter than I'd imagined.

Suddenly, a flame surged above Beau's head. It shimmered like a promise of love. My own bond blazed inside me, and when I glanced up at Radley and Felix, I could tell by their own flushed cheeks, that they could feel it too.

The bonds were complete and finally, we were united.

Then the flame faded.

We were together, bonded, and fated. I'd never wanted to live so much for my lovers, and I'd never had so much to lose.

"What does fated mean?" Felix's voice was quiet in the hush. "We looked it up but still...why us?"

"I wish I knew." Laurel still didn't let go of Beau like having found him at last, he was too precious to risk losing. "I've been thinking about it ever since the flames appeared. I'm royal, which means that it's possible but... It's so rare, even I thought that it was a myth. Perhaps, it's a prophecy that we'll save your people or just that we're fated to rule my land well...?

You do get that you're now *princes*? At least, you will be once the official ceremony happens."

Okay, I hadn't thought about that. Marquess had felt too much of a responsibility. Would I one day be able to rule beside a *Queen*?

I pushed myself up, holding out one hand to Laurel and the other to Beau. "Princesses and princes shouldn't sit on the floor."

"Newsflash, royalty can sit in dungeons as easily as commoners." Laurel allowed herself to be swung to her feet next to me. "I guess you know that."

I squirmed. "Sounds familiar."

When I wrapped my wings around Laurel, she laughed. Then the rest of my bonded swept around us in a claiming heat of wings and kisses. I thought that I'd burst from joy.

Until a Nephilim with milky-white skin and deep brown eyes stalked out of the trees. He was flanked by a gang of female vampires, including the one with Barbie-pink nails, who shot me a nasty grin.

Neither Oscar nor Barley were with them.

Perfect, the asshole Paranormal Prefect Patrol had arrived to discover us snuggling with the counselor.

Yet what were the Prick Patrol doing in the dangerous woods in the middle of the day? They didn't usually patrol like this. They couldn't have been following us since we'd been invisible.

Don't let the Dean have set his spies on Laurel...

"How entertaining." The Nephilim ran his hand over his golden hair. "A magic trick. The Countess and the counselor go into the wood, but then *poof*...the Countess vanishes, and the House of Fae's wickedest appear instead."

"You should see the one I do with the saw, the magic wardrobe, and the dwarf," Felix smirked. "Now, if you've had your fun, why don't you leave?"

The Nephilim's eyes narrowed. "Because you're here, and it'll be even more entertaining to watch your punishment."

"Excuse me, have you forgotten that you're students? How dare you talk to me like that?" Laurel put on her best stern voice. *Was it wrong that it still made my prick perk up?* "I'm a staff member, and I'll be reporting you to the Dean."

"We're not breaking any rules." I moved in front of the Laurel, despite the fact that she had a hundred times the power as a professor than me. "We have Chores Passes. They're like Get out of Jail cards, only you're still in jail."

"I didn't realize that they granted you permission to have orgies," the Nephilm said, primly.

"Look, asshole," Radley growled, "I don't know what lame *orgies* you've been to, but we're dressed. I prefer my kinky fun wild, dirty, and *naked*." The Nephilim vibrated with rage, when the vampires snickered. "Who were you following?"

"Our orders were to keep an eye on the Countess. Where is she?" The Nephilim demanded.

"Oh, hanging around somewhere," I offered, sweetly.

*...in pieces...*I didn't add.

"What you haven't figured out about this school is that there's only one way to survive, and that's *not* to fight the system. The Dean promised me if joined this patrol, then I'd be guaranteed to graduate."

When the Nephilim sauntered closer, the vampires circled.

"So, what happened to Oscar?" I asked, casually. "Or Barley? Do you think they'll graduate?"

The Nephilim stiffened, and the vampires whispered fiercely amongst themselves. "I won't fail like them. You think that rebelling will save you, but it won't. I'll prove it. I'll take you and your *love bird* counselor back to the House of Fae. She's your weakness." *No, no, no... Why did the asshole have to be right?* "Your Head of House will discipline you for corrupting the Court Fae as much as his counselor, and I can't wait to watch as you're finally tamed."

CHAPTER SEVENTEEN

**Wicked Reform School, House of Fae, Orchard
Thursday 29th April**

My shoulders slumped in the intense afternoon heat. Even under the shade of the All Spells Apple Tree, the warmth was like a smothering blanket. I dragged in ragged breaths.

My knees ached, and my thighs burned from the hours that I'd been forced to kneel on the grass, since the Paranormal Prefect Patrol had marched my lovers and me back to the House of Fae. Wells had ordered us into this public kneel, while the rest of the fae watched on curiously and farmed the neat ranks of vegetables.

I almost missed their patented sneers.

So far, the fae had only managed the jerk level of

the Nephilim who'd marched us back to the House of Fae as prisoners between his Prick Patrol and then disappeared inside the golden turret with Wells.

I needed to get them to brush up on their sneering skills.

Yet they must've been intimidating enough because the gang of vampires had fled as soon as the Nephilim wasn't with them. Even kneeling in shame, the Fae Lords' reputation was still enough to freak out the other Houses.

I gazed over the farm, pond, and further to the blue-haze of the mountains. This had been my home for a decade and in just over a day, I'd be leaving in one way or another.

Wow, I wouldn't miss this place at all.

If I had a party hat, I'd be wearing one.

My outstretched wing bushed against Felix's, as he knelt next to me. He shot me a quick smile, before sneaking his hand from behind his back and stroking across Apollo's head.

Apollo fluffed up his feathers. *"It's an honor to kneel with you for one last time, My Lord."*

"Swans don't kneel, remember?" I said, fondly.

"Then I sit next to you in solidarity." Apollo raised his beak. *"I'm proud to always be by your side."*

"Let's call it a sit in." Radley grunted, shifting on his knees to ease their ache.

Beau's wings quivered. "I wasn't aware, all those

times that I watched you being shamed at Court, how painful this was."

"Oh, this is nothing." I tried for flippant but I failed. "Try it for two days in a row because you magicked the Countess' wings to flash: **Kiss Me, I'm Horny**."

Felix chuckled. "Still worth it."

When my stomach growled, I groaned. Then I glanced longingly at the overflowing baskets of apples that Wells had placed around the tree. To see them and be unable to bite into their sweetness was torture, even if I knew better than to willingly eat a spelled apple.

Wells knew how to punish without the Countess' brutality.

"Hey, if you guys don't concentrate, then I'll kick your asses at the Spot the Skvader game," Laurel's voice called from behind me.

Strictly speaking, we should've been contemplating the sins of loving our counselor and the disgrace that we'd brought on our House. By the public nature of being placed symbolically under the All Spells Apple Tree that represented the Court, our humiliation alone should've transformed our wickedness.

Instead, we were playing a game of Spot the Skvadar *with* that counselor. Worse, she was considerably better at it than we were.

"You already *are* kicking our asses," Radley said.

"I didn't want to be the one to point it out…" Laurel laughed.

I sneaked a glance over my shoulder at her. The branches of the All Spells Apple Tree had lashed her to its trunk. Pink blossoms rained around her. She leaned against the tree like she owned it, rather than was a prisoner.

How hadn't I seen that she was a princess?

Laurel arched her brow. "I spy Mr Bunny peeping at us from behind the red apples. That makes ten. I win, huh?"

"I dutifully pass on my skvader crown." Felix sighed.

The skvader squeaked, hopping along the branch. He turned and waved his tail at us.

"Furry asshole," Radley snarled.

I grimaced. "Another image that I'll never bleach from my brain."

"And here's one more," Beau hissed. "My father, his evil swan, and that fascist of a Nephilim have left the tower and are marching towards us. I know father, and he looks as grim as if he were going to war."

"Bring it on." Radley's eyes blazed.

"Even worse news," Beau added, "he's gathering soldiers at his wing."

My chest tightened. I clasped my hands tighter together behind my back.

Why were the other fae falling into ranks behind Wells and following him like cygnets behind the cob?

The fae encircled the All Souls Apple Tree, until the sun was shut out, trapping us in a green and gold night.

My lovers and I were caged.

My heart thudded, and my breath was too rapid. Nothing good ever came of Wells' gathering of the House: rituals, executions, and shamings.

Why couldn't there be an occasional rave thrown in?

When Wells stalked towards my mates and me with his back so straight that it looked like it could snap, I raised my head.

Whatever happened next, *I* was the leader. My lovers might be wing by wing with me, but the one thing that I'd learned this week was that I couldn't run from the responsibility of my rank and title and I wasn't ashamed of it.

I *was* the Marquess of Spring.

Wells scrutinized us intensely enough to make me squirm. Lincoln stood smartly at his heels.

Then Wells reached out his hand and brushed it down Felix's bruised cheek. "Who hurt you? Was it the thugs in the Paranormal Prefect Patrol? I shall report them to the Dean and ensure that they're most severely dealt with. No other House has a right to bully my fae."

The Nephilim's smug smile vanished, and his mouth opened and closed in shock.

Brilliant.

Felix took a moment to consider (just to give the Nephilim a taste of his own terror), before he shook his head. "You can't bully someone who's invisible."

Wells blinked. "I don't have time to deal with your existential crisis. In fact, your *counselor* should've been helping with your delusions. Instead, she took advantage of your trust."

"Just like you requested." Laurel's voice was low and dangerous. "I take it that we're being honest now? *They know.* Why not let them choose who they love, when the Day of the Wicked is so close? It's only part of my method."

Even though I knew that she was lying, it still hurt.

Wells' eyes became ice-cold. "I'm not inclined to believe you. You're protecting them. I know love; I've tasted it. And I *know* that you have too. You love them, as much as they do you. Is that part of your method, counselor?"

"It never was," Laurel's voice shook. "I loved them from the start."

"That's a shame. I truly regret it for your sake because I've mourned, and living after the death of your lover…" He broke off, looking down. *Was he about to cry?* Yet when he raised his gaze again, his eyes flashed with rage. "But you weren't hired to mesmerize my *son*." Wells grabbed Beau's hair, wrenching back his head. When Beau cried out, I started to push myself up, but the ring of fae drew their scimitars. Reluctantly, I subsided back onto my knees. "So, you wish to have some honesty…?" When he shook Beau, I winced. "I hid my son, so that he'd remain invisible, untouched, and pure. In the vain hope that he'd grow to become like his mother. But you've turned him into a *whore*."

On the name of Belenus, make him take it back…

When tears chased silently down Beau's cheeks because he'd even been trained to cry without being a bother, I craved to kiss away each one.

"You don't have the right to talk about your son," Laurel raged. Her anger vibrated through the bond. The All Spells Apple Tree shook from it, until it cried blossom tears itself onto us all. "I love him, and he *chose* to bond with me. If you hurt him even once more, then you'll discover why everyone fears succubi."

"*Bonded…?*" Wells whispered, letting go of Beau and backing away. "What have you done, you wicked boy?"

Beau cocked his head. "I've chosen love over duty. I should feel shame, I believe. But I don't."

"*Aye, you tell him.*" Apollo flapped his wings.

Wells stared at Beau, before glaring at Laurel. "How have you corrupted him? *All of them?* I'm certain that you have no idea how special a bond is for a Court Fae. You succubi have your harem of bonded incubi, but Court Fae mate with a single lover for life. You've stolen that chance from my son, can't you see?" *Were his lips trembling?* "The fae who…Beau's mother…was murdered by a Seelie. I shall never be able to love another. You don't understand that sort of love."

When I twisted on my knees to Laurel, her expression was troubled.

"You're wrong. Just because we love differently, doesn't mean that we love less." She caught my gaze and smiled. "I'll love them as much as you loved your wife."

"Impossible!" Wells snarled, and Lincoln hissed in outrage. "When she died—"

"You ceased to see me." Beau pushed himself to his feet. He shook with more anger than his father, and his wings flared. "Do you think that mother would've *wished* you to neglect me? That she'd hear you calling me *whore* and be delighted? When she died, *you* died too because you gave up. You stopped being able to love...even me." He advanced on his dad, and to my shock, Wells stumbled back. "But that's nothing to do with being a fae and everything to do with being *my* father."

Wells fell over a basket of apples, landing on his ass. The apples spilled out in a multi-colored stream.

Beau was panting hard like he'd just fought a war himself.

I slunk to my feet, holding out my hand to Felix and then Radley. I wouldn't kneel for a moment longer. Apollo stretched out his wings, bustling towards Lincoln who *honked* in alarm and flew into the branches of the tree.

Coward.

The fae watched in tense silence. They were my tribe, and it didn't matter what Wells said, I'd take them back.

"This is *your* doing." Wells pointed at Laurel, awkwardly shoving himself to his feet and stumbling on the loose apples.

Perhaps, he should become a clown.

"Hey, you did this all yourself." Laurel's smile was sharp. "You know, it's not too late to turn this around, don't you?"

My lover was smart.

Just for a moment, I thought that she had Wells. Then his gaze stiffened to its haughty mask.

Wells flicked blossoms off his uniform's sleeves. "I should send you back in disgrace to the Succubi Court." I stiffened at the same time as Laurel. "But I'd rather you stayed and watched the fae die on Saturday." *Wow, that was dark even for Wells.* His smile became sly. "Unless, they choose to reform and make it easy on you." I was surprised by the earnest way in which he marched to me, grasping me by the shoulders. "Are you going to make her witness your execution? I'd have done anything to spare my bonded. Are you cruel or just not really in love at all?"

I clenched my jaw. *Feathery heavens, he was a jerk.*

Already, my lungs burned, and I was dizzy in the heat. Now, under the pressure of his question and the scrutiny of my lovers, I knew that there was no correct answer.

Wells wanted to prove that *my* type of love was lesser than the Court type.

I clenched my hands, desperately not looking at Radley or Felix.

"Don't answer me now," Wells said with a faux kindness. "After all, the Dean's gone to all that effort of building the guillotine. He'll be disappointed if we don't offer him some sort of spectacle on the Day of the Wicked. Plus, I've heard that there are a number of betting pools going around as well." He stroked a strand of my hair behind my ear, and I fought not to flinch. "Just repent, reform, and return home with Beau and me on Saturday."

I drew in my breath. *This was it.*

Let my bonded understand...

"On two conditions," I stated.

Felix gasped.

"Stick your conditions where the sun doesn't

shine," Radley growled. "What crap are you trying to pull?"

"Go on," Wells encouraged.

Laurel's bond burned through me, easing the pain in my lungs. Even as she stared at me in shock, her love helped me live.

"The first condition is that all the fae survive the culling," I forced myself to say.

Wells nodded like it was the simplest thing in the world.

I gritted my teeth. "The second condition is that Laurel's not hurt *at all* and isn't kept as a prisoner."

"Don't you dare do this," Laurel hissed.

"Done." Wells *clacked* his boots smartly together.

The branches that were lashing Laurel to the tree slithered away, freeing her. When she slumped, Felix and Beau rushed to catch her. She glared at me, and my balls ached like she'd pressed the wedgie ward on my pants.

"You're in for some serious non-kinky trouble," Laurel warned.

"Yeah, I figured."

Radley snatched me by the shoulders, dragging me away from Wells. "What on Belenus' glowing cock *are you doing?*"

"We tried, but Wells has won."

"Ah, I see." Felix gave me a knowing look. "We

must listen to our leader. He's only giving our Head of House *what he wants*."

Beau's head shot up, at the same time as Apollo let out a delighted hiss.

I fought to hide my smile.

Number Two on the Wicked Bucket list coming up...

"My sensible wicked boys." Wells didn't attempt to hide his smile or his relief. After all, he'd been working towards this for a decade. If he hadn't hurt Beau, there'd be a *tiny* part of me that felt sorry for him. The tiny part that remembered all the times Wells had protected me from the Countess. "At last you understand your position. I've longed to know that you were safe. You do know that my flock of hundred are precious to me?"

"Oh, I feel precious." Felix rolled his eyes.

I stuck on a mixture of my holy and pious face. *On my feathers, let this work...* "Your Grace, just grant me one thing."

Perhaps, I'd overdone the double whammy of faces because Wells peered at me suspiciously. "Highly unlikely."

Radley patted my shoulder.

I tried again. "You've tamed me. I'm reforming, but you know that I'm wild and free and... I need a way to say goodbye to that. A last chance to get it out of my system. It's Beltane Night tomorrow..."

Wells snorted. "Hundred percent for effort, Lord Spring, but not a chance."

"Please," I begged. Wells' eyes widened, as I grasped onto his sleeve. The other fae had sheathed their scimitars and their wings were beating in excitement even at the mention of the Beltane. They could sense it too: the call to the ancient magics. "Let my tribe worship their god one last time. At Court, we'll never be allowed to again. We can welcome in the summer and then, after that, we're yours." Wells looked conflicted, as his gaze met mine. "Look around at this flock that you call precious. Can't you see how important it is to them?"

Wells glanced around at the fae and then uncertainly, back at me. He cleared his throat. "*Hmm*, so you're asking me to call in a huge favor with the Dean just for the House of Fae."

I tilted my head. "Then ask for a Beltane Dance for the entire school. The Dean can make out that he's rewarding them for... I don't know... throwing less elves than normal to the kraken or something. Look, you've taken everything from us. Let us say goodbye to our old life, so that we're ready to say hello to the new."

I could be as poetic as Apollo when I tried.

Wells' lips pinched. "That was a good speech. If only you put as much effort into following the Dictates."

"Now let's not go mad."

Wells' gaze became flinty. "Talking of Dictates, where's our Countess? The Nephilim over there told me a strange story, but what's your version?"

I shrugged. "I don't know where she is and I don't want to think about her. I'll be seeing enough of her after Saturday, right?"

Wells' expression softened. "I'll talk to the Dean about the dance. Perhaps, you do deserve to celebrate your last night here."

The fae cheered, breaking ranks, and swinging each other around in joy. Their laugher was like bright musical notes, which shimmered in the heat. I'd never heard such laughter in this orchard before.

Why should something so beautiful be suppressed? Stunned, Wells forgot to yell out how many Dictates they were breaking.

The Nephilim stormed forward, snatching up a green-and-pink apple from a basket and hurling it at me. I hissed as it struck my temple. When I reached up, my finger was painted with scarlet.

I swayed, and Laurel dashed forward. She caught me, wrapping her tail around me.

"This was meant to be a shaming." The Nephilim stuck his snooty nose in the air, as he grabbed another apple. His voice shook with rage and pain. "Why do you believe them? Command your fae to hurl the apples at them, as we agreed. They're outcasts. I've taken every dirty mission from the Dean for decades, and he hasn't rewarded me with so much as a gold sticker. Yet now you intend to grant this rebel an entire *dance*?"

The Nephilim lobbed the second apple, and it struck Apollo's back.

The fae fell silent.

The hush in the circle was deadly. My lovers along with the rest of the fae drew their scimitars with a lethal *swoosh*.

When I looked at Wells, as he prowled towards the cringing Nephilim, I realized that I'd never seen him truly angry before.

"How arrogant you are. Your compulsions don't work on fae, yet you'd still try and *command* me? You dare in *my* House to attack both a marquess and a sacred swan?" Wells grabbed the Nephilim by the neck. "They may be wicked but they're fae. You're nothing but the Dean's puppet."

"Everyone's the Dean's puppet," the Nephilim gasped.

"Not anymore." Wells tossed the Nephilim at Radley's feet. Radley's eyes lit up like a dog with a new chew toy. "Have fun."

Yet before I could enjoy the sight of the Nephilim scrambling amongst the apples, my throbbing head joined with the burning of my lungs, until I could no longer stand. My knees buckled.

Why was everything so dark?

Dizzy, I reached for Laurel, who was hollering something, but I could no longer feel her, even though she was holding me up.

My head fell back, and my eyelashes fluttered. My breath was raspy and uneven.

I couldn't breathe...

My eyes closed.

Would this be the time that the darkness claimed me, and I never woke up? Had I at last been caught by death?

CHAPTER EIGHTEEN

Wicked Reform School, House of Fae Staff,
Bedrooms
Friday 30th April

When my eyes fluttered open, I squinted against the light that ghosted halos across my retinas.

Had I died? *Was this heaven?*

I was lying on something silky and soft. I was still wearing my pants but I was bare chested. My temple no longer throbbed from the apple's blow, and there was an exotic sweetness in the air like paradise.

Except, without my lovers, it could only be hell.

I clenched my hands. Whatever happened next, I knew that my bonded would wish me to face it like they were still wing by wing with me.

Even if they would never be again.

"Hey, if you're awake now Sleeping Beauty, can you help me do up my dress?" Laurel's voice called.

What on Belenus' shining balls…?

Weak still, I struggled onto my elbow, blinking to clear my sight.

The room was windowless but bright with hundreds of candles that magically hung upside down from the ceiling like wax bats. White gardenias grew from the walls, tangling in blooms, which explained the Garden of Eden scent.

This must be one of the staff bedrooms in the tower. But why was I in Laurel's personal rooms? I glanced down at the silk sheets that were bunched in my hands.

The last thing that I remembered was losing consciousness, and now Laurel was acting like we'd had such disappointing sexy times that she'd decided to pull on her dress and make her excuses?

Perhaps, that was why I was deliberately forgetting the intervening hours.

"Sure, I'll get right on that, as soon as I remember why I'm sprawled in your bed." *Where was Laurel?* When I glanced around the room, I noticed a spiral staircase that led down. Wow, they truly were spoiling her if she'd received a suite of rooms or at least, Wells had been desperate to hire her. "And just so we're clear, that's in no way a complaint."

Laurel climbed the staircase, appearing in degrees like a striptease. She was naked. Her hair hung wild and loose, and her tail swung behind her. I longed to lick her tail, sucking on the tip to make her moan.

I was glad that the sheet covered my bottom half, or Laurel would've known just how excited I was to see her. Wait, succubi could sense pleasure. *She already knew.* By the smug smile on her gorgeous face, she was flattered and feeding.

I shrugged. *Who wouldn't get hard at the sight of those tits?*

Laurel carried an evening gown over her arm. "Professor Wells had a moment of compassion when you fainted, and allowed you to be carried here with me."

"Did it hurt him?" My eyes narrowed. "I collapse; I don't faint. It's more manly."

Laurel smirked. "When you *collapsed* in my arms in a *manly* way, I asked Professor Wells if I should take you to the Medical Center, but he said that *this* is normal for you." She stalked towards the bed. "Tell me, fae should be able to *breathe*, right?"

Just for a moment, I *couldn't.*

I choked, as my fingers tingled, and my back arched.

Laurel's eyes widened in alarm, and she tossed her dress onto the end of the bed, before crawling over to me and gripping my face. "I'm sorry. You're okay.

Don't faint…collapse…again because of me. You've already slept for a day and it's almost time for the dance."

I drew in a deep breath, forcing myself to hold it and push down the burning in my lungs.

I *would* dance with Laurel tonight.

I knew now that Number Eight on the Wicked Bucket List would be to dance on the Night of the Beltane.

Belenus, in the name of the forest, let me live to worship you one final time.

"I've wasted an entire day…?" I panted, struggling to get up.

"Hey, take it easy." Laurel eased me to sit propped amongst the pillows.

"I'll just take a nap, shall I? I mean, it's not like Belenus expects there to be certain rituals completed with flowers and blessings and... Okay, now I'm hyperventilating again and I haven't even got to the part where I promised to put on a prom for the entire school. The witches will transform me into a toad, if I take away their chance to let down their witchy hair. Could you love me as a toad?" I grasped Laurel's hand, earnestly.

She squeezed my fingers. "Nope, I'd probably just sell you as a familiar." Then she laughed at my shocked expression. "Trust me, if I can love you lying in my bed worrying about being turned into a toad, then I'd love you if you were a frog, lizard, or even a skvader. You're mine."

"Thanks for that." I smiled but struggled to swing my legs out of the bed. "But also, I'd rather remain a fae. On my wings, I owe this to every student."

Laurel's tail whipped out, pinning me to the bed. Then she straddled me, grinding her naked ass against my prick, which hardened further.

"And what do they owe *you*?" When Laurel slid her hands down the sensitive edges of my wings, I trembled. "Don't you get it? You're bonded now. I've been caring for you inside, and out there, your bonded mates have been working those rituals to prepare for the Beltane. The duties aren't yours alone anymore. Tonight's going to be the most special of our life because it's our official bonding." Then she squirmed against me. "*Hmm*, is that your scimitar I can feel or are you just pleased to see me?"

I spluttered with laughter, adjusting my sword safely away from her. "I love you," I murmured. "I love all of my bonded."

"We know." Laurel's lips curled into a smile. "Honestly, the entire House of Fae didn't even need to be asked to help because they're so excited and grateful. Then Radley press-ganged the rest of the school with the aid of a Dance Committee. Guess the name of the dick who volunteered to lead it?"

"Well, in this school that doesn't narrow it down."

Laurel chuckled. "Oscar, the pure blood. I thought he hated you?"

I remembered the way that Oscar had looked in the Dean's office with his shaved head, and how he'd expected nothing but humiliation. Then his surprise, when I'd helped him, instead.

Perhaps, the other students did have a chance to save themselves.

"People can change," I said. "Plus, I've come to see that sometimes we don't know people at all."

A fleeting look of worry chased across Laurel's face, then she nodded. "So, you only need to shrug into your coat, help me on with my dress, and turn up to the ball, sexy wings."

I grinned. "I can't wait to show you the most magical night of my world. The veils will break. I remember the excitement of never knowing what'd happen. It's dangerous, but I've dreamed of worshiping this way again. If Radley and Felix set up the rituals, then this night will be special to us. Whatever you see, you'll be safe.'" When she paled, I circled her hip with my thumb. "Don't be frightened."

"You don't get it. I'm not scared for me." Laurel's fingers tightened in my feathers, as if I might vanish. "I can't go to the dance with you, until I know what's really up with you."

I winced, avoiding her gaze. My lungs burned on

every intake of breath. When I slid my hand up her side, it shook.

Laurel had a right to know. Yet I'd hoped not to have to say the words out loud because then they'd become real.

I only wanted to experience love without death overshadowing it. *Why couldn't I have that?*

"The magical illness hasn't got a name. At least, not one that anyone has told me." I closed my eyes because it was easier to speak to the darkness than Laurel. "Unless you simply call it..." I wet my dry lips. "I'm dying."

Laurel's fingers bit into my wings hard enough to hurt. "Open your eyes. Don't tell me something like that and..."

I forced myself to open my eyes and study Laurel's face, which was ashen and determined.

"You won't die," she insisted.

"I'm your subject in all else, princess, but I can't obey that command. I've been dying my whole life, even though the other fae merely think that I'm ill." I looked down. "I was the Hostage Lord and youngest son. It never mattered that I wasn't strong."

"You're the strongest fae I know." Surprised, my gaze snapped up to Laurel's. Suddenly, she looked younger than me. "When...?"

"I've never known, only that my magic is attacking itself and can't last much longer." When a tear chased down Laurel's cheek, I wiped it away. "It could be today, tomorrow, or six months. But I will die. I've fought this hard against reforming because I didn't want my last memories to be a forced bond to a woman who's done nothing but try to change me. She wanted to break Radley, Felix, and me. I swore a promise to my mates that I'd never bond, but strictly speaking, what we longed for was *love*."

"On my tail, you have it." Laurel curled closer to me; her eyes gleamed. "Just don't leave me."

"It's the will of the forest." *Why couldn't I stay with Laurel forever? Why did the forest demand my sacrifice?* "On the Day of the Wicked, I'll get to be a leader like my brother, Quinn. I've craved to experience that, even if it's only once. Because no matter what happens, I'm not one of the survivors. I've always known that."

"Quincey," Laurel's voice was raspy with tears, as she rested her forehead against mine.

Her use of my first name slashed me as sharply as a blade. I blinked back my own tears. Yet she looked more hurt than me.

"I'm okay with that," I murmured.

"I'm not." Laurel's lips were hot against mine. Her scent of fiery ginger wound around me like she could protect me from my own words. "I'll never be okay with it." Then she kissed me, and when I'd expected passion, there was loving gentleness. Finally, she drew back. "Do you feel alive now?"

My wings folded around Laurel; I held her tight to me, until I could feel the thud of her heart against mine. "Your psychoanalysis of me was brilliantly wrong, by the way. I don't want to die. I've just always known that I was going to… That's why I've been trying to *live* every day."

"Then live for me." Laurel kissed along my jawline, before sucking down my neck.

I arched, as her hands palmed the fabric of my pants over my prick and then slipped open the buttons, sliding inside. In turn, I traced my own hand down her stomach. Her eyes dilated, and she quivered. I teased up her inner thigh with my other hand.

When we smiled at each other it was once again with the relaxed joy of two lovers free and *alive* in the moment.

I'd feed Laurel with pleasure and then I'd take her to the Beltane Dance that'd sing with magic. That was why *my* prom would be the best either the Wicked Reform School or this princess had ever seen.

Competitive, Laurel upped the ante by running her finger up my prick and circling the ridge. When I gasped, her gaze became predatory.

Prick, for the honor of the Forest Fae, you won't come first…

When Laurel blew in my ear and wrapped her soft

tail around my balls, I almost lost that honor straight away.

Sneaky succubus.

But then I could be sneaky too...

When I slid my hand to Laurel's clit, circling it with two fingers to match her rhythm on my cock, her mouth fell open on an 'o.' When she sped up, so did I. Her breath gusted across my cheeks. I panted in time with her own moans.

Then Laurel's gaze burned with a steely determination, and I swallowed.

Uh-oh...

Laurel fondled my balls with her tail at the same time as she tugged on my prick. My balls tightened, aching.

Let me come, let me come, let me...

I wouldn't lose this game.

When I flicked the finger of my other hand around Laurel's clit, she moaned. In that moment, I knew what I wanted more than to win.

I wanted us to come together.

I stroked the soft feathers of my wing between Laurel's legs and across her clit at the same time as her tail squeezed my balls and just like that, we were both coming.

Laurel glowed as she fed on both our pleasure; her eyes sparkled ruby. Her back bowed, and she screamed.

My wings outstretched, and I shuddered.

It *was* heaven. There was nothing but Laurel, and the blinding-white of our love.

Okay, and the stickiness in my pants. Perhaps, I'd have to get cleaned up before the Beltane Dance.

And just like that I was laughing. Laurel laughed too, falling on her side next to me, curled on my wing.

"Now I feel alive." I kissed Laurel's shoulder, tucking her hair behind her ear. "Take me to the dance."

"I don't know." Laurel's grin was more malevolent than my best effort. "That was an experiment. I reckon we need to try *at least* once more to be certain."

My limp prick twitched in interest.

"I really can't wait to do that because experiments must be repeated to confirm results. But won't we be late?"

"Only fashionably." Laurel wiggled her ass. "What's your fantasy, sexy wings?"

My eyes lit up. "The Night of the Beltane is officially the best night of my life…even if I die."

WHEN I WANDERED TOWARDS WHAT SHOULD'VE BEEN the Training Grounds behind the dining hall and in front of the House of Demons, I slowed. Only Laurel's hand in mine pulled me on. The night was warm, and the moon shone from the velvet of the sky. Phoenixes flew like shadows, swooping with the bats; the phoenixes' cries were eerie but heartbreakingly joyful.

Ancient magic thinned the air, winding through my own. My skin prickled with the sense that I'd fallen into a wonderland. The Training Ground looked like a Beltane woodland re-imagined for the twenty-first century with gold trees, strobe lighting, and bowers of yellow roses, where the roses had been magically spelled to bloom at night (had even Tom helped out?).

This was a true Beltane Night, and not prisoners playing at it.

The bleak modern buildings and barren grounds had been decorated and brought to life. This was no longer a school but a ball complete with a dance floor where elves danced with mermaids.

I'd expected the cold elves to be more the *hang moodily around the bar* type. It just showed that I'd never truly known any of the other Houses.

This many students had never gathered together before, however, without guards and killings. Strictly speaking, the guards were here, but the ogres were bogeying right in the center of the dance floor. I didn't imagine that the Dean had intended them to join in the festivities when he'd ordered them to attend tonight.

Oscar's Dance Committee deserved their night of freedom because they'd done us proud. I knew that I was smiling like an idiot with no patented sneer in sight but for once, I didn't care.

Let the Fae Lords be loved, rather than feared.

Yet most of all, I cared that I was loved by the princess on my arm. Laurel was beautiful in an evening dress that swept the floor like white flames. I still tingled at the thought that she'd needed *me* to help her into it in a secret moment, which had been shared only between us.

Later, I'd dance with her because this was our night.

Laurel pulled me towards a table, which was draped in gold silk. It groaned underneath burgers, chips, and cakes. For this school, it was a feast.

Just like in the Beltane Rituals.

A large bowl of...suspicious...punch simmered in the middle.

Radley and Felix leaned against the table. Beau clasped Apollo and watched the dance with amazement. I didn't imagine that a haughty Court Fae had ever seen anything like it before or witnessed anyone showing so much emotion, let alone been surrounded by a bunch of locked up young people suddenly offered one night to let down their hair.

If their species *had* hair, of course.

Felix didn't wait for me to reach him, however, but bounced towards me.

He gripped me by the shoulders, dragging me away from Laurel. "Isn't it incredible?"

"Awe-inspiring. You guys are incredible. I don't tell you enough."

Felix grinned. "Oh, you don't. But we forgive you."

When I reached the table at Felix's side, my stomach growled.

How long had it been since I'd eaten?

I stuffed a cream cake into my mouth and sighed at the explosions of tastes. The warlocks must've baked these; they tasted hot, spicy, and *magic*.

When I reached for another one, Radley slapped away my hand. "You're late."

I shot him an aggrieved look, before nabbing a second cake anyway and munching it.

Ah, there was the goodness. "Only fashionably."

Radley grunted.

Felix selected a chocolate cake and then held it up to Laurel's lips like an offering. She nibbled on the cake, making sure to nibble on Felix's fingers as she sucked the cake between her lips.

Felix sighed happily.

Beau stepped closer; his eyes gleamed. "You're breath-taking." Then he flushed. "She is."

I studied Laurel. "I'm not disagreeing here."

"*Aye, but she's as beautiful inside as she is out. I never knew that anyone could love My Lord as much as I do. I did wonder whether I'd have to peck out her pretty eyes."* When Laurel paled, Beau *tutted*, tightening his hold on Apollo. *"But you love him with the same fierceness that I do. I thought this fated business was only so much fuss but I believe in it now. I believe in you, princess."*

Laurel slunk closer to Apollo, allowing him to rub his head underneath her chin. "I love you too, sweet swan."

Apollo ruffled his feathers in mock outrage. "I'm *beautiful* and *sacred*. I'm not sweet."

Laurel's lips curled mischievously. "Sweet."

Radley only tapped his chin. "I bet my wings that you weren't wearing that hot dress when you became *late*."

I masked my laugh with a cough.

Laurel scanned the dance. "So, what's the signal? What are we waiting for?"

"The wild-fire." Felix's eyes were wide with excitement. "It'll light and then it'll lead us to where the secret ceremony of Belenus will take place. At that magical time, we'll be truly hidden from the rest of the school."

My breath caught. *This was it.*

"As I'm a gentleman, let me get you a drink." I reached for the ladle that stuck tantalizingly out of the punch, which looked more like a hissing witches' brew.

Radley grabbed my arm. "I wouldn't."

Beau's lips thinned. "We saw the witches spike it. We're doing our best to guard it and stop...accidents. Unfortunately, we were too late to stop a pack of wolf shifters drinking."

"What does it do?" *Why did I want to drink it now more than I did before?*

Oh yes, wicked Rebel fae...

"We believe that it lowers inhibitions." Beau pointed out onto the dance floor.

A pack of naked wolf shifters were bopping to a Justin Bieber song and singing along at the top of their tone-deaf voices. A ring of snickering witches surrounded them.

Okay, that was something that you didn't see every day...*or at all*...or would ever be able to forget.

I ran my hand along the table. It was decorated with shells and ribbons. All of a sudden, the memory of helping Quinn sort through shimmering shells for the festival, as I played with fluttering ribbons, before I was old enough even to walk, shot through me.

When I raised my head, Felix caught my gaze.

"You r-remember t-too?" Felix bit his lip. "It's l-like returning to the f-forest and our l-lives before."

"Really, thank you for this." Even though I was gesturing at the decorations, I knew they understood that I meant *everything*. "And I've just been lying around all day."

"*Enough of that. Only you could describe being unconscious like you were being lazy.*" Apollo flapped from Beau's arms into mine.

I caught Apollo, and he snuggled closer.

"All the Houses helped. The Dean's astonished face was the funniest thing I've seen." Radley smirked. "Even the dwarfs pitched in."

For once, I didn't mentally tag on *the dicks*.

Then I noticed that white bats were flying between the dancers. Except, they weren't bats, they were *skvadars*. They swooped and spun, lost in the music. I'd never thought to see that. But then, I'd never believed that Natalia and the golems would attend a dance either. They looked more nervous than the other students like they hadn't truly been invited and any moment would be kicked out as gatecrashers.

Come on, start dancing...make the choice...you can do it...

Finally, Natalia grasped one of the golem's hands, spinning him onto the dance floor.

My heart soared at the sight. Natalia didn't belong to the Dean because no one could belong to someone like property. Felix *whooped*, when the rest of the golems dived into the sweaty fray.

As I watched the Houses united in dancing the Macarena, I allowed myself to believe that they could be united in rebellion on the Day of the Wicked.

But first, I had a Wicket Bucket List to complete. My final dance with the woman I loved.

"May I have the honor of this dance?" I turned to Laurel.

Apollo preened. *"I thought you'd never ask, My Lord."*

Felix snickered. "Come on, we'll dance."

When Apollo swooped to Felix, I held out my hand to Laurel. Then I pulled her close. She smelled fiery. When she pressed her cheek against mine, her skin was hot.

At last, we'd dance together.

Then a sudden roaring filled my ears, the scent of charcoal flooded the night air, and ghostly flames swung in an arc above me.

There was no time for dancing. The wild-fire had arrived to lead me into the dawn.

CHAPTER NINETEEN

Wicked Reform School, Main Campus, The Beach
Friday 30ᵗʰ April

The wild-fire hung above the ocean waves. I breathed in its scent, which was like the ancient bonfires of my ancestors. I thrilled, holding out my wings to catch the eddies of air. At my side, Felix and Radley gloried in the night just the same as me. Apollo flew above our heads; he circled, as if he never wanted to land.

Beau and Laurel held hands, watching with wide eyes. They'd never felt such wildness clawing their throats. Yet they were walking this Beltane journey with the Forest Fae. They were safe by our wing.

At least, I'd *thought* that they were, but the wild-fire had led us weaving to the back of the school and towards the coast. This was the furthest edge of the grounds from the House of Fae. Yet the Beltane ritual demanded the combining of the elements: we had fire, earth, and wind. I should've known that it'd also need water, and our dramatic god would desire something more primal than the pond.

I'd followed the ghostly flame away from the Training Grounds, past the House of Elves, and through a thicket. The music from the prom had faded the further that I'd walked.

Now, I was standing on the edge of a sheer cliff. My heart thudded against my ribcage. I stared in shock, as the flame quivered over the ocean below.

I peered down at the jagged rocks that stuck like fangs out of the waves.

The flame wiggled its ass like it was tempting us to jump.

I blinked. "Knock the gold from my wings, first I don't get to dance with Laurel, and now my own god wants me to jump to my watery death."

Laurel patted me on the shoulder. "Hey, we'll dance tonight, I promise."

"And what about the watery death part?"

"*Don't be so dramatic*," Apollo called. Since when was *I* the dramatic one? "*He's asking us to trust him, My Lord. Like I've always trusted you.*"

"Easy for you to say. You can fly...and swim. Wait, *most* of you can."

"That's not the point. Perhaps, *you* can tonight." Felix cocked his head. "This is Belenus. We have one night to worship him. We've all worked to grant you this, remember?"

I knew what Felix was saying.

Radley and he had spent their lives as my protectors. Yet they'd also been trying to grant me as good a life as they could *because I'd die before them.*

"The veils are down between the worlds." Beau let go of Laurel's hand, staggering to the edge of the cliff. For one heart stopping moment, I thought that he was going to throw himself off then and there. When he held his hand up to study it, it was shaking. "I can sense it. The magic's rushing through me like..."

"True magic." Radley's grin was dark.

When Radley held out his hand to Felix, and Felix took it, I knew what he meant to do. He'd never let me fall, and he wouldn't now.

"Everything's transformed for fae tonight." Felix waved his other hand at me.

I grasped Felix's fingers between mine, before hooking my hand in Laurel's. She was breathing too fast, and when she laughed, it was high and excited.

Beau turned to study us. His expression was torn. Then his shoulders relaxed, and his wings spread out with a beautiful elegance. I'd never seen this side to him; he brimmed with a newfound confidence as he strolled to Radley and snatched his hand.

Beau's lips twitched. "Let us jump to our watery deaths then."

The wild-fire flickered. *I'd bet that it was laughing.*

I took a final look over the precipitous edge at the waves.

We were crazy...

"In Belenus' name...without wings," Radley boomed; his voice echoed through the dark.

Apollo *honked.*

Laurel's grin was feral. "Five...four...three...two...*one!*"

And as one, we leaped.

I screwed shut my eyes. My stomach lurched. I waited to be hit by the freezing shock of the night waters.

Instead, a whirlwind caught me like I was a feather, softly twirling my mates and me. Laurel gasped.

For a moment, caught under the stars and above the waves, I *was* flying.

It was the best gift that I'd ever received.

At last, as if a giant's breath was blowing us, we spun further along the coast.

Then I landed.

Except, that shouldn't be possible. There was no beach on the grounds. The reform school was built along a sheer cliff to trap us.

Yet now I stood, dazed, on the soft sand of a beach that'd never existed before. Felix and Beau laughed, dropping to their knees and running their fingers through the sand.

We'd never been to a beach before. This was a week of surprises and firsts, and to my surprise, not all of them were deadly.

I wrenched away from the others, twisting around. "Where on Belenus' cock *are* we?"

"I believe," Felix's voice vibrated with joy, "that Belenus has created a magical pocket within the school for us because of the ritual. This is a beach that shouldn't exist, but our Celtic god has commanded even the ocean."

I stared out at the sea, which had been driven back and now lapped at my feet. Huge hippocampuses leapt from the waves. They held their horse-like heads high, and their bodies flashed with gold, before they dived back under with a splash of finned tails. Seahorses gleamed beneath the moon's light. When eerie horns were carried to me on the wind, I shivered.

Anything could happen. For one night only, on this beach, we were free.

"Is it okay with you," Laurel breathed, joining me at the water's edge, "if I now have a thing for this god of yours?"

"*He makes me hot too.*" Apollo landed behind me.

At a sudden *whoosh* and rich aroma of bonfires, I

twisted around, resting my hand on my scimitar. My magic burned hotter inside.

I was being called home.

I choked, struggling for breath.

A bonfire sprang up at the base of the cliff. Its flames roared higher than any natural fire. I shuddered, glancing at Radley and Felix because I knew that they understood.

Every Beltane night had its fire, which was the light and warmth to cleanse the world.

When Felix *whooped*, Beau let out a gasp of shocked laughter. Radley didn't drop his gaze from mine. I knew that we were both remembering the same bonfires when we were kids. Radley had loved watching the flames. He *still* loved roasting warlocks on their own flames if they hurt me.

Perhaps, it gave him happy memories…?

Before I'd been taken as a Hostage Lord, I'd gathered kindling for the Beltane Bonfire with my brothers, even though I'd only crawled in their shadows. Later, the clearing in Hope Forest would he alive with glowing embers and the scent of charcoal. Quinn would lead the fae in jumping over the flames as part of the games.

On my wing, I'd forgotten how much I missed being with my family and tribe. How much I'd lost myself.

This night was bittersweet. But it could never have ended better than this.

I allowed myself to pretend that it was the smoke from the bonfire stinging my eyes and making them water.

"You know what'd make this perfect?" Felix held out his arms to Apollo who flew into them.

"Sparklers?" I ventured.

Felix glanced at Laurel. "Let's see if you're lucky enough to meet all your bonded tonight...without collars."

Felix's Fortune Magic snapped open Apollo's emerald collar, and it fell to the beach floor.

Immediately, Apollo shifted into his human form. Laurel's pupils dilated at the gorgeous sight of Apollo's naked muscles, high cheekbones, and the cute way that he clung to Felix like he thought that Laurel might reject him.

Apollo was a beautiful swan, but he was a *hot* man.

Felix shoved Apollo towards Laurel. "Go woo her. You're not usually short on romance, Romeo."

Apollo ran his hand though his wavy hair. "It's not so easy when she's..."

Laurel rushed towards Apollo, snatching him into a kiss. She wrapped her arms around his shoulders, and he moaned. Then she drew back.

I longed to kiss both their lips: one petal soft and the other fiery hot.

"Does that make it easier?" Laurel murmured.

"Now you know me, would you still choose me?" Apollo asked. "I'm no Lord but I'm loyal. I'll stand wing by wing with you in love and life...if you want me, princess."

"Honestly, you've just won the Romeo Award. And you're my bonded. I'm never letting any of you go." I didn't miss Laurel's sharp glance at me.

I shifted uncomfortably.

When Laurel traced down Apollo's chest, stroking over his pink nipples (and I knew from experience how sensitive they were), his blue eyes sparkled.

"You've no idea how much I long to kneel and taste between your sweet thighs, until you scream," Laurel's eyes widened at Apollo's seductive tease, "but we're on a hidden beach for the first time in a decade. The daft Fae Lords have a battle campaign to plan. After that, we'll talk making the bond official."

"Sex on the Beltane is sacred. It's part of the Great Rite," Radley pointed out.

Felix nodded. "It's a symbolic joining."

My prick nodded its agreement too. "Or that's our excuse, and we're sticking to it."

Laurel's eyes glittered. "What makes you boys think that I need an excuse to screw you all senseless at the same time?"

Ah yes, succubus.

I hid how enthusiastically my prick was nodding to *that* plan, by gesturing towards the bonfire. We gathered around its heat, sitting in a huddled circle. There were worse places to plot than under the stars in the cradle of ancient magic.

"Honestly, it was easier than I'd expected to find out how to take down the wards on the gate, the spells on the cyclops guardians, and the magical barrier over the sky." Laurel gave a smug smile, but she'd earned it. *How in the feathery heavens had she managed that?* "It was all down to Natalia, the Dean's secretary. The Dean trusts her too much because he created her, which makes him underestimate her. The asshole thinks she's the only one who could never betray him. Well, the dick's wrong."

I gaped at her. *Natalia...?*

Beau furrowed his brow. "But golems can't think for themselves."

"Like you can't because you're conditioned that way...?" Laurel asked. Beau ducked his head. "I simply told her that it was you, Lord Spring, who needed help."

I sat up straighter. "She did it for me because I told her to believe in herself?"

"Natalia has a crush on you."

Was this the first time that a golem had ever rebelled against their creator?

"It's not enough." Radley drew a rough picture of the stage in the sand. "Even with the barriers down, the Dean and his guards can use weapons or spells to shoot us down if we try to escape. We're sitting ducks."

"Talking of birds," Felix nudged Apollo, "the witches have spelled the cygnets not to fall from the swans' backs, when they escape. Odile and Lil Swan will be safe. Plus, once we're free, the collars will open on all the swans, and they'll be able to choose whether they shift into their human form or not. It was the witches' thank you for the dance."

"You're taking all the shifters with you?" Apollo gasped.

I grinned. "We're *freeing* them. Did you really think that I'd leave behind such sacred creatures?"

Apollo threw his arms around my neck, before whispering into my ear, "*As soon as we escape this school, I'm going onto my knees and sucking you off, until you scream.*"

I shivered. *Okay, I was fine with that.*

"Will the other Houses fight tomorrow?" I asked.

Radley shrugged. That said it all.

"And you have me." Laurel smiled. "Your secret weapon."

I swept Laurel to her feet. "I also have a Wicked Bucket List and a promise of a dance."

I pulled out my iPod, selecting Massive Attack's hypnotic "Teardrop".

Laurel's eyes lit up. I gripped her by the waist, pulling her close. Then in the light of the fire, we danced to the heartbeat of the throbbing music. She slid up and down me, rubbing her cheek against mine. She was more than sensual: she was the wild-fire alive and burning *inside* me.

She was mesmerizing.

I turned to catch her lips with mine; I could feel her power tingling beneath my skin. Could she sense my magic as well? This *fated* bond...? When I glanced around my bonded, who were watching us with intent gazes, it was like each of us was connected in the dance.

I spun Laurel, liberated. She laughed, and I pulled her close again. "No matter what happens tomorrow, I can't regret that we met."

Laurel shook her head. "I'll never regret it."

I flung out my wings like I truly could take flight, before pulling her tumbling on top of me in the middle of my mates. They caught us and in the coiling night's magic, we were a frenzy of kisses, licks, and stroked wings.

Laurel was the center of it all: our chosen princess.

Beau pressed kisses along her tits, just as Apollo slipped up her dress, sinfully peeking at her from underneath his eyelashes. Radley pulled her head back by the hair to give Felix access to suck and mark along her neck, and I kissed her on her lush lips. In turn, she slipped her hand into my pants to rub my prick.

Above me, the stars burned in the black sky.

Number Seven was the only one left on my Wicked Bucket List. Yet as I stared up at the silent stars that completed my list to make love underneath them at the same time as fulfilling Number One (making this an official bond), it was the only number that mattered.

The list was finished.

As Laurel's hand circled the silky head of my prick, I was aflame.

It was too much.

It felt like the heat from the fire had jumped down my throat. My own magic was burning me up from the inside. The smoke was choking me.

I was the guy being burned to ashes on the bonfire.

I gasped, attempting to warn my bonded, but Laurel thought that I was simply caught up in the passion like her and tightened her hold. Her nail pressed into my sensitive slit. I arched, scrabbling my fingers through the gritty sand.

Then all at once...it stopped.

The world exploded to dark.

I fell backward but I didn't feel what I hit because there was...*nothing.*

Darkness and nothing.

I could hear shocked voices but I didn't even know who they belonged to.

Everything softened like maybe it hadn't mattered with the bright sharpness that I'd once believed it had.

What's wrong with him?

He's dying. Do something.

Shining Belenus, help us!

Please, Quince, you can't...you can't just leave us...

I wished that I'd had longer with these people who I loved. But I wasn't sad. I'd bonded. I'd even completed my Wicked Bucket List. I'd known that I'd been loved, as well as celebrating the Beltane for one final time.

I trusted my mates to save my tribe.

That was more than most younger sons could ever hope for.

All of a sudden, I had a sensation like I was fading and a white light blazed in front of me.

In the name of the forest, he's burning up...

Save him!

Fire seared through me. Yet it didn't hurt because weirdly, I knew that I was dead.

Then a moment later, my eyes snapped open, and light seared them again. This time, it *did* hurt.

I screamed, struggling like a new-born in the arms

of the huge man who was cradling me and leaping out of the fire on his chariot.

Wait, his chariot...?

When the god, who gleamed in golden armor, smiled at me, it was shocking that such a fierce warrior could look soothing.

I was held in the arms of *Belenus*.

And I'd thought that dying would be the biggest thing to happen to me tonight.

The wind whipped the oceans to foam, and the earth shook and shifted. Rocks skittered from the cliffs.

The world was tearing itself apart.

Belenus pulled the reins on the chariot and his fire horses (which looked like they'd burst from the sun), reared above my mates. Their tear streaked faces stared at Belenus and me in amazement.

At last, the wind quietened, and the rumbling earth settled.

I spluttered, rubbing at my cheeks. Then I stared at my fingers; they were covered in ash. I was coated in it. Something else was different too.

What had changed?

"My son," Belenus said, tenderly.

He wiped away a smear of ash from my cheek.

Did Belenus call *all* fae his sons?

Frozen, I still forced myself to return his smile.

When your god snatched you from the jaws of

death and took the time to cross the veils to appear to you, then the least you could do was be polite.

I didn't know why I felt so comfortable held by Belenus, but I didn't hate being in his arms.

One by one, my lovers pushed themselves to their feet. Radley and Felix exchanged glances as they unsheathed their scimitars. I'd never seen Laurel look so deadly, as she stepped up to the god, as if Belenus was merely a misbehaving student.

Laurel's eyes flashed. "Put Lord Spring down."

Well, that was how to stun a god.

Belenus glanced down at me in his arms and then back at the ring of paranormals around him. "Is that any way to talk to a god?"

Radley's grip tightened on his sword. "Oh, fair shining one, please put him down, before I scalp your golden hair from your beautiful head."

I don't think that Radley entirely understood the memo on politeness.

The fire horses snorted, but he didn't move back. I shook at the thought that Radley would even take on a god for me.

"I don't believe that I've ever heard that threat before. Most bold." Belenus raised his eyebrow. "But I'm the Wild God and this is *my* night. Nothing you can do will harm me, so don't make *me* harm *you*."

Hurriedly, Beau stepped in front of Laurel, at the same time as snatching Radley's arm to hold him back. "Wild God, we thank you for gracing us with your presence. But we've just watched the fae who we love die and then reappear from the bonfire carried in your arms. So, excuse us for not being at our best."

"Even if you're a Court Fae," Belenus smiled, "for such an answer, I'll let you live."

Beau paled. "Most gracious."

Okay, that was enough. Even if this was my god, no one scared Beau.

"Good job on the...whatever just happened...but I'm not actually your kid, so if you wouldn't mind putting me down...?" I begged.

For once, I missed the Dictates. At least they'd have told me how to act when I met my god.

Belenus circled his thumb on my forehead like a blessing. "What happened is that you died...just for a moment…and then I brought you back. You're better than new." *Now I was even more creeped out.* Yet I finally got what was different. I felt better than I ever had: stronger, more powerful, and fitter. My breath caught. *The illness that'd plagued me all my life was gone.* "And you *are* a kid, at least to me."

"Aye, because his noble behind is so young compared to your ancient one…?" Apollo ventured.

Belenus *clicked* at his horses, and they trotted forward. Then he lowered me into Radley's arms.

Instantly, I was surrounded in a cocoon of my lovers; their tears were wet against my cheeks. Laurel wiped the ash away from my lips and then kissed me like she'd forgotten my taste.

On my feathers, she'd thought that she'd never kiss me again.

Belenus drummed his fingers against his chariot impatiently. "This was a onetime deal. Don't go calling for me and expecting me to save you. I only have so much patience even for my children."

There he went again.

When I peered up at Belenus, it struck me with sudden wonder that I was studying my god, but that he was studying me with equal interest. He looked almost like he was about to demand to see my report card.

Wow, I hoped that he didn't.

I wet my lips. "Now, when you say children...?"

Belenus *tsked*. "Do they teach fae nothing nowadays? Your mother prayed for fertility on the Beltane. She'd birthed your brothers before but couldn't conceive you, the last child. I granted it to her, but the magic that conceived you makes you *mine*. I can sense when someone will play an important role in your world."

"*Fated*," Laurel gasped.

I pushed back into the hold of my lovers like that would anchor me against everything that I'd believed being torn away from me. "My father...?"

"You're a demigod." Belenus' golden eyes flared.

"The Court Fae trapped you without the rituals and access to the ancient magics like the Beltane, which would've freed the fire inside you. It's what weakened you and stopped you from transforming or flying."

"Quince, you can fly with us at last!" Felix's eyes gleamed with tears.

I didn't dare meet his gaze in case mine would too, but my wings beat in desperation to test it out.

"A demigod?" Radley looked at me blankly. "That explains his attempts to pull rank."

Belenus' expression gentled. "You needed to die, in order to become my true son."

All at once it was too much. Fury roared through me. My new power thrummed.

"And you couldn't have told me this, I don't know, when I was a kid?" I demanded. "How about before I suffered in agony or believed every day that I'd die?"

When Belenus' horses *neighed*, smoke flickered out.

Belenus tugged his chariot in a circle. "I appear when my sons prove themselves. How long has it been since you called out to me and meant it? When did you last trust yourself?"

"Tomorrow's the Day of the Wicked." My new magic sparked through me. My power no longer attacked itself. It was wild and free like Belenus. "It's when the Forest Fae either reform or die."

Belenus' smile was as malevolent as mine. "You're

a demigod. You don't choose between someone else's options. You make your own third way." Then he roared, "Run wild like the fire."

Belenus snapped his reins, and the chariot dived into the bonfire. The flames surged up, burning Belenus and his horses and taking them back to their side of the veil.

Our god was vanished, I was a demigod, and in only a couple of hours, the sun would dawn over the Day of the Wicked.

CHAPTER TWENTY

Wicked Reform School, Trial Area
Saturday 1ˢᵗ May

It was the morning of the *true* Day of the Wicked. Wells would insist that either I reformed and graduated or remained wicked and died. But unlike the mock run-through on Monday, this time I'd created my own third option: *escape*.

The other fae didn't call our tribe *Rebel* for nothing.

I squirmed on my spot in front of the guillotine. I was safe, however, snug between Radley and Felix. When their shoulders nudged mine, power sparked through me. My wings crackled with golden magic.

Why was I thrumming to incinerate the Dean's guillotine and his smug demon face along with it?

Ah yes, demigod.

My power surged through me for one moment longer, then I forced it deep inside: *hidden.*

Last night, my bonded and I had screwed in as many ways as we could imagine (and Laurel knew more ways to fit our sexy parts together than I'd ever dreamed, which was the benefit of a succubus as a lover). By the end of the night, we'd broken over fifty Dictates.

Next time, I'd shoot for a hundred.

Beau had groaned, collapsing back. Laurel had glowed with the energy, on which she'd fed. Exhausted, we'd laid in each other's arms, until the fire had died to embers and dawn had streaked the sky.

We'd watched as summer had come in.

Then the world had lurched. The veils between worlds, which had been torn apart the night before, had mended themselves. I'd missed the scent of ancient magic.

Would I see Belenus again?

Wells would've been crazy with worry that we hadn't returned to our dormitory after the Beltane Dance, but as revenges went, it wasn't up there with Radley's worst.

After all, how would Wells make us suffer for breaking the rules? Threaten to chop off our heads...?

Then the world had grown hazy. I'd gasped, panting. When I'd blinked away the haze, I'd found myself sprawled with my lovers on top of the cliff that we'd hurled ourselves off the night before.

I'd crawled to the cliff edge and peered down. Then I'd shivered at the sight of the waves crashing against the rocks.

The beach had disappeared like it'd never been there.

Yet I'd known by the way that I'd burned with power rather than pain just how much it *hadn't* been a dream. Now I had to save the lives of all my tribe.

I glanced across the stage at the fae, who stood in gleaming ranks. They didn't appear afraid. Their chins were tilted up, and their gazes burned with something that I hadn't seen in them in a long time...*hope.*

The other Houses crowded the stage along with the staff. They buzzed with anticipation, and I didn't think it was just the excitement of their bets. Since the method of execution loomed in iron behind us, the most popular bet appeared to be on who'd die first.

Yet the mood in the crowd had changed. The vampires jostled the shifters, but they didn't fight back. When the mermaids chatted to the witches, I raised my eyebrow.

Anticipation was thick in the air. The other paranormals weren't here to witness our deaths. At least, most weren't.... *Okay, 60:40.*

Shining Belenus, let it be enough.

I shuffled my boots on the stage, scrunching my nose up against the tangy scent of blood. Was it stronger than before or were my senses simply better? Since I'd been reborn, everything was brighter, louder, and more intense.

The world felt reborn right alongside me.

The fountains *tinkled*, the air was fresh, the sun beat hot against my head. Above, phoenixes swooped across the sky, singing haunting *goodbyes.*

My wings fluttered like they couldn't wait to take flight. Radley shot me a look that caused them to wilt. In the name of the forest, I mustn't risk the staff guessing that I'd become a demigod.

I ducked my head, attempting a contrite face.

"Aye, that's right," Apollo glanced up at me through his thick lashes. Naked, he knelt in front of me. I'd refused to put his collar back on him. Conveniently, I'd *lost* it on the magical beach. When he next shifted, it'd be because he chose to and not because he was forced. It'd be the first time in his life that he shifted for himself. I itched to witness it. "Remember that this is the day we're returned to Court, My Lord. That'll cool your wings."

My wings wilted further, curling around me. I'd never return to the poisonous black court with its narrow corridors and sneering fae.

It'd kill me for real.

"That's the face we need," Felix muttered.

I searched the audience for Laurel. *Where was she?* What if Wells had locked her up or refused to allow her at the ceremony?

Unfortunately, scanning the crowds meant catching the Dean's eye. He shot me a beaming smile. The asshole thought that I was tamed and as controlled as his golems. I couldn't wait for him to discover Natalia's strength. When Natalia waved at me, I fought hard not to wave back.

Where was Laurel?

My pulse raced. Surely, Wells wouldn't have trapped her in the dungeon? Perhaps, we should've worked out a Plan B...

Yet Wells would enjoy forcing her to watch us being returned to the Court. He wanted to prove that his method of reforming was the correct one.

Then a pair of phoenix twins strolled to one side, and Laurel pushed to the front. Her fiery ginger scent wound around me, and I longed to kiss her. I'd never have enough of her because to the tips of my wings, I knew what being bonded meant now. It was loving someone so fiercely that you'd protect and fight for them, but that you could never live without them.

I understood Wells' grief for his dead wife.

My draw to Laurel stole the breath from me. Yet my bond wasn't complete without my fae and shifter lovers as well. Plus, if we ever had children, then I'd love them with the same fierceness. I'd never forget them like Wells had Beau.

I'd done that once. Never again.

When my gaze caught Laurel's, my wings perked up again as much as my prick. Her smile was strong and reassuring, rather than sad like when I'd first seen it. She didn't doubt me for one moment.

So, I didn't doubt myself.

Ogres ringed the crowd. Their swords were raised in preparation. When one slunk past Laurel, leering at her, I noticed the way that she assessed him. Those assholes who thought with their pricks (another image that I'd have to scour from my mind), wouldn't be hard to control.

Wells stepped to the front of the stage with Lincoln trotting proudly at his heels. Wells' uniform had been brushed and polished until it gleamed midnight black. Beau stood at Wells' shoulder, fiddling with his cuff. He was pale, but his haughty mask was fixed in place.

Wells was relaxed, however, and he smiled benevolently at me.

Okay, now I felt icky.

Wells needed to believe, however, that this ceremony was only a formality because I was going to say *yes...*

Yes, I was reformed. Yes, I'd return to the Court. Yes, I'd be forced into the bond.

Then my tribe would follow me, even though I'd renounced lordship rights.

It was a shame for Wells really that I had a whole lot more than that to say.

"Where's my requested drumbeat?" Wells asked conversationally, but there was a dangerous bite to his tone.

The fae remained still. They didn't beat their wings together.

The audience fell to a sudden hush.

Anticipation. Readiness. Threat.

My magic wound around my lovers like a shield. Danger scented the air. Suppressed violence simmered close to the surface from so many paranormals, and it set my teeth on edge.

The Dean wasn't smiling anymore. Instead, he glanced around himself in confusion. Not even the beserkers had made a move yet, and they were dumb. They all knew to wait for the signal.

Wells cleared his throat like he hadn't just been publicly ignored by his own House. "The Marquess of Spring, step forward. It's time to judge the wicked."

I allowed my hair to swing forward, covering my eyes. The less Wells could see of me, the less chance he had to guess the truth. Radley and Felix swaggered forward at the same time, flanking me. Apollo crawled sexily in front of us. I'd never imagined that it was possible to crawl in a dominant way, but Apollo pulled it off.

Wells blinked at Apollo. "And this naked creature is...?"

"A sacred shifter." Apollo knelt, sitting back on his heels. "Plus, beautiful," he added as an afterthought, "and like the one that you still have collared at your feet. You wouldn't know how gorgeous I'm certain he is, since you've never freed him, right?"

For once, Lincoln didn't hiss. Instead, he stared longingly at Apollo and then up at Wells.

Wells shifted uncomfortably. He avoided meeting his swan's accusing glare. "Once we're back at Court, you'll be a pampered pet too. Shifters are beautiful, elegant, and acceptable in swan form only." He waved his hand at Apollo. "*This*, on the other hand, is not."

When Apollo shivered, I stroked my hand through his hair, before fluidly dropping to my knees in front of Wells. Radley and Felix knelt either side of me. One last time, we'd be wing by wing in this school.

"Don't you have a tribal dance for me?" Wells drawled. "A Shakespearean sonnet? Surely you at least have a sarcastic quip?"

I shook my head.

"I don't need Shakespeare to tell you that every Forest Fae and even every human (who you despise), are more civilized than *you*." Felix's eyes were steely with determination. I loved that he didn't stutter. "The mysteries of the world are wasted on the small-minded."

"Boom!" Radley grinned.

I stroked along Felix's neck with my wing. "Well said, Lix."

Wells' gaze darted between us, before settling on me for a long moment. My shoulders stiffened.

Don't let him guess...

Then Wells pulled out a graduation scroll from his pocket. "Aren't you at least going to turn this to ash? I never thought that I'd miss your drama."

When Wells glanced at the Dean, I knew that Wells was playing to the crowd. If he needled us, he could prove how *reformed* the Hostage Lords now were. He could show the entire school that our emotions had been wrecked in a single week.

Who I was to let down an audience...?

I clasped my hands together. "In the name of the Queen, I regret our despicable behavior on Monday. I beg your forgiveness." Wells scrutinized me; his expression was conflicted. He was desperate to believe me, but then, he'd known me for a long time. "Why? Are you disappointed?"

Finally, Wells allowed himself to let out a bark of laughter that made Beau jump. "*I'm delighted.* You shall make the most outstanding Court Fae."

Gold sparked my feathers, and rage coursed through me. It was the pain of my ancestors and the pride of my fathers. It was everything that I was and had been ripped away from me.

I was a Rebel Fae. This was *my* Day of the Wicked, and I'd be proud to claim my heritage and not the Court's.

"Thanks for that. But first, let me tell you a story. This is my graduation, after all. Won't you all listen to the myth of how our Rebel tribe gained their name?" When I glanced at the ranks of fae, they beat their wings. Wells jumped, then frowned. *Had he realized yet that the fae were no longer taking orders from him?* The ancient drumming of the fae's wings was no longer to urge me towards death but in solidarity of the tale. When a breeze gusted through my feathers, it was like the breath of every one of my ancestors. "The Court Fae say that it's a mark of shame that the color has been bleached from our wings in fae form. But in fact, us Forest Fae know that our wings are a mark of pride. We're called Rebel because our ancestors were the first to rise up against the tyranny of the Seelie. Every Dark Fae owes us gratitude. Rebellion sets you free...even your Queen."

"Enough stories and treason," Wells growled.

Beau tapped Wells' shoulder. "You've just broken **Court Dictate 203**: *No snarling or growling*."

Wells growled again.

Despite myself, I snickered.

"Where's the Countess?" Wells questioned. "She

should be here to witness your graduation and then complete your bond. You have no conception the trouble that I've suffered at her hands because she's desired to tame you. Do you know how long she's wished to bond with you?" I shuddered because *yeah, I did*. "I'm not inclined to believe that you're innocent as to her whereabouts."

Felix cocked his head. "That certainly sucks for you."

When Wells circled us, the hairs on my nape rose. "If she doesn't arrive by the end of the ceremony, her claim on you, Lord Spring, shall be forfeit. And that delights me as much as you reforming does." I twisted to Wells in shock. *He'd never wanted me to bond with the Countess?* "Do you believe me still so unloving towards my flock? I've never been free to make my own choices. But I detest cruelty between lovers. My bonded never raised her hand to me or..." His gaze rested on Beau. "...Her son. I swear that I shall do everything in my power to ensure the Queen chooses a Court Fae who'll treat you with the same kindness..."

Wait, he intended for my fate to rest in the hands of the *Queen*? She'd wanted to bond with Quinn. What if she saw me and decided simply to take the younger brother?

Focus, Quincey, you're already bonded to royalty...

"I've just found a way to save you the bother. Do

you remember your counselor? She's here, willing, and kind," I suggested.

Wells' lips twitched. "Good try."

"It was worth a shot. She's prepared a goodbye gift." I gazed hard at the ground, as my heart thudded in my chest. *This was it.* "It's a special end to the ceremony."

"That's not appropriate."

"If you've tasted love," Felix said, quietly, "then you'll understand what this means to us."

Wells hesitated.

Please, please, please...

At last, Wells stepped back. "Be my guest. Does she intend to pull a skvadar out of a hat?"

I forced myself not to grin. "Something like that."

Wells startled, when Beau clapped his hands. Instantly, the fae separated, carrying forward folding chairs that they put out along the front of the stage as if for a show.

"What's going on?" Wells demanded.

Felix, Radley, and I pushed ourselves to our feet, slipping our hands to the hilts of our scimitars.

"The performance of our lives." I steered Wells to the middle seat, pressing him down.

Wells blinked in confusion as the fae, led by Sour Face himself, dived into the crowd and dragged up the reluctant staff to fill the seats. Even the Dean strolled to take his place like it was a throne and he was being offered a treat.

I couldn't wait for him to choke on it.

The ogres didn't want to be left out, sheathing their swords and strutting to stand around the edges. My nose wrinkled at the stench of mud that hung around them.

Finally, Laurel stalked onto the stage. Her dress fluttered behind her like she was so white-hot that she flickered with flames. *She was decidedly hot* and made warmth pool inside me. Particularly, at the way that her eyes lit with predatory danger.

Laurel was about to battle for her bonded, and a succubus was deadly when protecting her harem.

Right now, however, she was going to dance.

When I slipped on "Glory Hole" by Portishead, Laurel matched the song's spooky sensuality, as she danced in front of the staff. I wanted to screw her hard and fast and make love to her slowly at the same time. She raised her hands above her head, swaying her hips and glancing over her shoulder at them.

She was a temptress. A flame sprung to life. *Everything.*

My mates banded around me, my wings beat, and the anticipation in the crowds grew.

This was the signal.

Laurel threw her succubi power to mesmerize, which had been boosted by our marathon sex session the night before, at the gathered staff. They couldn't resist. In a daze, they sat under her thrall.

How deadly could Laurel be with such a power now that she was bonded to the five of us?

I was starting to get the *fated*: a succubi princess, demigod, sacred shifter, Marquess Court Fae, and two Rebel Lords.

Yet when I studied Wells, there was just enough of a spark in his eyes for me to wonder if Laurel's spell was truly working on him.

I nudged Beau. "What's going on with your dad? How could he resist that level of power?"

Beau worried at his bottom lip with his teeth. "He once said that no succubus could tempt him with their *dirty emotion*. I believed it to be nothing more than Court prejudice. Yet perhaps, this is what he meant and why he felt safe to hire one. You know, she could compel us to do anything, if she wished."

I shivered. Yet Laurel had never abused her power. She'd never forced anything on us.

"Then why is Wells pretending?" Radley snarled.

Apollo grasped Radley's hand. "Leave off growling. Despite it all, the rascally bastard might want to give us a chance to experience freedom. It sounds like he never has."

When my gaze shot to Wells, he coolly met it. He wasn't mesmerized. Yet he hadn't tried to raise an alarm. For the first time since I was a kid and he'd helped the Countess to foster and tutor me, Wells was allowing me to make my own choices. Like Belenus, he wanted me to prove myself.

Then Natalie gave me the thumbs up, and the wards snapped down. At the same moment, the glowing runes on the coat lapels of every single fae, faded.

We could fly.

Instantly, it was chaos.

The gates crashed open. The wolf shifters howled, and the witches shrieked with delight. I hoped that the spells had broken on the cyclops guardians as well.

Oscar nodded to me from underneath his dark hood, before he led the vampires darting across the lawns and towards the gates. Even the phoenixes landed, crashing into the mermaids and elves, in a wild sprint for freedom. They didn't know that the invisible barrier in the skies had also been lowered.

A twinge of regret shot through me.

The other Houses would be hunted through the woods and mountains. Most would be caught. But then, they'd known that when we'd passed on the message about today. Escape for them was far-fetched because they were the distraction. Yet this was their chance to rebel and flick off the professors and Dean who'd oppressed them. And it was still a chance.

From now on, they'd never stop trying.

The faes' wings outstretched, before they glanced

at me. I'd been an outcast only a week ago. The fae wouldn't even let me sleep with them at night. But now, I was their leader.

I grinned, and there wasn't even a hint of malevolence in it. "Get your fae asses out of here!"

My grin widened, as they transformed into their fae form. Like a cloud of white butterflies, they rose towards the sun.

At a sudden *honking* above, I squinted at the flock of swans, who flew between the fae: black danced between the white.

Apollo twisted to me. His eyes were bright. "My lord, let me choose to fly with my brothers and sisters."

"You never have to ask again."

Apollo transformed in a spray of glitter, beating his wings to rise into the sky. His long neck stretched out in joy, as the other shifters *honked* joyful greetings.

"We *live* for our brothers." When Radley touched his wing to mine, golden power sparked between our wings, until my magic wove through him as well.

The words had never held such meaning before. I longed to howl them.

Felix touched his wing to mine as well. "Brothers in wings."

When my power pulled him closer to me, he gasped.

"Fae Four." Beau brushed his wing across each of ours in turn.

"Mine," I said, simply.

Then I glanced across at Laurel. Her dance was as mesmerizing as before, but her steps were clumsier. She was tired. The dance needed to end sometime, which meant that we'd reached the risky part.

I pulled back from my mates and then marched to Laurel. I dragged her into my arms.

At the same time, I hollered at Radley, Felix, and Beau, "Go!"

They transformed into white fae and a single black fae, fluttering around each other like blossoms.

Yet the peace of their escape above the barrier was broken by the Dean's fury, as he awoke from Laurel's spell. His chair smashed backward, as he threw himself up, cussing at the dazed ogres and dragging Wells up by his lapels.

Wells ignored the Dean, however, raising his hand to the sky, before letting it fall with an aching sadness.

In the confusion, I grabbed Laurel around the waist. She rested her head against my shoulder. Tremors ran through her, and her knees buckled. She'd given every shred of herself to save us. She still pressed a kiss to the base of my neck.

She'd done it. *We'd* done it. But although the swan shifters and fae were saved, Laurel and I were yet to escape.

Shining One, let me truly be able to fly...

I reached inside myself for my new power. It couldn't be the cruelest prank of all that I was a demigod, right? Intense sensations vibrated through me. My back burned with searing tendrils. Then I screamed as my wings burst out longer and larger than ever before. The feathers sizzled with golden magic.

Let me fly...

Wells shouted out in shock and awe.

Laurel shivered. "Have I told you that you're the most beautiful creature I've ever seen?"

I smiled. "Not today."

"Then let me add that you're also the best leader, lover, and friend." She held on tighter. "And I'll never let go."

I flapped my wings in a single powerful beat, rising above the stage.

I was flying.....*in the name of the forest*...I was flying.

Down below, the Dean shoved professors and guards after fleeing warlocks and rampaging beserkers. The rebellion on the ground stopped him noticing the one in the skies.

I swooped higher, higher, and higher. I followed the wave of fae and swans. The Wicked Reform School soon became so small that it looked nothing but a child's play set.

In my arms, Laurel's glamor fell away: her golden

hair became red, her face heart shaped, and her eyes larger. She no longer needed to wear a mask. Our rebellion had freed her as well.

Then I laughed as loudly as I wanted because for the first time since I'd been handed over as a hostage, there was no one to control my emotions.

I was alive, loved, and a demigod in a fated bond to a princess. I wished only that Prince Lysander wasn't still trapped in Rebel Academy.

Yet finally, my fae had rebelled. Who decided whether that was *wicked* or not?

All that mattered was that we were no longer prisoners. I didn't know what we'd do next. As long as I was with my bonded, I'd travel across realms because I was no longer under the shadow of death.

I was free.

THE END... FOR NOW

Continue the adventure with the Rebel Fae, Prince Lysander, in **REBEL ACADEMY: CRAVE** in Book One of the Wickedly Charmed Series **NOW** https://rosemaryajohns.com

Thanks for reading **REBEL: HOUSE OF FAE!** If you enjoyed reading this book, **please consider leaving a review on Amazon.** Your support is really important to us authors. Plus, I love hearing from my readers!
Thanks, you're awesome!

Rebel: House of Fae with its magical and sexy fae, swan shifters, and demigod who's reborn on the Night of the Beltane is an idea that I've been sitting on for years, waiting for the perfect setting. I LOVED placing my Rebel Fae in the Wicked Reform School! Forbidden romance, fated love, and both Court and Forest Fae were exciting to write. I fell in love with Lord Spring, especially his Wicked Bucket List...

The idea of the coven-run college for supernatural bad boys (where Prince Lysander is sent) — **Rebel Academy** — has been with me as long.
At the heart of the paranormal prison is the wickedest witch of them all. It's a twist on academies like you've never seen before. I can't wait for you to discover the ghost witch who haunts Oxford's secret college and

her delicious immortals (including Loki's son), as well as the prince fae and elves.

You're total stars for your recommendations, word of mouth, and reviews because it's how my books reach new readers. I'm truly grateful to you. Even a single line review raises the series' visibility.
Thanks, you're awesome - my Rebel family :)
Rebel here, yeah?
Rosemary A Johns

Sign up to Rosemary A Johns' Rebel Newsletter for two FREE novellas. Also, these special perks: promotions, discounts, and news of hot releases before anyone else.
Become a Rebel here today by joining Rosemary's Rebels Group on Facebook!

I caught Willoughby's mouth with mine, and he pressed me against the wall. I wrapped my legs around his waist.

"Strip, fae," Loki's son commanded, grasping Prince Lysander by the neck.

Lysander flushed, and his golden wings flapped. His fingers hesitated over the buttons of his pants. But he wouldn't call the bluff first.

We were playing a deadly game between Immortals and Princes. Desire, rivalry, and temptation. It would crush us all.

Discover now what happens to the Court fae prince who was sentenced to the deadliest academy...

USA TODAY BESTSELLING AUTHOR
ROSEMARY A JOHNS

The werewolf's lips brushed across mine, and I jolted. "May I caress you…here?"

I nodded, shuddering. He drew circles over my skin, and I heated like he was touching me inside, coiling the pleasure higher.

Lower…please, touch me lower…

When I squirmed to encourage his fingers below the fabric of my ball gown, he chuckled but only continued his maddeningly slow teasing.

"Kiss her neck, prince," the god ordered; his voice was like winding silk.

The incubus' eyes sparkled. He was feeding from the order and my pleasure.

My crimson magic burst out, whilst I experienced each of the men's pulsing, panting pleasure.

"Hold the witch's hands above her head," the god commanded. "She won't be able to stay still for what comes next..."

Escape into the world of bad, bad wolves and wicked witches in REBEL WEREWOLVES...

READ THE COMPLETE REBEL ANGELS SERIES!

The vampire's fangs shot out, and I shuddered, as he grazed them along my neck.

"I love you, Violet." Ash's pupils were blown, and his gaze was desperate. "I know that you don't want my protection." He kissed my neck; his large hands stroked up my spine. "But just once…pretend. I'm not a hero but I could be—"

"I don't need to pretend." I caressed Ash's bare chest, and his wings fluttered.

When my fingers moved towards the waistband of Ash's jeans, however, his breath hitched.

"How can you touch me?" He rested his head on my shoulder. "When you know what I am?"

"You're mine." If Lucifer killed us tonight, at least we died claimed and together. "You're family and the Brigadier. No one can take that away."

I'd show Ash just how much I craved to touch.

I pushed open the button on his jeans, and although his breathing became harsh, he didn't stop me this time.

I slid my hand lower again…

Binge-read the addictive **REBEL ANGELS: THE COMPLETE SERIES** by the USA Today best-selling author Rosemary A Johns TODAY for FREE with Kindle Unlimited. **DISCOVER WHAT HAPPENED TO QUINN, LORD SPRING'S BROTHER, IN THE REALM OF GODS AND MONSTERS…**

Grab this magical, dark, and sizzling hot vampire and angel Romance with gods and fae!

Number One: Experience a true bond
Number Two: Celebrate the magical rituals of
Belenus on Beltane Night
Number Three: Free the cygnets
Number Four: Outrage a vampire
Number Five: Fight a bear
Number Six: Bond with fae and shifter lovers
Number Seven: Make love underneath the stars
Number Eight: Dance on the Night of the Beltane

House of Fae

Lord Quincey Spring, the Marquess of Spring, Forest
Fae, Unseelie and demigod

Lord Radley Brooke, Forest Fae, Unseelie and
Hostage Lord

Lord Felix River, Forest Fae, Unseelie with Fortune
Magic

Lord Beau Wells, the Marquess of Wells (the Duke of
Wells' son), Court Fae, Unseelie

Swan Shifters

Apollo, Lord Spring's shifter

Lil Swan, Lord Brooke's cygnet, Odile's sister

Odile, Lord River's cygnet, Lil Swan's sister

Paranormal Prefect Patrol

Oscar, pure blood vampire

Barley, bear shifter

Nephilim, half-angel and half-human

Staff

Dean Aero, demon, Dean of Discipline

Natalia, golem, Dean of Discipline's secretary

Tom, ghost, cursed gardener

Professor Emerald/Princess Laurel, succubus,
Emotions Counselor, House of Fae

The Duke of Wells, Unseelie, Court Fae, Head of
House of Fae

Professor Pond, the Countess, Unseelie, Court Fae,
Deputy Head of House of Fae

Ms. Farah, banshee, librarian

Supernaturals

Prince Lysander, Unseelie, Court Fae, sentenced to
Rebel Academy

The Duke of Spring, Quinn, Lord Spring's brother,
Forest Fae and leader of the Love Rebellion
High Queen, Court Fae, Royal House of Swan
Chief Myrmidon, leader of myrmidons

ABOUT THE AUTHOR

ROSEMARY A JOHNS is a USA Today bestselling and award-winning fantasy author, music fanatic, and paranormal anti-hero addict. She writes sexy angels and werewolves, savage vampires, and epic battles.

Winner of the Silver Award in the National Wishing Shelf Book Awards. Finalist in the IAN Book of the Year Awards. Runner-up in the Best Fantasy Book of the Year, Reality Bites Book Awards. Honorable Mention in the Readers' Favorite Book Awards. Short-listed in the International Rubery Book Awards.

Rosemary is also a traditionally published short story writer. She studied history at Oxford University and ran her own theater company. She's always been a rebel…

Want to read more and stay up to date on Rosemary's newest releases? Sign up for her *VIP* Rebel Newsletter and grab two FREE novellas!